"An interesting meditation . . . on the changing foundations of love. In many ways it challenges the first and only soul mate concept that is so prevalent."

—*Dear Author*

"I anxiously await every new Cindy Gerard release. I've always thought there was nobody who wrote romantic suspense better, able to seamlessly blend romance and action while creating strong heroines and macho yet caring heroes."

—*Fiction Vixen*

"Gerard is an author whose stories I always have an easy time falling into and thoroughly enjoying. . . . You can never go wrong with the Black Ops world."

—*Happily Ever After-Reads*

"Gerard simply excels when it comes to writing action-packed scenes that are highly detailed and infused with passion and fun. Similarly, her heroes have been some of the hottest in RS that I've read."

—*Under the Covers Book Blog*

KILLING TIME
Nominated for the *RT Book Reviews*
Best Romantic Suspense Award

"Cindy Gerard writes such fun books. Full of tons of action, witty lines, and plenty of sexual tension, *Killing Time* totally lived up to my expectations."

—*USA Today*

"Gerard's name has become synonymous with high-stakes and high-action adventures that don't skimp on either the romance or the thrills. A Gerard novel is always worth the time and money invested, and this one is no exception."

—*RT Book Reviews* (Top Pick!)

"From the intensely captivating opening scene to the last tender moment, Gerard takes the reader on an emotionally complex yet action-packed roller-coaster ride of romance and conflict, capitalizing on both sexual and situational tension."

—*Kirkus Reviews*

"Danger-fueled romantic tension . . . [and] sizzling chemistry."

—*Publishers Weekly*

"The first chapter infuses sexual tension (and frustration) with exotic locales and a little spark of forbidden danger. It works so well in capturing the readers' attention that they are helpless but to dive right in. . . . Gerard not only took me on a wild ride of my life, but she also introduced me to my future book boyfriends, made me laugh and suck in shocked gasps, and of course, made me fall in love."

—*Under the Covers Book Blog*

"This book was everything I could have asked for. . . . Gerard really is unmatched for quality of characters and writing in the genre."

—*Smexy Books*

"This story started off with a bang and continued throughout."

—*The Book Nympho*

"I've been a LONGtime fan of Cindy Gerard's work and this book more than lives up to her reputation as a master of building suspense and creating believable, three-dimensional characters that leave you both racing to reach the end and sorry to turn the last page. . . . I always have her latest book on preorder."

—*Writer Mom's Blog*

CINDY GERARD

The Way Home

POCKET BOOKS

New York   London   Toronto   Sydney   New Delhi

Pocket Books
A Division of Simon & Schuster, Inc.
1230 Avenue of the Americas
New York, NY 10020

This book is a work of fiction. Any references to historical events, real people, or real places are used fictitiously. Other names, characters, places, and events are products of the author's imagination, and any resemblance to actual events or places or persons, living or dead, is entirely coincidental.

First Pocket Books paperback edition November 2014

POCKET and colophon are registered trademarks of Simon & Schuster, Inc.

For information about special discounts for bulk purchases, please contact Simon & Schuster Special Sales at 1-866-506-1949 or business@simonandschuster.com.

The Simon & Schuster Speakers Bureau can bring authors to your live event. For more information or to book an event, contact the Simon & Schuster Speakers Bureau at 1-866-248-3049 or visit our website at www.simonspeakers.com.

Cover design and art by Tom Hallman

Manufactured in the United States of America

10 9 8 7 6 5 4 3 2 1

ISBN 978-1-4767-3521-4
ISBN 978-1-4767-3522-1 (ebook)

Unknown faces, unknown names, far from home on Christmas Day, protect us with unwavering vigilance so we can gather with our families around tables laden with holiday goodness and hearths warming us in the chill of winter.

This book is dedicated to them and to the families who miss them. And to the ones who return the same yet forever changed. You have my unending gratitude.

Soldiers are dreamers; when the guns begin
they think of firelit homes, clean beds and wives.

—SIEGFRIED SASSOON

Prologue

Afghanistan, July

*I*t wasn't the memory he would have chosen—not
when he couldn't even remember his own name—
but he knew that he used to have nightmares about
vampires. Hiding under his bed and in the dark closet.
Swooping down on their Dracula wings, sinking their
fangs into his neck, and sucking out his blood.

How ironic, then, that he'd become a vampire of
sorts: a creature who lived in the night, hid from the
light, and sucked sustenance as if it were blood from a
young Afghan woman, who despised him but wouldn't
let him die. She brought him food, water, and medicine. And opiates that she liberally laced in all three.

He watched her now through a drug-induced haze,
physically incapacitated and totally dependent on her.
He knew that her name was Rabia and that she could

ill afford the things she brought for him. He also knew that if he were caught while she harbored the escaped American soldier a horde of Taliban warlords were searching for, not only would he be tortured, interrogated, and finally executed, but so would she.

So he didn't know why she continued to help him, but he had no option but to accept it. Just as he had no choice but to believe what she'd told him in heavily accented English about who he was . . . because he didn't remember. He didn't remember being an American soldier, or what had happened to him, or how he'd escaped from the Taliban and ended up here.

The panic and anguish that stalked him whenever the opiates wore off were as huge and dark as the cave where she hid him. So he gladly relinquished both to the apathy induced by the poppy. Apathy was painless. Apathy made it tolerable to know that weeks, maybe months, of his life were gone. His memories . . . gone.

Only the vampire dreams remained of who he'd been. And only the woman kept him alive.

He studied her now as she prepared his meal in the dim light of an oil lamp, in a silence that embodied their uneasy and unnatural bond, as shadows danced along the curved rock wall and dust swept into the cave on a wind that never quit blowing. He knew scattered words in Pashtu but didn't know why he knew them. She had a passing command of English but rarely chose to use it. She was the only constant in a life that had been reduced to pain, fear, and the vertigo that crippled him even more than the opiates. And he didn't know whether to thank her for keeping him alive or hate her as she hated him.

Moving his head slowly to avoid triggering another vertigo attack, he pulled the ragged blanket around him against the chill of the cave floor.

Because he was so weak, she had to feed him the lukewarm soup that kept him alive. He could never see her features beneath the burqa covering her face. He could only see those eyes, onyx black, winter cold, and void of any emotion but weary disdain.

It had been the same thing every day for twenty-three days. He'd used a small pebble to scratch a mark on the rock wall each day since he'd regained consciousness. She would appear wearing dark, baggy trousers beneath the black burqa that covered her from head to knees, hiding her body beneath yards of coarse cotton. The scent of the summer heat and the scorch of the sun that she brought with her were reminders that a world existed outside this cave. A world that wasn't dank and dark and cold. A world that was hostile and foreign and where, she told him, he was not safe.

For twenty-three days, she had been the only soul he'd seen, and she had yet to look him directly in the eye. He wouldn't recognize her if he saw her on the street. Not that he would ever leave here. If the pain and the vertigo didn't keep him flat on his back, the ankle shackle that chained him to the rock wall would.

And then there was the poppy. Who knew how deeply he'd been dragged down that rabbit hole?

Some days—the lucid ones, when he couldn't fight the fear—he would lie here shivering and wish for death. When pain ripped through his head, when the crippling dizziness reduced him to lying rigidly still, hugging the rock floor in a desperate attempt to stop the nausea, that's when despair crushed him. And he would beg her to let him die.

But always, she refused. She continued to risk everything to make certain he stayed alive, and he had no idea why.

He only knew that every time she appeared on quiet feet and condemning silence, he felt both shame and gratitude, because she hadn't forgotten him . . . the way he'd forgotten everything but the need to leave this place that even God had forsaken and find his way back home.

If he only knew where home was.

Chapter

1

Northern Minnesota, July

*T*oday, of all days, Jess Albert needed routine. Most days, she got it. Shop keeping wasn't exactly a glamorous, exciting occupation. In fact, every day was pretty much a repeat of the day before and the day before that. Little mini Groundhog Days, stacked up like cordwood, one on top of the other.

"Until tomorrow, my little lotus blossom. Dream of me." Boots England, one of her regulars, wiggled his busy white brows and blew her a kiss.

Jess grinned as he tucked his newspaper under his arm and limped on his recently replaced knee toward the front door of the Crossroads General Store.

"One of these days, Marcia's going to show up with a shovel and bash one of us over the head, if you keep flirting with me like that."

"Ah, but what's life without a little danger?" He let himself outside on a hot rush of July air to drive back to his lakeside cabin for his afternoon nap and his wife of almost fifty years.

The bell above the front door dinged softly behind the irrepressible old flirt, sounding the same as it had since Jess's father had first set up shop almost fifty years ago. She loved the sound of that bell. It was comforting and comfortable, the bedrock of her childhood, as ingrained in her psyche as the scent of sunscreen, bug spray, and the cherry nut ice cream she'd already scooped gallons of this summer.

She'd spent her youth playing on this scarred pine floor, then working behind the counter when she got older. And after burning out as an ER trauma nurse, she'd taken over the store when her parents had retired to Arizona three years ago. So, yeah, she loved the sound of that old bell. Especially because every time it rang, it meant business, which was good, because her quarterly taxes were due soon and, as always, she was a little short on cash.

Today, she also loved it because it meant she had another customer to help keep her mind off the fact that this particular day would be tough to get through. She glanced at the framed eight-by-ten photo of her and J.R. on the wall behind the cash register. Suntanned and smiling, their whole lives ahead of them . . . And then it wasn't. At least, not for J.R.

He would have been thirty-five today. If he'd been home and not deployed, she would have baked him a cake, and some of his buddies on the post would have stopped by for a few beers.

But the last birthday J.R. celebrated had been thousands of miles from home. He'd been thirty-two. Eight months later, he was dead.

"Too late to add these to the bill?"

She looked up at the young father making some final purchases before he and his son headed out for a week of camping and fishing. He'd added a map and two black ball caps with "Lake Kabetogama" embroidered in red across the bills to their stack of supplies.

"Not a problem." She gave him a bright smile and harnessed her attention to the business at hand. "Anything else?"

The Crossroads General Store was a north woods version of a Walmart, on a much smaller and less state-of-the-art scale. The store had been supplying goods to locals and travelers alike for more than eighty years. You needed boots? Whiskey? Bait? Groceries? DVD rentals? Anything you could think of, the Crossroads provided.

"Yeah, throw in half a dozen C batteries, and we'll call it good. Right, son?"

The boy looked to be around ten, with flashing brown eyes and buzz-cut blond hair. He was the image of his father and clearly antsy to start their grand "just guys" adventure.

"Do you think we'll see a bear?" Equal measures of hope and trepidation filled the boy's question.

"It's a good possibility," Jess said, feeding his excitement. "At the last DNR count, more than a hundred and fifty black bears called this part of Voyageurs National Park home. Where are you camping?"

The dad dug into his breast pocket and checked his camping permit. "Blue Fin Bay."

"Ah. Then there's a pretty good chance you might spot one."

The boy's eyes grew as big as bobbers.

She couldn't help but laugh as she continued ringing up their sale. "Make sure to police your campsite every day, and store your food in the bear-proof lockers the Park Service provides. You'll be fine."

The bell above the door rang again, and Jess glanced up from the cash register in time to see broad shoulders and the back of a baseball cap disappear down the center aisle toward the live-bait tanks.

It was a sight she saw dozens of times a day during the summer season. Another fisherman burning with fishing fever, hoping to get lucky and needing some bait. Since she was on her own until Kayla Burke, her mainstay summer help, got back from a bank run, she let the newcomer figure out what he wanted while she finished ringing up twenty gallons of gas, a mocha cappuccino, a root beer, and the rest of the groceries for the campers. She gave them directions to Wooden Frog Landing, where they could put their boat in, and wished them good luck as they headed out the door.

Coming out from behind the counter to check on Mr. Ball Cap, she nearly tripped over Bear, her twelve-week-old Labrador pup. All glossy black fur, big clumsy feet, and happily thumping tail, Bear had "assumed the position" and napped soundly by her feet.

"No, don't get up." She grinned at the oblivious dog and headed down a row of shelves stocked neatly with everything from canned goods to marshmallows to fishing lures, toward the place where she'd seen the top of the ball cap disappear.

"Sorry for the wait. What can I get you?" she called.

"Not sure. What do I need to catch the big ones?"

The voice stopped her cold. And routine, mundane, and comfortable shifted to excitement and chaos in one heartbeat. Although the stocked shelves hid him from view, she knew exactly who was back there.

Tyler Brown.

Holy, holy cow.

It had been a year ago February since she'd met this man and exchanged a very few words with him. No way should she have remembered the timber and the pitch of his voice so clearly after . . . eighteen months? Yet she was one-hundred-percent certain it was him before she hesitantly turned the corner to face him.

"Surprise." He smiled, hopeful and expectant and even a little shy. Coupled with his very large, very striking, and very unexpected presence, it set off a handspring of emotions in her stomach.

"Yeah," she finally managed, along with a return smile that felt as forced as it felt necessary. "You could definitely say this is a surprise. Hello, Ty."

She started to extend her hand, thought better of it, and stuffed it into the back pocket of her shorts. "Wow. You're a long way from home."

A very long way. And not just from Florida but a long way from his life. A *heck* of a long way from the cold winter night when he'd swooped in and out of her life like the storm he'd blown in on.

And now here he was, back again. One of the men who'd been part of a dangerous rescue. A man who had made enough of an impression on her that she'd opened up her gun safe to him and three other virtual strangers based on his word alone.

Unable to stop herself, she stared at Tyler Brown. Although he looked nothing like J.R., she suspected he was like him in every other way. Every way but one. Ty Brown was alive. J.R. wasn't. Her husband had died thousands of miles from home, fighting a war she'd never quite understood, hadn't truly sanctioned, and hadn't been able to keep him from fighting. Looking at Ty—who'd made her think of J.R. the first time she'd seen him—unsettled her as much as it confused her. And, unfortunately, excited her.

Yup. Her day had gone from mundane to totally bonkers to the tune of a bell above the door.

"So." He looked expectant when she just stood there. She guessed he'd finally decided one of them needed to say something, and since he'd brought this game into play, she was fine with it being him. "Thought I'd do some fishing."

Florida is no longer surrounded by an ocean full of fish?

Because he had this little "If you buy that, I've got some farm land in the Sahara desert I'd love to sell you" smile, she avoided the obvious questions, such as: What was he *really* doing here? And the most damaging one, Why did it seem to matter so much?

"Early July's not the best time of year." Two could play this game. "But I'm told fishing started to pick up a bit this week." She pasted on her shopkeeper smile and pretended her world hadn't been tipped on end. "You want live bait?"

He grinned, looking both thoughtful and amused, as if he knew that she knew he hadn't come all this way to fish but was willing to play it that way until she got used to the idea. "Live bait. Yeah, sure. Why not? Live bait would be good."

She moved behind the bubbling minnow tanks, hoping she didn't appear as off-balance as she felt. "Got a sale on flathead chubs."

That spurred a soft chuckle. "My lucky day."

She couldn't look at him because, for God's sake,

live bait had not brought him back to Kabetogama. Neither had fishing, but she wasn't ready to process that yet. Head down, she started scooping up minnows. "Couple dozen do you?"

"I don't know. *Will* a couple dozen do me?"

He was laughing at her now . . . not unkindly but as if he found her entertaining, which meant he saw right through her.

Lord, she hoped he didn't have her figured out. Or maybe she did. Then he could tell her exactly what was going on in her head, because she didn't have one solid clue.

Well, maybe one. There hadn't been a man in her life since J.R. And there'd never been a man who triggered the physical reactions this man had at first sight, all those months ago. Reactions he triggered again today.

It had unsettled and puzzled her that she'd experienced such a strong, instant physical reaction to him. She'd chalked it up to a cold, isolating storm, the threat of imminent danger, and a lot of long, lonely nights alone in her bed.

Then he'd disappeared from her life as quickly as he'd come into it. Which had been good. Which had been fine. She'd actually been relieved when he hadn't called, even though he'd said he would—at least, that's what she'd told herself. She didn't want to get involved with anyone. She especially didn't want to get involved with a man like Tyler Brown, who was just like J.R.

Special-ops soldiers, whether on active duty or retired, were always warriors. They would always be the men leading the charge, putting themselves in danger, living for the adrenaline rush, and dying for God and country and the guy next to them in the trenches.

She'd lived with that man. She'd loved and tried to understand that man. But neither love nor understanding had been enough to keep him home, keep him happy, or keep him alive.

Chapter

2

*A*ware that Ty watched her in a curious silence, Jess poured the minnows and enough water to sustain them into a clear plastic bag, filled it with air from the pressure hose, and fastened it with a rubber band.

"Need anything else?" She held out the bag, still doing her best to avoid eye contact.

The long silence that followed had her tensing muscles she wasn't sure had ever been tensed before. When he finally shifted his weight and reached for the bag, she thought, *Here it comes*, and waited on an indrawn breath.

"Maybe a pole?"

That finally brought her head up. "Excuse me?"

His blue eyes flashed with amusement as he

glanced from her hair to her mouth, then back to her eyes. "A fishing pole? I've heard it's mandatory."

Right. OK. A fishing pole was absolutely mandatory. If he'd actually come here to fish. Which, clearly, he hadn't.

Or maybe he had, and she'd read everything wrong. People traveled to Lake Kabetogama from all over the country. The scenery was stunning. The national park bordering the lake was pure and pristine. You wanted to get away from it all? You came to the North Country, where you could fish and camp and, yes, maybe even see a bear.

So . . . what if he *had* come here with fishing in mind, and all this absurd schoolgirl hormonal activity was a result of a sad case of wishful thinking? Which was another surprise, because she'd had no idea she'd been wishing for anything. Her life was good. Maybe a little lonely. Especially today.

And maybe she needed to get a grip, because she really didn't want to travel *that* road.

"Let's get you set up with a pole, then," she said, working hard to dismiss the notion that she suddenly felt more disappointment over the possibility that he'd actually come here to fish than apprehension over the notion that he hadn't.

All purpose and pretense and business, she headed for the back wall, paneled in age-yellowed knotty pine and lined with dozens of fishing rods and reels.

"So, how've you been, Jess?" he asked softly from behind her.

She stopped mid-reach, then slowly pulled a rod off the rack, turned around, and handed it to him. "Good. I've been good. You?"

He studied the rod, tested its flex, then met her eyes on a long, slow blink. "Good. Yeah. I've been OK."

It was only a blink. But it did things to her. Things that created a silence that became a little too lengthy and compelled her to take a stab at filling it. "You and your brother and your friends . . . you're quite the legend around the lake, you know."

He looked a little disappointed that she'd decided to keep up the dodge-and-weave game, but one corner of his mouth finally lifted in an ironic smile. "I thought you had to be dead to become a legend."

"Since the biggest news this far north generally involves fishing and the weather, stories don't need as much time to marinate."

He got very quiet then. Thoughtful quiet. Troubled quiet. The kind of quiet that seemed personal and made her want to fill it. Again.

"So what are you fishing for?"

His grin came back slowly. "Um . . . isn't that a redundant question?"

How could she not smile at that? He made it very easy. "What *kind* of fish? Walleye? Northern pike? Bass?"

"Ah. How 'bout we shoot for the walleye? Do they all come with saddles?"

An involuntary laugh burst out before she could stop it.

Across the road from her gas pumps stood a gigantic fiberglass walleye, complete with a dozen steps for the kiddies to climb up and sit in the saddle strapped to its back so Mom and Dad could snap their pictures. As a tourist gimmick, it was pretty corny, but since the lion's share of the businesses around the lake depended on fishing for revenue, it was also highly effective in drawing travelers off the main highway.

"Last I knew," she said, "only the big guy has one."

"Good to know."

Darn, that smile did things to her. Things she felt woefully unprepared to deal with. Just like it was hard to deal with his presence. He'd been dressed in winter gear when she'd seen him before, but even the bulky quilted outerwear hadn't been able to hide the fact that he was fit and fine. Today he wore a pristine white T-shirt and worn jeans that proved she'd been right about his build. He was tan and tall and strong in the shoulders, and she didn't have to guess if his snug T-shirt concealed a set of six-pack abs to go with the biceps that bulged beneath his sleeves.

He had such an easy way about him. A man comfortable in his own skin. A man unimpressed by himself and by the reaction he most likely got from women. But as this drew out, he also looked uncertain—and that got to her more than how physically striking he was. A man who looked like him shouldn't feel insecure around a woman like her.

She was no fashion plate. She didn't have the time or, since J.R. died, the inclination to be. Makeup generally equaled tinted lip balm. The last time her plain brown hair had seen a pair of scissors, they'd been in her own hands. She kept it short out of necessity and softly curled because of heredity. She was tan from working outside in the sun, because shorts, tank tops, and flip-flops were her uniform this time of year.

By no stretch of anyone's imagination would she be considered voluptuous, but she was proud of her toned limbs, which he'd been eyeing. And whoa, the silence had stretched out too long again as she'd wished that she'd put on a little mascara and done more than finger-comb her hair after her shower.

"Are you staying on the lake?" she asked, half afraid of his answer.

"Hadn't thought that far ahead yet. Seeing you was as far as I got with the plan."

Hokay. There it was. The part that made her heart pound. No more pretending that he'd come here to fish.

And he had a *plan*.

She should tell him, very sensibly, that this was not a good idea. That he should go back to Florida and leave her peace of mind and her equilibrium and her fragile sense of stability intact.

Except the truth was, none of those things had

been stable or whole since she'd lost J.R. All of those things were raw and frayed and so far from healed that she had no convincing argument that his departure would make it better.

She really looked at him then. At this man who had blown in on that snowstorm and whom she'd never thought she would see again but had foolishly thought of so often since then.

Too aware of his gaze on her and feeling a sudden need for distance, she moved around him to return to the front of the store. "You should be all set, then. All you need is a fishing license."

His footsteps made the floorboards creak as he followed. Not crowding her. Trailing her slow and easy, giving her space and time to think as she slipped behind the counter, so distracted that she nearly tripped over the sprawled pup again.

"Jess. Let's get this out in the open. You don't seriously think I came all this way to fish, right?"

She faced him from behind the safety of the high countertop. Scratched Plexiglas covered a sales-tax chart, a map of the lake, a copy of the fishing regulations, and a dozen old cartoons her dad had cut out of newspapers dating as far back as the '60s—all of which she couldn't tear her gaze away from.

Well. If she hadn't figured out that he'd come here to see her before, the sudden rasp in his voice and the nuclear explosion taking place in her chest were major tip-offs.

OK. So this was really happening. But it shouldn't be. And she needed to make that clear.

"Ty. This is . . . well . . . I'm not . . . I don't . . ." She stopped, suddenly incapable of finishing a thought, let alone a sentence, because anything that came out would sound presumptive or cowardly. She looked toward the door, willing someone to step inside. Someone who needed fuel. Or was lost. Or wanted a lottery ticket or a fishing license. Anyone who could save her from having to face the inevitable.

For God's sake, grow a pair, Jess.

"Jess."

The softness of his voice finally brought her gaze back to his.

"Relax, OK? No pressure here. I know my showing up like this is way out of the blue. I know I caught you off guard. But I wanted to see you. I hoped maybe . . . I don't know. I thought we had a connection that night."

She swallowed hard, and suddenly, her heart pounded with an anger she hadn't known she'd been harboring.

"You mean that night more than a year ago, when I gave you guns and you went out and made a pretty good stab at getting yourself killed?"

The legend surrounding "that night" was more fact than fiction and had been fodder for stories around the lake ever since. In certain "good ole boy" circles, where regulars like Boots and his cronies gathered in a restaurant booth or around a potbellied stove with their mugs of strong coffee or bottles of Scotch, the tale of the "shoot-out at the Nelson cabin," where Tyler Brown and two other former spec-ops soldiers and the daughter of the secretary of state had ended up in a life-and-death face-off with a team of hired assassins, had been told, retold, embellished, and revered. When all the facts had come out, it had been pretty clear that he *had* almost gotten killed. And that he'd been a hero.

Well, she'd been married to a hero. Look how that worked out.

Why, today of all days, did *this* hero have to show up?

He wasn't smiling when she met his eyes this time—probably because her voice had risen before she'd been able to check it. He slowly nodded. "Yeah. That night. I'm sorry. I know what happened was up-setting."

Apt word, *upsetting*.

He let it settle for a moment. "You saved our lives. Letting us have those guns . . . it was a brave thing you did. Trusting us. Trusting strangers."

"Some have different words for what I did." Her brother-in-law, Brad, in particular had a lot of words . . . words like *stupid*, *insane*, *reckless*.

"You trusted me then. I hoped you might trust me again, this time with nothing nearly as scary."

Oh, but this was scary.

"I've thought about you, Jess. I've thought about coming back to see you for a long time now."

It was on the tip of her tongue to blurt out, *Then why didn't you? Why have eighteen months gone by without so much as an e-mail?* He'd asked for her phone number and her e-mail address. She'd thought he would call. Who was she kidding? She'd been certain he'd call. The way he'd looked at her. The way his eyes had spoken to her.

Even knowing he was the last kind of man she ever wanted in her life again, it had hurt when he hadn't contacted her. And she'd felt foolish for thinking about him too much. The way she felt foolish now.

"I hoped maybe you might want to see me, too," he said, breaking into her thoughts. "Can we start with something that simple?"

As if there was anything simple about this.

Tell him to leave. Just say it and end this.

But he'd come so far. Made such an effort.

"Yeah," she heard herself saying, despite the warnings banging around in her head. *God help me.* "I guess we could start with that."

He looked so relieved that some of her own tension eased out on a tight smile. "So we're clear, though, you're still paying for those minnows and the tackle."

He laughed and dug into the hip pocket of his jeans for his wallet. "Fair enough."

Before she could think it through or second-guess herself, she picked up the phone and dialed.

"Shelley. Hi. Yeah. It's Jess. Hey, I've got a fisherman here in need of a place to stay." She glanced up at him, at his watchful eyes, then quickly looked away when she felt her cheeks redden. "Got any vacant cabins?"

Shelley and Darrin Lutz were her friends and the owners of Whispering Pines Resort—and yes, they had an available cabin.

"Thanks. I'll send him your way, then. Name is Brown. Tyler Brown."

She couldn't quite meet his eyes after she hung up. And she already hoped she wouldn't live to regret making that phone call, because here was the deal. Ty Brown showing up out of the blue this way might represent a life-changing moment for her. A moment she didn't want, a moment she actually feared but hadn't realized she needed until she'd heard his voice in her store and the sound of it had made her knees go weak.

He handed over his credit card as the door burst open to the ring of the bell. A gaggle of sunburned and giddy teenage girls tumbled inside, smelling of suntan lotion, laughing and joking, and headed straight for her wireless Internet station.

"What time do you get off?" he asked, low enough not to be overheard.

Here, at least, was a small reprieve. "You forget. I own the place. I live here." Her apartment was above the store. "I'm here until lights out."

Since taking over the store, she had never regretted that she worked long hours, day in, day out, during the summer. It kept her busy. And she needed to be busy. She needed to be dog-tired exhausted each night when she went to bed to have any chance of outdistancing the thoughts that kept her awake most nights since J.R. died.

J.R., who would have celebrated a birthday today.

She had a moment of deep, aching regret that until this instant had never been coupled with guilt. But suddenly, she did feel guilty. For being alive. For *feeling* alive in a way she hadn't in a very long time. And she felt guilty because for the first time in three and a half years, she realized she wanted to look forward to something instead of always looking back.

"Figure something out," he said, tempting her toward that future. "Have dinner with me tonight."

Chapter

3

*Y*ou're sure you can handle things until I get back?"
Jess walked back into the store after watching
Ty's taillights disappear down the road. She already
had second thoughts about letting him talk her into
dinner and leaving Kayla in charge of the store.

"You have to eat," Ty had pointed out when Jess
had insisted she couldn't leave until closing time at
nine P.M. "Besides, you're the boss. Don't you have
someone who can cover for you for a couple of hours?"

She might have been able to stage a stronger
argument if Kayla hadn't bopped through the door
about that time—all five feet and one inch of her, a
college freshman who looked about thirteen instead
of nineteen, with her bouncing brown ponytail, short-
shorts, and halter top, and telling Jess, "Go. I can

handle the dinner hour and close up for you. And if it gets too busy, I'll call Blake or Lane. Those two always want extra hours. Hailey, too. She's saving for an iPad. Cripes, boss. We've got you covered. Now, take a break. It's been forever since you took any time off."

That had pretty much ended the discussion, except for the part where Ty had said he'd be back to pick her up around six.

"So who's the hot guy?" Kayla asked.

It would get out sooner or later, so she might as well tell it straight. While tourists came and went from the store in droves, men who asked her to dinner didn't. At least, they never asked her more than once, because she always gently told them no. Still, in the small lake community, word would spread like wildfire. This would be her only chance to temper that fire before it took on a life of its own.

So she told her.

"OMG. He's one of those commandos who shot up the bad guys at the Nelson cabin." Kayla started digging into her hip pocket for her iPhone to spread the word.

Jess rolled her eyes. "Hold off on the smoke signals, Pocahontas. In the first place, he's not a commando. In the second, I really don't see the need to broadcast that he's here. Let's respect his privacy, OK?"

"So why *is* he here?"

Jess snatched Kayla's phone out of her hand, then tucked it back into the girl's hip pocket. "You know, I honestly don't know," she lied, hoping to sidetrack Kayla's curiosity. "Maybe business brought him."

"What kind of business?"

"I don't know that, either."

"Maybe *you're* his business," Kayla said with a suggestive grin.

That may have been true, but there was no way she'd let Kayla know it. "Don't even go there. All I know is that he said he was in the area and he'd like to thank me for helping them out—"

"With the commando stuff," Kayla interrupted with a leading look.

"Whatever," Jess said. "So he's taking me out for a bite to eat."

"To say thank you." Kayla reiterated Jess's statement, making it clear she thought there was a whole lot more than a thank-you involved.

"Yes," Jess said firmly. "To say thank you. Now, you said you wanted to work, so quit drilling me and work. There are two boxes of freight in the back room I haven't had a chance to get to yet today."

"Because Commando Cutie kept you otherwise occupied?"

Jess lifted a finger and pointed to the stockroom. "Go."

Kayla giggled and headed out but not without one last parting shot. "'Bout time you had a date."

"It's not a date," Jess said mildly, determined to deny, deny, deny. Only she couldn't deny to herself.

Just as she couldn't stop wishing she had something upstairs in her closet that hadn't been washed and worn a hundred times. "I'm going up to take a shower."

Kayla poked her head out of the stockroom door, grinning like a goon. "Make sure you use some of that sexy-smelling lotion I got you for Christmas last year."

"It's not a date," Jess ground out one more time, and headed up the stairs, trying to remember where she'd stashed the bottle of lotion.

✶

THE CROSSROADS GENERAL Store sat between nowhere and the end of the earth at the junction of Highway 53 and a cratered blacktop road that led to a Minnesota lake with a name Ty hadn't yet figured out how to pronounce. And as he pulled out onto the road, he wondered if maybe he should have played it differently with Jess Albert. Maybe he should have fudged and told her he was in the area on business and decided to stop by and say hi. See how she was doing. Thank her again for the help that long-ago winter night. Maybe she wouldn't have been as jumpy. But that plan had felt as dishonest as it was, and in the end, he'd decided to play it by ear.

She was wary of him. Maybe even a little angry at him. Last time she'd seen him, he'd let her believe he would call, but he hadn't, so she had good reason to be both. Still, she hadn't run him off. She'd given him directions to the Whispering Pines Resort, where she'd arranged for someone named Shelley to hold a cabin for him.

Which meant he was staying. Which hadn't necessarily been part of his plan when he'd arrived, because, as he'd told her, he didn't really have a plan—except to take his cues from her.

And those cues so far were pretty mixed. It wasn't only wariness. There was that underlying anger he'd sensed, maybe even a little fear, in her. Definitely resistance. Yet her eyes had told a different story from her body language. Enough to give him hope. She was glad he'd come back. She just didn't want to admit it.

He glanced in his rearview mirror as the store faded from sight. The last time he'd left the lake and the store, the snow had been flying, and he'd had the shakes from an adrenaline crash following a siege on a wolf pack of hired assassins. As soon as he'd gotten his act together and had been debriefed by the federal alphabet agencies and thanked by the new secretary of state herself, he'd had every intention of calling the pretty little widow with the beckoning brown eyes.

Jess Albert had saved lives that night. She'd taken a long, hard look at him and his brother, Mike, and a very desperate Joe Green and his wife, Stephanie, when they'd shown up in the dark, stomped snow all over her floor, and asked for the impossible. Blind trust.

She'd led them to a back room, spun the combination to a gun safe, and opened it up to four strangers.

Inside, a pair of AR-15 rifles sat alongside several hunting rifles, shotguns, and handguns.

"They were my husband's," she'd said, crossed her arms over her breasts, then stood back and invited them to take whatever they wanted.

There had been a critical word in her statement. *Were?*

She'd hesitated. "IED. Afghanistan. J.R. was spec ops, too," she'd added with a tight smile. "And yes, I can spot one of you guys a mile away."

Some might think she'd exhibited a kind of trust normally reserved for fools or dreamers that night. She'd made it pretty clear, however, that she was neither.

He swiped a hand over his lower jaw as he steered his rental—a black Jeep Cherokee—down the bumpy asphalt. Complicated. This was every bit as complicated as he'd thought it would be.

Yet here he was. Determined to take it slow, feel his way along, and see if there was anything more than wishful thinking on his part where the vulnerable and oh so tempting Widow Albert was concerned. If it turned out to be wishful thinking, he'd take it on the chin, cut his losses, say good-bye, and get on back to his life. Maybe he'd even take his brother, Mike, up on his offer to join a top-secret spec-ops team and go back to fighting the war on terrorism.

But if she was interested . . . well . . . if she was interested, he had a feeling he might be in this for the long haul because even with everything that had happened since he'd last seen her, he'd never been able to get Jess Albert's all-American-girl face and dark brown eyes out of his head. Those eyes had haunted him and told volumes about her. About how brave she was, how alone she was, and how determined she was to keep all of her feelings tucked away. Only she hadn't been successful. He'd seen interest in those eyes. And no matter how many times and how many ways he'd tried to convince himself he didn't want the complication of getting involved with a woman who most likely still mourned the death of another man, what he'd seen had compelled him. He'd intended to call.

Then his whole life had changed.

"Do you have a clue what you're doing, Brown?" he muttered, as second and third thoughts about his harebrained idea to fly up here nipped him in the ass.

"Not lately, no," he admitted aloud, and wondered when he'd started talking to himself.

About the time he'd left the store, very much aware of Jess's softly curling hair and strong tan limbs as she stood in the open doorway, a shoulder propped against the jamb, arms crossed beneath her breasts, watching him pull away with a troubled furrow between her eyes. Eyes that said he had the power to hurt her, which probably made him a selfish bastard, because he really didn't know where this was going.

He only knew that she'd been there. In the back of his mind, tucked in a corner reserved for unfinished business. Business that would have stayed unfinished if life wasn't full of so many curves.

He hoped this didn't end up as one of those "sounded like a good idea at the time" experiences he'd live to regret. Or that she would.

Losing Maya was something he regretted. Hell, losing her had pretty much knocked him down. But he kept thinking about Jess. Of how she'd soldiered on.

In all honesty, he wasn't one-hundred-percent certain when he'd decided to come back here if the reason was to heal or that he'd simply never forgotten her. He needed to find out. And he needed to be honest with Jess about that.

He needed to be honest about Maya, too. He'd loved her, and he wasn't looking to replace her. He was looking to move on. Jess Albert was a good place to start. She was a special woman. And he'd grown weary of grieving. He figured she had, too. And if not, hey, he'd been due for a change of scenery.

And boy, howdy, had he gotten it. The Crossroads General Store, with its three gas pumps, time-worn exterior, and cute-as-a-button proprietor, was a far cry from Key West. It looked a lot different in daylight from when he'd first seen it through the low beams of a rented pickup in the dead of winter on the hunt for a pack of predators hell-bent on killing some people he cared about. At least, he cared about them now. Now that he'd gotten to know them through his brother, Mike.

The terrain was as far from palm trees and sand as you could get. Dense pine and birch forest crowded within ten feet of the road's shoulder in spots as he followed Jess's directions, which he'd plugged into the onboard navigation system. Huge boulders and rock outcroppings popped up in the middle of a rare open meadow. He passed a couple of driveways that he assumed led to houses tucked back in the woods, a tidy log restaurant and bait shop—with an eye-roll-inducing marquee sign inviting travelers to "Eat here and get worms"—a small country church, a very rural fire department, a marina, and Albert's Guide Service.

He wondered if that Albert was related to Jess's husband. The nav system dinged softly then, followed by the dulcet tones of a computerized woman's voice. "Turn right onto Gamma Road in two-tenths of a mile."

He drew a deep breath and flipped on his turn signal, although this deep into the forest, there wasn't another vehicle in his line of sight.

"Turn right."

Turn right toward what might be a new chapter in your life . . .

It was time.

Chapter

4

*L*iving on Lake Kabetogama was like living in a fishbowl. There were no secrets. Kabby was a small, tightly knit community of shopkeepers, innkeepers, carpenters, and loggers mixed in with the summer residents and a steady rotation of tourists, many of whom were repeat resort customers summer after summer. Everyone looked out for everyone else—to excess sometimes—and word of a change in the norm moved faster than Kayla's fingers across the keypad on her iPhone.

There were several restaurants on the lake within ten miles of the store where they could go for dinner but nowhere close where Jess wouldn't run into someone she knew—from the owners to the waitresses to the regulars. So when Ty picked her up promptly at six and asked where she'd like to eat, she hadn't hesitated.

"Would you mind terribly making the twenty-minute trip back to the Falls?" Since International Falls had the only airport within eighty miles, she'd figured he'd rented his Jeep there. "We can swing over to Rainey Lake. There's a pretty good restaurant right on the water." In this land of ten thousand lakes, there was always a restaurant on another lake within driving distance.

"And a pretty good chance no one will find out you're on a dinner date?"

He got points for being intuitive. "It would be nice to think so, but that ship has already sailed, I'm afraid."

"Kayla?"

She smiled. "The girl has a network that would make Ma Bell green with envy."

"Am I causing trouble for you?"

Oh, she'd have to contend with dozens of "drop-ins" within a day or so, people stopping by the store on the pretense of needing a loaf of bread or a case of soda or any number of excuses, but in truth, they'd all be angling for information. Nothing she couldn't deflect.

J.R.'s brother, Brad, however, would be a different story. Brad had been wonderful since J.R. died. Helpful, supportive, and kind. But she knew exactly what his reaction would be when he heard about Tyler Brown. He'd be resentful. Angry, even. He'd loved his brother. He cared about her, but he would consider her interest in any man a betrayal—even after three years. More than once, she'd heard him say, "Mallards mate for life. If the drake dies, the hen never pairs up again." Brad believed the adage applied to human marriage, too.

"No trouble," she lied, and put Brad out of her mind. She'd deal with him when the time came . . . which, if Kayla's grapevine was humming, would probably be sometime tomorrow morning.

Tonight was about what happened tonight. Now that she had acclimated herself to the truth—Tyler Brown had come a long way to see her—there were things she wanted to set straight both in her mind and in his. Starting with the dressing down she'd given herself as she'd showered and gotten ready. Having dinner and polite conversation with this man was fine. But she was a pragmatic person. She knew that was as far as it was ever going to go—dinner and conversation—regardless of what he might be thinking. Regardless of how flattering it was. Once he thought about it, he'd realize it, too.

She'd reaffirmed that as they made the drive, and now, with her head on straight, she looked across their table near the window with Rainy Lake shimmering in a wide, glistening swath across the northland, glad she'd picked this place. Even though many people she knew frequented the Thunderbird restaurant, they usually reserved their dinners there for the weekends or during the off season. So she figured they had about a ninety-percent shot at anonymity on a Wednesday evening at the height of the tourist season.

"You look very pretty," Ty said, breaking into her thoughts.

She didn't know about pretty, but she did know it pleased her a little too much that he'd said she was. She'd turned up a soft white cotton knit top with a deep U neckline and little capped sleeves that was almost new and fit her like a glove, then tucked the shirt into a summer print skirt she'd bought for one of the Bradley boys' weddings two summers ago. The skirt hit her mid-thigh, and between it and a pair of woven sandals with wedge heels, her legs looked long and toned.

She hadn't given a thought to removing the wedding ring that felt like it had always been a part of her. In fact, it felt like a protective barrier of sorts tonight. A reminder of many things. She'd seen Ty's gaze stray to her left hand when she'd gotten into the Jeep, wondered what he'd been thinking and embarrassed by her hands, which were work rough, with short, no nonsense nails. Nothing she could do about that, but she'd been glad for Kayla's jasmine and musk lotion. It had taken a couple of applications to smooth out her hands and moisturize her arms and legs to a dew-soft glow.

There wasn't a lot she could do with her hair, but for once, the curls fell softly around her face and were actually kind of flattering. Or maybe it was the eyeliner she'd lightly smudged on her lids and the bit of blush she'd brushed on her cheeks. It had been so long since she'd made herself up and dressed for a man—even though it was not *that* kind of a date—and she actually felt a little foolish for making the effort tonight.

It hadn't stopped her, though. She'd traded her standby gold studs for a pair of dangly copper earrings sculpted into the shape of feathers. Her necklace matched. The local artisan who had made the set had called the necklace a cleavage piece, and as Jess felt it warm against her skin, she felt a tiny stirring of arousal that self-consciousness quickly undercut.

Maybe she shouldn't have worn it, because not only had she noticed Ty's gaze on her left hand, but once or twice, it had also drifted to the feather between her breasts before he'd quickly looked away again.

And whoa, he was watching her face now, she realized, about the same time that she realized she'd been so busy second-guessing the effort she'd taken to look nice that she hadn't responded to his compliment.

She met his eyes across the table and blurted out the first thing that came to mind. "You look pretty, too."

"Thanks. I think."

They both smiled at that, and she worked hard at stalling a blush. His dark hair wasn't overly long, but the tips had been wet when he'd arrived, which had conjured an immediate and vivid picture of him naked under a steamy spray—along with a jarring olfactory memory of how wonderful a man smelled fresh from a shower.

She'd be lying if she said she didn't think about and miss sex. And yes, nights when the bed felt so empty and she ached with loneliness, she'd call on a memory or a fantasy and make the occasional solo flight, and oh, boy, she needed to steer clear of that arena right now.

Except that the man watching her with compelling and inquisitive eyes made that next to impossible. He really did look pretty. She'd told him to dress casual—everything in the summer in northern Minnesota was casual—and he'd taken her at her word. He'd traded his white T-shirt, jeans, and deck shoes for a soft butter-yellow T-shirt, olive-drab cargo shorts, and brown leather sandals. When he'd pulled up, he'd been wearing aviator shades that hid his eyes—eyes that had latched on to her from behind those dark glasses for several long, humming seconds that started up that muscle clenching she didn't seem to have much control over when he was around.

He was tan and buff and self-assured, and if that wasn't enough, every time he smiled, something inside her melted a little bit more and reminded her, again, that while Bear had taken away some of the sting of being alone, a snuggly puppy was no substitute for a man.

However, a man like Ty—so much like J.R.—was fine for dinner and conversation, but beyond that, he was way too risky.

He'd ordered a bottle of red wine, and she reached for her glass. "I meant to ask earlier. How are your friends? And your brother? Mike, right?"

A smile came over his face that conveyed how much he loved his brother. "Joe and Stephanie are fine. And Mike—well, Mike is Mike. There's not a lot more to say . . . except that he's living in the States again, so I get to see him a little more often."

"What is it that he does, exactly?"

Another fond smile. "Let's leave it at Mike has one of those jobs where if I told you what he does, he'd have to kill *me*."

"You two don't work together?"

"As a rule? No."

She didn't miss the implication. All Mike had to do was call, and no matter what he needed, Ty would be there. Yup. Way too risky. Been there, done that. Had the condolences of the U.S. military to prove it.

Time for a new topic. "Did Shelley get you settled at the resort?"

He lifted his wine, too, and something about the way his strong, lean fingers wrapped around the delicate stem of the glass captivated her.

"She did. Nice lady. Very nice resort."

"Shelley and Darrin—her husband—run a tidy ship." The Whispering Pines boasted twelve rustic log cabins with varying numbers of bedrooms, all charmingly furnished with an eclectic mix of new and antique furniture and art that Shelley had collected locally over the years, and all with gorgeous lake views.

"Been a long time since I breathed deep and all I smelled was pine. Makes me think of home."

She stopped with the wine almost to her lips. "Florida's not home?"

"It is now, yeah. Key West. But I grew up in Colorado. Very rural. Our log house was a lot like the main lodge at the resort. Huge native stone fireplace, open beams, big wraparound porch."

The wistfulness in his voice and the soft smile on his lips told her that home for him was a very fond memory. "You miss it."

He shrugged. "Like I said. Been a long time since I've smelled air this fresh. Substitute horses for motorboats, and I'm almost back there."

"Are your parents still there?"

"Yeah. Saw them last month. They're doing great."

"So why Key West?"

He settled back in his chair, looking very male and very comfortable with himself. "That's where my business is. Air cargo."

It had taken several months for the full story to emerge about the events of the night Ty and his brother and Joe and Stephanie Green had rescued Stephanie's parents—her mother was now secretary of state—from would-be assassins. "We can't comment for reasons of national security," had been the answer most given when reporters had knocked on doors attempting to ferret out the facts. But a local reporter had been dogged about digging up all the details he could. Airport personnel had confirmed that Mike Brown had indeed successfully landed a small private jet at the International Falls airport in the midst of a blizzard and that Ty had been his copilot.

"You were military." She'd known the first time she'd met him that he was or had been in the service. All it had taken was a look. J.R. had been Special Forces. All those guys had a look about them. Edgy, intense, focused.

"Right. Navy."

"Navy what?" Every man in uniform was a special man, but again, she had recognized him from the beginning as something more.

He looked out over the lake, then back at her. "HSC-23. Wildcards."

She shook her head. "Sorry. I'm not familiar."

"Air ambulance. We choppered casualties in and out of combat zones in southern and western Iraq to supplement the Army's Dustoff operations."

Because she'd been married to a Green Beret, she was semiliterate in spec-ops speak, but this was a new term for her. "Dustoff?"

"A credo attributed to a guy named Kelly—Major Charles L. Kelly. Back in the Vietnam era." He stopped. Shook his head. "But you don't want to hear this."

"Actually, I do. Tell me about Kelly and Dustoff."

He shrugged. "Kelly—Combat Kelly—was commander of the 57th Medical Detachment, helicopter ambulance. He was some kind of man. 'Dustoff' was his call sign. When there were wounded, in came Kelly, no matter what. July sixty-four, Vietnam, he approached a hot area to pick up wounded, as usual, and started taking fire. The red cross on the bird's fuselage made a nice bull's-eye," he added, with the insight of one who knows and has been under fire himself.

"Anyway, ground support called him off over and over, but he didn't listen. 'When I have your wounded,' he told them. Not long after, he was killed by a single bullet."

Ty became quiet and reflective for a moment. "Anyway, Kelly's gone, but 'Dustoff' became the call sign for all aero-medical missions in Vietnam. And since then, 'When I have your wounded' has become the personal and collective credo of all Dustoff pilots who followed him."

While he'd said very little about himself directly, he'd revealed a lot. J.R. used to tell her about the bravery of the medical-evac crews. Because the Army and Navy air ambulance birds have a red cross painted on their sides, the Geneva Convention rules don't allow them to arm themselves with machine guns or mini-guns. Pilots like Kelly and Ty flew into hot zones with nothing but personal weapons—M-4 rifles and handguns—for protection against RPGs and small-arms fire. This practice was supposed to ensure humanitarian treatment of wounded during war, making aircraft, ships, corpsmen, trucks, facilities, and anything else displaying red crosses off-limits to enemy fire. Big surprise, the Taliban and Al-Qaeda—like the Vietcong in Kelly's era—were not signatories to the Geneva Convention, so they use the red crosses as targets.

"My husband held the medical crews in very high regard. He said what you did was the equivalent to tap dancing blindfolded into a minefield."

Another throwaway lift of a shoulder. "Everybody's got a job to do."

He looked at her then. "Your husband . . ."

"J.R.," she supplied when he hesitated. "Army. Special Forces."

She toyed with her wineglass. Another change of subject seemed in order. "So . . . you weren't a career man?"

A slow shake of his head. "Wanted to be." Another shrug. "Didn't work out."

The statement begged for a follow-up, but the distant look in his eyes told her it might be best not to go there. That maybe it was a confidence he didn't want to share and she didn't need to hear. Not on a date that was not a date.

Clearly, though, his military career had been cut short. She wondered if he'd been injured in some way—couldn't tell by looking, although now that she thought about it, she had detected a slight limp when he'd first gotten out of the Jeep. She'd chalked it up to a long plane ride in one of the cramped commuter jets that routinely flew in and out of the small airport in the Falls.

"So enough about me," he said with a quick smile. "Why a general store in the middle of Nowhere, Minnesota?"

It was her turn to shrug. "I grew up here. Kabby, Lake Kabetogama," she clarified, "it's home. Crossroads was my mom and dad's store. When they retired in Arizona a few years ago, it seemed like taking it over was the right thing to do at the right time."

"Before that, what did you do?"

"I was an ER nurse. Last place I worked was Womack, the Army Medical Center near Fort Bragg—it was the last place we were stationed."

He looked impressed, and she tried not to let it please her. "You miss it?"

"Nursing? No. At least, not yet."

"Burn out?"

"Some, yeah," she admitted. "But it was more than that. After J.R. died . . . I guess I needed to come home, you know?"

She could see in his eyes that he did know.

"Anyway, on any given day, I end up treating anything from sunburn to sunstroke to removing fish hooks embedded in . . . well, you can imagine some of the places those things get stuck. So I still keep my fingers in the pie, so to speak."

"Sort of a local Dr. Quinn, Medicine Woman?"

She grinned. "Closest doctor is twenty, twenty-five minutes from the lake. Everyone knows I'm a nurse. So I'm going to turn them away?"

"No, I don't imagine you would. You didn't turn me away."

Not that winter night. Not today. She didn't regret what she'd done that night. She hoped she wouldn't regret not sending him on his way today.

The waitress had brought their salads several minutes ago, and they'd both been halfheartedly working on them when he finally posed the question about something she'd been too chicken to ask.

"Why haven't you asked me what took me so long to come back?"

She looked across the table—and saw in his eyes that the small talk was over.

Chapter

5

Ty watched Jess carefully as she set her half-eaten salad aside to make room for the steak he'd convinced her she needed to order. After several long moments, she finally answered his question.

"I didn't figure I needed to ask."

That's not what her eyes said. "You weren't surprised when you didn't hear from me?"

She picked up her steak knife and fork, let them hover over her plate, then set them down again. "A little bit, maybe. Until I got to thinking about it. I mean, seriously. Things were a little intense that night. It was difficult to get a true read on anything but the danger. Besides . . . I live here. You live half a continent away. We lead very different lives. So a little time, a little distance, a lot of perspective, and you coming back didn't look like such a good bet on paper. I chalked it up to a passing chance encounter. Hardly something to—"

He covered her hand with his and stopped her with a soft chuckle. "OK. I got it. Good points. All taken. You can stop rationalizing now."

And protesting. Too much, maybe, judging by the sudden flush on her cheeks. He couldn't remember the last time he'd seen a woman blush. He found it endearing and pretty and sexy as hell. Reluctantly, he pulled his hand away.

"You weren't even a little bit disappointed?" It was a shameless fishing expedition, but he didn't feel guilty about it. He'd thought he'd get a smile out of her. Maybe an admission.

He got far from it when those big brown eyes met his. "Look, Ty. The fact that you came back . . . asking me to dinner . . . it's all very nice. But nothing's changed. We both know nothing's going to come of it. And wow, didn't that sound presumptive and sadly hopeful?"

"Whoa. Wait. Presumptive? Hello . . . I'm here. I think it's safe to *presume* I came back for a reason. And when has *hopeful* ever been sad?"

Her eyes grew a little wide, a little wet. "When representatives from the Army show up at your door to inform you that your husband was killed in action, and you sadly and futilely hope there's been a horrible, horrible mistake."

She looked mortified, suddenly, by what had come out of her mouth. And there wasn't even a touch of color in her cheeks now. Her face had gone deathly pale.

"Excuse me." She shot out of her chair. "I need to use the ladies' room."

He stood, thought about going after her, but in the end let her go. It wasn't as if he could follow her in there. And it wasn't as if he knew what to say if he did.

She needed a minute to collect herself. For that matter, so did he.

Maybe this was a bad idea after all. By his calculation, it had been three and a half years since her husband was killed. Should her wounds still be this raw? Or was there something wrong with him that he was ready to move on so soon after losing Maya?

He'd poured more wine and contemplated downing the whole glass when she came back to the table, composed and apologetic.

"Sorry I went all weepy widow on you there. I don't know where that came from. I don't usually—"

"I know you don't," he interrupted, because he felt both relieved and sensitive to her embarrassment. "You hold up. And you didn't do anything wrong."

He was the one in the wrong. He should have realized he made her nervous. After all, the last time he'd seen her, he'd used her dead husband's gun to kill a man.

✳

JESS FELT BEYOND grateful that Ty had the sensitivity to let things go. At that point, she somehow marshaled the wherewithal to shift into "Board of Tourism" mode and change the subject to a lengthy and oh so educational and oh so *boring* history of the area and the chain of lakes. She told him all about the Boise Cascade plant that was the region's biggest employer and about the intriguing NOvA project, the world's most advanced neutrino experiment, which, if successful, would have profound implications for understanding the structure and evolution of the universe. She talked about anything to keep from talking about something that might lead back to a personal dialogue about her life in general and her husband in particular.

She was a coward. She knew it. Ty, apparently, accepted it and made every effort to keep her engaged in generalities. Somehow, they made it through a dinner that felt as endless as the ink-black sky that greeted them when they finally left the restaurant to drive the twenty miles back to Kabby.

She didn't even remember what she'd babbled about on the half-hour drive; she only knew that she had babbled, and by the time they pulled into the Crossroads parking lot, she felt one-hundred-percent certain that one Tyler Brown would be on the phone first thing in the morning booking a return flight home, as relieved as a caught-and-released walleye to be getting away from the crazy, gibberish-talking widow he'd had the bad sense to think he wanted to get to know.

She was an uptight, nervous flake who hadn't even realized until he had shown up and shaken her insulated little world that she still felt so raw and ruled by her feelings about J.R. and his death. She should have moved on by now—or at least be working on it. She hadn't. She wasn't. And regardless of the fact that she would not let herself even think about moving on with a man so much like her dead husband, Ty's ability to shake things up this way proved how badly she needed to get on with the business of living.

Since embarrassment didn't even scratch the surface of how she felt about her behavior, he'd barely rolled to a stop when she shoved open the passenger-side door. The overhead lamp wasn't harsh, but she felt ten times more exposed for the coward she was when light flooded the front seat.

"Thanks for dinner. I'm sure you're tired. Long flight and all that. Good night."

"Jess."

His soft voice stopped her from jumping out of the Jeep.

"Wait. For God's sake, wait a second."

He sounded frustrated yet infinitely concerned.

"Shut the door, OK? The bugs are getting in."

Although Kayla had closed up and left only a security light on inside the store, a light burned over the giant walleye figure on one side of the road, and the lights from the fuel island burned on the other. The vapor bulbs drew mosquitoes the way the North Pole drew snow.

She shut the door. Folded her hands on her lap and stared straight ahead.

"Do I really scare you that much?" he asked, so softly and with so much disquiet that she felt ashamed of her spinelessness. Ashamed enough to admit it.

"Yes," she confessed, still not looking at him. "Yes, you do."

"How can I make that go away?"

She pushed out a harsh laugh. "You can't."

✱

TY STARED AT the profile of this woman whom he absolutely could not figure out. Then a belated thought hit him hard and low. "Oh, man. Are you involved with someone?"

"No," she said quickly. "No. I'm not involved with anyone."

Only curiosity outdistanced his relief. "No one since your husband?"

She slowly shook her head.

What? Were the men around here blind or just plain stupid? Or were they maybe not as persistent as they needed to be? This was a woman who clearly knew how to redirect the attention from herself and avoid talking about anything remotely personal. Core-deep, her involuntary reflex was to deflect. But you bottle things up long enough, and eventually, the cork is going to pop. Like at dinner, when her emotions got the best of her.

"Don't you think maybe it's time you changed that?" he asked gently.

"That's the problem," she said to her hands. "I don't know what I think. Until you showed up this afternoon, I didn't have to think."

Her low groan made it clear that she'd realized something about herself. They were making headway. "Ah. So it's not me. It's the idea of change."

She closed her eyes and let her head fall back against the headrest. "So it would seem."

"Well, that's something I *can* do something about."

She rolled her head to look at him. "What can you do that I haven't been able to do in three and a half years?"

Because she looked so lost and defeated, he lifted a hand, let the back of his fingers brush along the ridge of her cheekbone. He told himself the touch was for her. To steady her. But the truth was, he'd been wanting to touch this woman since the first time he'd seen her. "I can give you a reason and enough time to get used to the idea."

She shook her head and sent the copper feathers at her ears trembling. "Right now, it doesn't feel like there's enough time in the world."

"But we both know different, right? How does the Bible verse go? To everything there is a season? A time to weep and a time to laugh, a time to mourn and a time to dance. Maybe it's your time to dance."

She glanced at him, confusion creasing her brows. "I don't get you."

"You're not supposed to. It's part of my charm."

Before she could check herself, she smiled. "Seriously? You want to stick around after that dog-and-pony show I subjected you to tonight?"

"What? I found the history of the Smokey Bear statue in the middle of the city center riveting."

A weak laugh tempered another groan.

"Hey. You were nervous. My mom is a nervous talker. I get it. And my brother, Mike? Get him in a dicey situation, and he literally can't keep his mouth shut. It's a defense mechanism. Me, I get quiet. Makes me think we might work well together. Yin/yang? Black/white? Day/night?"

She shook her head again. "I'm a mess. And I didn't even know it until you showed up. You should be running in the opposite direction. Why aren't you?"

"Because if I go back that way? I'm going to end up just like you."

She shifted in the seat, then searched his eyes. "What are you talking about?"

He looked down at her hands. Then back at her face. "One more time. Ask me why I didn't come back until now."

Several tense, lengthy seconds passed before her curiosity won out over reluctance. "OK. Why didn't you come back until now?"

"Because shortly after I went back to Florida . . . I lost someone, too."

Chapter

6

It's been a long time since I've been out on the lake." Jess dug deep with her paddle early the next morning as she glided alongside Ty's matching kayak. The surface of the water glistened, glass-smooth and reflecting a cerulean-blue sky dotted with bridal-white clouds. "You grow up around something—even something as beautiful and unblemished as Lake Kabetogama—and you take it for granted. I've really missed being out on the water."

Last night, as she'd sat in the Jeep with Ty and realized they had much more in common than she'd ever thought, she hadn't been capable of telling him no when he'd asked her to spend the day with him.

"Get Kayla to cover for you again," he'd said, pressing his advantage. "Spend tomorrow with me. I'll tell you about Maya. And you can tell me about J.R."

Chalk it up to nerves or the fact that she'd been prepared for him to tell her just about anything . . . anything except that he'd lost someone, too. Or maybe it was the momentary flash of pain she'd seen in his eyes, a pain she'd seen in her own eyes too many times over the past few years when she'd caught sight of her reflection in a mirror.

Whatever the excuse, she'd said yes. So today, Kayla and two of her high school part-timers were minding the store, and Jess was doing something she hadn't done in years with a man who, in turns, made her nervous and comfortable and excited and hopeful.

The hopeful part of the equation worried her most, because one thing would never change. She would not get involved with a warrior again. It didn't matter that he was retired. What mattered was the mentality, the reckless disregard for their own safety, the unalterable alpha gene embedded in their DNA. The right cause, the right call, and he'd be gone. He'd be in danger. And he could end up dead.

In any event, kayaking—in separate kayaks— seemed like a pretty safe bet. The weather forecast had sealed the deal. The temp would climb into the low eighties by noon, but this morning, it was a cool, breezeless sixty-five, the air so crisp and clean it almost burned her lungs with its purity.

She'd advised Ty to dress in layers, so they both wore long-sleeved shirts and pants. By noon, when she planned to break for a shore lunch, they'd be ready to strip down to shorts. A swim might even be in order. Something else she missed doing.

"It's rare to see inland water this clear." Ty kept an easy pace beside her, expertly handling his paddle.

"Kabby's a glacial lake. The lake bed's as rocky as the shore unless you get into one of the backwater bays, and then you'll run into some sand and mud flats."

Kayaking had always been one of her favorite pastimes. With twenty-five thousand acres of water, almost eighty miles of shoreline, and two hundred islands, there were limitless places to explore.

They'd borrowed a pair of Shelley and Darrin's kayaks and left shortly after first light, with an intrigued and smiling Shelley waving good-bye from the dock. Her friend hadn't asked any questions, but Jess knew the day of reckoning would soon be upon her. One thing had been very clear: Shelley approved.

In any event, that had been about two hours ago, and they'd paddled steadily and crossed a major stretch of open water. In retrospect, Jess realized that part of the reason she'd agreed to take Ty out on the lake first thing in the morning was that she wanted to avoid the confrontation with J.R.'s brother, Brad, which was certain to be unpleasant. But that had only been part of the reason. Truth was, she wanted to hear the rest of his story.

Spend tomorrow with me. I'll tell you about Maya. And you can tell me about J.R.

"Do we have a destination?" Ty's question brought her back to the here-and-now.

The way he asked made her smile. "What's the matter? You getting tired already?"

She knew otherwise. With upper-body and arm definition like his, he could paddle all day and not wear out. Besides, zero wind and calm water made their trip practically effortless.

"Just getting curious about your plan. We've passed some interesting islands. Makes me want to get out and explore. I'm thinking Native American artifacts galore. Ojibwe, right?"

"Somebody's been doing some reading."

"Blame it on your friends. The cabin is full of reading material on local history. I even learned some things that you didn't tell me about at dinner last night."

She laughed at his good-natured teasing. "Yeah, well, that was the free lecture. You want more details, you're going to have to pay for them."

"Fair enough."

He was very easy to be around, this man. Easy to smile for. Easy to talk to. Easy to look at. And she had been looking. He had a nice stroke, competent and capable, and he knew how to handle himself around the water. No doubt, he knew how to handle himself in any number of situations.

While safety laws required that they wear life jackets, a thought did occur to her. "You do swim, right?"

"Am I going to have to?"

"It's not in the plan, no. But the weather can be unpredictable. I've been out on the lake before when a squall came up and we had to race for cover."

"I can swim," he assured her.

"Good. Because it's about forty-five feet deep right below us."

They'd passed Picnic, Ram and Sheep Islands in the first hour, paddled on past Harris, and were about to round the wide end of Sugarbush when Jess balanced her paddle over her lap and motioned for Ty to do the same. She reached into the dry storage hole, pulled out her dry bag and the pair of binoculars she'd packed along with lunch and a first-aid kit she never went anywhere without.

After a quick check to confirm what she saw, she motioned Ty closer. When their kayaks gently bumped, she handed him the glasses.

"Two o'clock. Off the tip of that jutting stretch of shore." She held the kayaks together as he lifted the glasses. "Past the white rock. In the water heading toward shore."

He focused, searched, and grinned. "Bear."

"Yup. A sow and twin cubs. They're swimming right behind her."

"Wow," he said, still grinning. "That is amazing."

"Blueberries are getting ripe, so they swim from island to island filling their bellies."

"Are they a threat?"

"Black bears? Not so much. Not unless you corner them or get between a momma and her cubs, which we definitely are not going to do."

He handed her back the glasses, and she took her turn watching the bears, even though they were close enough now that they could see them without the help of the magnification.

They watched until the lumbering trio disappeared into the island's thick undergrowth. Tyler took a pull on his water bottle while she packed the glasses away.

"And that just made my day complete." He pointed overhead.

A full-grown bald eagle bore down on them, its wingspan at least seven feet, talons extended.

"He's fishing," Jess said, and right then, the eagle swooped down to the water's surface about ten yards ahead of them, reached deep, and came up clutching a wriggling fish.

"Man, oh, man. That is so freaking cool!" Ty exclaimed on a laugh.

She agreed. It was cool. So was he. She liked it that he didn't try to hide his excitement. And she found herself taken again by how easy he was about everything.

"So you're a nature boy."

"Unapologetically."

"How is it, then, that you ended up in Florida?"

"Ever been to Key West?"

"Nope. North Carolina is as far south as I ever

got." She'd lived on a few military posts as an Army wife. Most of the time, it was she and the other wives holding down the fort while the men were deployed.

"There's more wildlife in Key West than you'd think. Especially at night." He grinned. "Truth is, while I like it there—crazy tourists, cruise ships, Keysie ways, and all—it's not the area I'd have chosen to set up shop. But I didn't pick it. It picked me."

"How so?"

"You really want to hear this?"

"I do."

They'd increased their stride again and were easily moving toward Nashata Point and Stalinsky Bay. The promised conversation about J.R. and Maya hadn't begun yet, but they had the rest of the day. Frankly, she felt fine talking about anything else except J.R., although she couldn't help but be curious about Ty's story.

"When I separated from the Navy, I was at loose ends for a while. Really didn't know what I wanted to do. I had some time on my hands and knew one of my old commanders had retired in Key West. And when I say old, that's a relative term. He was fifty. He'd always told me to come and see him when I got out. So I did. Turns out he'd started an air charter business a few years back, then expanded to air cargo."

A pair of loons surfaced ten yards to their left and, apparently not bothered by their presence, cruised around for several seconds before diving again.

"As it also turned out, he was looking for a pilot. He wanted to expand his fleet and his routes. Asked me to join him. So I did."

"How long ago was that?"

"Almost five years now. Three years ago, though, he got a wild hair and decided he wanted to pack it in and retire—for real this time—in Tahiti. He offered me a sweet deal on the business, so I bought him out, and that's how I ended up in Key West."

"It sounds exotic. Jimmy Buffett. Margaritaville. Surf. Sand. Sun."

"Humidity, hurricanes, spring break, and a nightmare of federal regulations that make my teeth ache. Don't get me wrong. I'm grateful. And business is good. But being here . . . well . . ."

He paused, and his silence compelled her to look at him.

"Being here is special," he said, with a smile that was far more intimate than a conversation about Minnesota should be. "And not only because of the wildlife and the scenery."

"There's a little beach where we can put in on the north shore," she said, knowing she was blushing again and hoping he'd think the exertion and the sun were at fault. "I thought we'd stop there and have lunch before heading back."

"Show me."

She pointed to an inlet about a hundred yards away.

He smiled that "I've got your number" smile again, and she felt that roller-coaster rush she experienced far too often since he'd shown up in her store yesterday afternoon.

"Race ya."

It should have come as no surprise that he'd be competitive. "You'll lose," she promised, and, glad for the diversion, she dug deep with her paddle.

Behind her, he laughed. "Who said go?"

"Already looking for excuses?" she yelled over her shoulder.

"No, ma'am."

She could hear his paddle rhythmically break water as he raced after her.

"Just so we both agree: winner gets to pick a prize."

"Fine. And loser gets to start the fire and roast the hot dogs." She didn't look back. She focused on the shore and gave it everything she had. "Hope you were a Boy Scout."

Another laugh. "Hope you're a good loser."

✱

TY WATCHED JESS'S very tidy backside as she bent over the round iron fire ring and lit a match to kindling. "You can tell a lot about a person by the way they handle a good trouncing."

"That was not a trouncing. You beat me by a nose."

"A win's a win." He smiled, knowing he shouldn't be enjoying this so much. The lady was a contender.

He liked it. But winning the race had cost him. He'd had to dig really deep, tested some muscles he hadn't tested for a while, and he could feel it in his lower back now. Not the smartest thing he'd ever done. Not that he planned to let her see he was in pain. "I could have let you win, but then you wouldn't have respected me."

She snorted and gave him an indignant look, but he could tell she enjoyed their little back-and-forth. "Should have warned me that you were a gloater."

"One of many things you don't know about me. Yet."

Yeah, that's right, he thought as she got real busy with the fire. *Get used to it. You're going to get to know me. And you* are *going to talk to me.*

Feeling pretty smug, he lay back on the blanket she'd produced from the dry hole in her kayak along with a soft-sided cooler filled with fresh grapes, hot dogs, all the fixings, and two cans of soda.

The woman was nothing if not resourceful. But then, he'd already known that. She'd brought kindling and newspaper and matches, the Park Service had provided the fire ring, and together they'd gathered enough deadfall wood to get a nice fire going.

"I like my dogs nicely browned, not burned, by the way."

"You'll like 'em the way I fix 'em." She straightened and dusted her hands together, then shot him a look that made him laugh.

"Yes, ma'am. I believe I will."

She sat down on the blanket beside him while they waited for the fire to get good and hot. They'd both worked up a bit of a sweat during the race. She'd stripped down to a tank top and shorts, and he'd tossed his long-sleeved shirt and pants aside in favor of the T-shirt and shorts he'd worn beneath them.

The day was postcard-perfect. As she'd promised, it had warmed up; the sun burned bright, and a gentle breeze stirred up and swept a little ripple on the water. What had once been a mirror of glass was now a softly crinkled surface sparkling like multifaceted diamonds.

"So what happened to your back?" she asked, breaking into his thoughts with the equivalent of a sledgehammer.

He wasn't ready to go there yet. "What makes you think something's wrong with my back?"

She pulled her knees to her chest and hugged them. "I'm a nurse, remember? I noticed the limp last night. And yes, you hide it well. You didn't do yourself any favors playing king of the kayaks, though, did you?"

He didn't want to talk about his back. Was angry that he'd given himself away. He looked back out at the lake. In the very far distance, a fishing boat skimmed across the water, leaving a white rooster tail in its wake. It was only the third boat he'd spotted since they'd left this morning.

"I also saw the scars," she said quietly. "Your T-shirt rode up when you shucked your other shirt. I recognize surgical scars when I see them. Is that what ended your military career?"

He set his jaw and wrestled with the idea of telling her.

"Sorry," she said, saving him from sharing the gory details. "I didn't mean to pry. I just want to make sure you're OK."

"I'm fine." And basically, he was. Now. Bottom line, though, if he expected her to open up, he'd have to do the same. "I'll tell you what. Since this whole outdoor adventure is about getting to know each other, and we're both reluctant to talk about certain aspects of our lives, let's do rock, paper, scissors to decide who gives up a secret first."

"Rock, paper, scissors? Seriously? I haven't played that since I was a kid."

He smiled. "My brother, Mike? That game was his way of solving everything. Come on. Live dangerously. Winner gets to ask a question. Loser has to tell."

"You're big into competition, I see."

Another engaging grin. "Go big or go home."

Chapter

7

*J*ess didn't give him an answer right away. Instead, she got up, stirred the fire, pronounced
it ready, and loaded a stick that he'd sharpened with
hot dogs.

He let her have time to think. She liked that about
him. OK. What didn't she like about him? Telling herself that no matter that her gut told her this was a good
guy, the truth was she didn't know enough about him
to answer that question.

So they talked about the lake, about the Park
Service—she was oh so good at the tour-guide
shtick—and then, with their stomachs full and the
sun warm, they both lay back on the blanket with a
comfortable distance between them and indulged in
the summer day.

"Where are all the mosquitoes Minnesota is so famous for?"

"They don't like the sun. Walk ten yards into the woods, though, and you'll find them—or they'll find you."

He seemed content to be lazy for a while. She liked that about him, too. J.R. had always been a neutron-charged mass of energy. He couldn't sit or stand still. Ty, apparently, had an off switch . . . or at least, a low setting.

She wasn't altogether sure, but he actually seemed to have fallen asleep. He'd thrown a forearm over his eyes and his other arm above his head. He had one knee cocked, and his breathing was deep and steady.

She could do with a nap herself. She hadn't exactly slept well last night. Truth was, she'd hardly slept at all.

I'll tell you about Maya. And you can tell me about J.R.

She kept replaying his words in her mind, too antsy to sleep. Being around him kept her on a mid-level adrenaline high. She was so aware of him. Of how his eyes softened when he watched her. How his smile came so quickly and how he could easily direct it at making fun of himself or teasing her. And this close beside him, she became hyperaware of the muscle and mass of him, the sweat and heat of him, the utter maleness that had been missing in her life for so long.

She rolled to her side and looked at him—the way she'd wanted to look at him for what seemed like a very long time. Only looking got her into more trouble, because there were so many physical complexities and perfections that it made her antsy in another way that had nothing to do with nerves and everything to do with chemistry.

She wanted him in her bed. There. She'd admitted it.

And that fact scared her as much as it excited her. And made her very, very warm, suddenly.

Careful not to wake him, she stood, then walked to the edge of the water. She'd worn her swimsuit beneath her clothes, so she stepped out of her shorts and tossed them and her top back onto the sand. Then she waded in slowly, biting her lower lip to keep from gasping as the cold water started to engulf her.

One thing about this lake. The air temp could be ninety degrees, but the water never got much above sixty. Swimming in Kabby was not for the faint of heart. Once fully submerged and with her body acclimated to the cold, though, it felt like heaven.

She was floating on her back and concentrating on not letting the water get into her nose when she realized she had company.

"Holy iceberg." Ty waded slowly toward her, shivering and briskly rubbing his arms. "Who added the ice cubes?"

She laughed and righted herself, treading water as

he waded deeper. "Just do it," she said. "Dunk. Much better to rip off a Band-Aid than pull it off slowly."

He looked doubtful, then took a deep breath and did a shallow dive in her general direction. He surfaced on a gasp.

She laughed again. "Not like the Gulf water in Key West, huh?"

He whipped the hair away from his face and sank up to his chin. "No. Not like the Gulf. You do this often?" he asked around chattering teeth.

"Used to. When I was a kid, we used to sit in an old-fashioned Finnish sauna for an hour or so, then burst outside and jump off the dock. Talk about a shock to the system."

And speaking of shocks to the system . . . the water was crystal-clear. She could see all the way to the bottom and every detail of the man standing in front of her. Which meant he could see every detail, too—and he was looking. Even though her black swimsuit was modestly cut, she felt self-conscious and exposed.

"I can see why you love it here."

"Summers are great. Winters are gorgeous but brutal."

"I remember winter."

She smiled. "It's not a climate for everyone."

"I miss snow," he said absently, and she could tell he was thinking of home again.

"Rock, paper, scissors, huh?" she asked, resigned and weary of stalling. She also wanted to know more about him suddenly, even though it meant she had to take a chance at giving up something of herself. She valued her privacy, but this wasn't about privacy. This was about trust.

He grinned and held up a fist.

She did the same. "One, two, three."

On three, she made a scissors. He made a rock.

"Rock breaks scissors," he said unnecessarily, and she steeled herself for his question. "Would you tell me about J.R.? How you met? How long you were married? What kind of guy he was?"

"That sounds like four questions."

"Only one, with some suggestions for fleshing things out."

She felt cold suddenly and headed back toward shore. She didn't have to look behind her to know he followed. Reaching into the cargo hold of his kayak, she tugged out another dry bag, unzipped it, and pulled out two towels.

She handed him one, wrapped the other one around her shoulders, and huddled beneath it as she sat down on the blanket.

"We were high school sweethearts," she said, taking the ripped-Band-Aid approach herself and spitting it out. "J.R. was the guy, you know? Captain of the basketball and football teams, cross-country skier. If it was physical, J.R. was in the mix. And he mastered whatever he decided to do."

"He sounds like quite a guy."

She nodded and used the towel to wipe her damp hair back from her face. "He was. It was like he was driven, you know? He didn't have the best home life. His mom left him and his dad and J.R.'s older brother, Brad, when J.R. was only five. His dad didn't make a lot of money—he worked in the Falls at Boise—and unfortunately, he drank up a lot of his paychecks. He walked out of a bar one night, got behind the wheel, and ran off the road into a power-line pole. The boys have been on their own ever since."

"That's rough."

"It was very rough. But Brad looked out for J.R. Taught him to hunt and fish and camp—in fact, Brad has his own fishing and hunting guide business here on Kab. You passed it on the road to Whispering Pines."

"How did J.R. end up in Special Forces?"

"His football coach, Mr. Latimer, became sort of a father figure for J.R. He was an Army vet who fought with Special Forces during the Vietnam War. He was also a storyteller. J.R. was enthralled by him. Ended up enlisting right out of high school instead of taking a full-ride football scholarship."

"Which broke your heart."

She crossed her arms over her up-drawn knees and laid her cheek on her forearm, then watched water droplets trickle off his hair and run down the broad expanse of his shoulders as the sun beat down and warmed them. "Yeah. Pretty much. But we kept in touch. I went on to U of M and got my nursing degree. We planned a wedding around his leave and got married in August, before nine-eleven. He shipped out to Saudi right before the Iraq invasion, ended up with a Bronze Star and a Purple Heart."

When he didn't say anything, she looked back out over the lake.

"I thought maybe he wouldn't reup after that. He was in the hospital for a couple of weeks and in rehab for three months. Didn't slow him down, though, and he'd found his niche. I tried to talk him out of it, but he applied for Airborne and then Ranger School—made both cuts with flying colors. I'd joined him at Bragg by then. Shortly after, he ended up back in Iraq."

"Those had to have been difficult times."

She ran the corner of the towel over her face. "Yeah. They were. But I was young and in love, and while I didn't like his decisions, I supported them. It wasn't like I hadn't known being an Army wife would be tough, but I hadn't been prepared for the loneliness and isolation. Or the fear. Always the fear that something would happen to him."

She sifted a handful of sand through her fingers and watched it fall back to the beach.

"I didn't even know he'd put in a request to apply for Special Forces. He'd been in training almost two years by the time I found out that he'd been fast-tracked through the system. He'd barely made it home from Iraq, and he was deployed to Afghanistan."

And never came home.

"I don't think anyone gives enough credence to how difficult it is for the wives and families," Ty said quietly. "The long deployments. And with spec ops, never knowing where they are, how they are. Anyway, I know it was hard on my folks when Mike was deployed to parts unknown."

"And you don't think they worried about you?"

"Of course, they worried, but he was in combat. I was—"

"Flying through fire with a target on your back."

He shrugged. "Like I said. Everyone had a job to do."

And his career had been cut short so he couldn't continue to do his. She had questions. She held up a fist. He gave her a crooked grin and did the same. She made scissors again. He made paper.

"Scissors cuts paper. My turn."

"OK, shoot."

She wanted to know about his back, but she had a bigger curiosity. "Will you tell me about Maya?"

Chapter

8

"*Maya was one of those people who kept showing up in my life, you know?*" Ty rolled to his side, propping his upper body on an elbow. "I met her in college, and we dated but drifted apart. I ran into her again when I was stationed in San Diego. We saw each other on and off but nothing serious. Again, we drifted. Then that winter? About a month after I met you? She showed up in Key West on vacation with a girlfriend. Had no idea I was there. And it was, I don't know. It was like we both stood back and took stock and realized we had so much in common—and then there was this fate thing, karma, kismet, whatever you want to call it, that kept putting us together."

He stopped. Swiped a hand over his jaw. "I don't want to minimize what she and I had, so please don't take this wrong. But it was kind of a right place, right time situation. She'd recently gotten out of a bad relationship. And frankly, you were on my mind. But the logistics—as you said—they didn't compute on paper. I was looking for a reason not to contact you. And there was Maya. My reason."

Another deep breath.

"That sounded horrible. It sounded as though I used her as a stopgap, and that is totally not the case. I loved her. I realized I'd probably always loved her to some degree. And she felt the same. So we decided to give it a try. And it was great. She was so . . . vital. Beautiful, intelligent. One of the most positive people I've ever known."

He missed her. He would probably always miss her, and thinking of her now made him realize how tragically unfair life was.

"What happened to her?"

"She had a brain bleed."

"Oh, my God. An aneurism?"

"Yeah. It was a shock. To say the least. She was the picture of health. Active. Took care of herself." He stopped, looked out over the water, still having trouble believing that a vital, beautiful woman had been there one day and was gone the next. "She woke up that morning with a headache. We'd only been together four months. She'd started a new job. I had a big charter that day. She told me to go. Assured me she would be fine. I got home that night and found her."

"Oh, Ty. I'm so sorry."

"Yeah. I'm sorry, too. She was an amazing woman. She died way too soon." He met her eyes and saw a world of compassion there. "They both did."

✳

THE WIND HAD picked up a bit and pushed against them all the way back to the resort, so it was close to eight that evening by the time they made their way back across the lake. Jess worried about Ty's back, but she didn't say anything, and he didn't, either. She felt both relief and an encroaching sense of loss when they finally reached the resort. Despite what had been a bit of a bloodletting for both of them when they'd opened up to each other about J.R. and Maya, she'd enjoyed the day. She'd enjoyed him.

Shelley greeted them with a smile and a wave when they beached the kayaks. "I'd started to think I might need to send out a search party."

"She gave me a workout," Ty said good-naturedly, as the bottom of his kayak skidded against the small, sandy beach. "Yet she tells me we only saw a small part of the lake."

"Big lake," Shelley agreed. "Where'd you go, Jess?"

Ty reached out and steadied her kayak when she stood. "Other side of Sugarbush—that little houseboat put in on the north shore."

"Yikes. You did give him a workout. Figured as much. And to that end, I thought you might be hungry.

Since you don't seem inclined to use that nice new fishing pole you bought, Mr. Brown, I thought you should at least get a taste of what you're missing. There's a platter of walleye keeping warm in your oven and a salad in the fridge. Hope you don't mind that I invaded your space."

"Are you kidding me?" Despite the wobbly kayak, he made his dismount look easy, although Jess noticed, again, that he had a little difficulty straightening up. "That sounds great. Thanks. And it's Ty."

"OK. Ty. As long as we're on a first-name basis, do me a favor. Don't let Jess leave without eating. I know her. She'll go back to that store, start working, and forget to fix any supper."

"Consider her fed. I won't let her out of my sight until she eats."

After helping Jess unload their gear, he dragged his kayak out of the water and flipped it upside down on the grass, then went back after Jess's.

"Why is everyone under the impression that I need a keeper?" Jess protested as she grabbed her dry bags.

"Not a keeper, sweetie."

Jess didn't miss the grin Shelley shared with Ty.

"Just a gentle reminder that you need to take better care of yourself."

Jess made a harrumphing sound, but when she met Shelley on the grass, she gave her a one-armed hug. "OK, *Mom*."

★

THE LAKE HAD shifted to a smoky blue platinum by the time they'd finished Shelley's delicious meal and half of the bottle of wine she'd left open and breathing on the table along with a bunch of wildflowers.

Shelley definitely had her matchmaking hat on tonight, Jess thought as she got up to clear the table.

"Leave it. I'll clean up later," Ty insisted, and re-filled their wineglasses. "Let's have one more glass and enjoy the sunset on the deck."

"I really should go," Jess said, but found she couldn't put much conviction behind it. "I need to relieve Kayla. Bear needs to go for a walk before it gets much later."

Because he looked thoroughly amused, she stopped. "What?"

"Only two excuses?"

He was right. She was digging, but the hole was already there, so she jumped into it. "I'm not making excuses. I feel like I'm neglecting my dog and my business."

"Because you took one day off? When was the last time you had some time off for yourself, by the way?"

"I take time off," she lied. "I don't want to take advantage of Kayla."

"Kayla is no one's fool. If she wasn't up for covering for you, she wouldn't have volunteered."

She set her shoulders and thought about another protest, but her heart wasn't in it. "One glass. Then I've got to go."

"See? That really wasn't so hard, was it?"

No. It hadn't been hard at all. In fact, it had been too easy. Like everything with him was easy. She should be wary of the way he eroded her defenses, but she simply couldn't marshal the will. Tomorrow. She would regroup tomorrow. Tonight she felt mellow and tired in the best possible way, and she selfishly wanted to indulge in it. So when he handed her the wine and then opened the door for her, she walked outside ahead of him.

Dusk had fallen softly over the lake. Lights glowed from cabin windows. The distant sound of laughter and the smells of a dozen different dinners mingled with the scent of pine and the soothing sound of water slapping gently against the shore.

He eased a hip onto the deck rail and looked out over the water. "Nirvana. A man could get used to this."

"Someday, I want a house right on the lake." She joined him at the rail and followed his gaze. "I've lived here most of my life but never directly on the water. Always above the store."

"I totally get why you'd want to be on the lake," Ty agreed, looking from his wine to her. "Colorado is beautiful, but this place gives it a run for its money. It's so pure and unpopulated. What I don't understand is where are all the people? The land development? The condos? Why doesn't everyone in the world know about this place?"

"I don't know, and I don't care. I want it to stay one of the best-kept secrets of all time."

"Even though more people means more revenue for you?"

"Even though. I get by. And I like Kabby the way it is."

"You'll get no argument from me. Thanks for showing me the lake today. I had a really great time."

"My pleasure." She sipped her wine, aware of him watching her. Aware that she felt too aware. Despite the warm summer night, a little shiver eddied through her, setting all of her erogenous zones tingling along with a few warning bells.

In the far distance on the north shore, the faint beam of a red signal light blinked on and off above the jagged, ink-black tree line. Someone had started a fire in the fire ring down by the shore, and a few people had gathered around. Their laughter blended with the mellow strumming of a guitar and the night sounds of lapping water and the hum of crickets and the steady breathing of the man standing beside her.

"We still have a bit of unfinished business to deal with, you know."

She knew exactly where this was going. Just as she knew that if she'd intended to stop him, she'd have been gone by now, instead of sharing the moonlight and the wine.

"Unfinished business?" Her voice sounded breathless, and oh, she hadn't wanted it to.

"The race? The bet?" He pushed off the rail and moved in closer.

"I cooked your darn hot dogs," she said, and made him smile.

"That was the loser's part of the bet. We never got to the winner's part. Loser made the fire and cooked. Winner got to pick a prize of their choice."

He'd moved in very close beside her now. She could feel the heat from his body. See his chest rise and fall beneath his shirt. Smell the lingering scent of sun and water and the sunscreen she'd insisted he wear.

"Ah . . . right. I forgot that part." That, too, was a lie. She figured she already knew what he wanted. Figured she'd probably let him take it.

"I didn't forget. Not for a second. I've been waiting for the right time to claim it."

She let him lift her wineglass out of her hand then and set it with his on the small table between the deck chairs. "I want to kiss you, Jess. I've wanted to kiss you since the first time I saw you."

He moved in to her then, wrapped his arms around her, and slowly pulled her close.

And she liked it. "You say the word, I back away. But I ask you to remember something." He smiled then, that oh-so-easy smile that made everything feel safe and right and so hot she thought she would self-combust. "You *did* agree to take the bet."

"That I did. I absolutely did."

When was it, she wondered as he pulled her closer, that she'd stopped reminding herself that she did not want to get involved with another warrior? When was it that wariness had transitioned to anticipation and yearning and obliterated her carefully thought-out arguments to keep a safe distance between them?

Honest truth? She didn't know, and in this moment, she didn't care. She wanted him to kiss her. She wanted it so badly she ached. And if he didn't "claim his prize" soon, she wasn't altogether certain that she wouldn't do some claiming of her own.

✳

TY FELT A slight give of muscle and resistance as some of the tension eased from her small body. He could feel her heat now. Feel both the anticipation and the indecision, and chose to believe the anticipation won out.

A bigger man might have given her more time to adjust to the idea. A bigger man would not have played the "You lost, I won, and to the victor go the spoils" card. He wasn't the bigger man. Not tonight. Tonight he was a man who held a beautiful and desirable woman in his arms. A woman who was skittish and uncertain but interested, and he'd be damned if he'd let her hesitation sway him.

When she turned her face up to his, he didn't hesitate. He lowered his head and drew her closer. Pressed his lips to hers.

And felt something close to magic.

Tentative. She was oh so tentative. He needed to remember that, and he needed to remember why. He needed to cater to her uncertainty as she got used to the fit of their lips, the melding of their bodies, the touch and heat and scent of his skin. It cost him. Holy God, it cost him, as he let her become accustomed to his mouth, to the warmth and the wetness, to the give and the take, reining himself in before things got out of control and he took this to a level that would probably scare them both.

His patience paid off. Her body seemed simply to liquefy as she finally relaxed into him, lifted her arms around his neck, and invited him to know her better. To know her mouth. To know the press of her breasts against his chest. The fit of their hips. And *please, God*, he needed to keep it together enough to let her set the pace when he wanted to indulge in the taste and the sweetness of her and the slow and steady melting of her guard as she gave up and gave in.

She kissed him back now. Now she asked for more. Her mouth open, tongue seeking. Her breath was warm and tasted of wine. Her heartbeat pounded, rapid and wild against his chest. Her skin warmed beneath his hands when he found her bare back beneath her tank top. And she smelled—*Lord*—she smelled of sun and pine and wood smoke and home, and he wanted to do things to her that would make her scream his name and beg him for more. He wanted to feel the depth of her passion and her fire and promise her that when they made love, it would be amazing.

Only this was supposed to be a kiss. Just a kiss. A friendly introduction to the prospect of many things in store. And it was up to him to dial things down before she panicked and bolted like a wild animal whose self-preservation instincts had kicked into high gear.

So he made himself take them both down slowly. He pulled back by degrees, easing them back to a place where it was safe and sane and his head wasn't spinning and she didn't have to worry about losing control. Hell, where *he* didn't have to worry that he'd pick her up caveman-style, carry her back into the cabin, and toss her onto the bed.

Finally, reluctantly, he ended the kiss and tucked her head beneath his chin. Then he held her while his heart slammed and she clung as if she needed him to hold her upright.

If he had any sense, he wouldn't feel so pleased with himself. He'd be more than a little alarmed by the way she'd turned him inside out with one single, simple kiss.

"Wow," he whispered, pressing his lips against her hair.

She sucked in a serrated breath and started to pull away.

"No. Not yet. You leave me like this, I may keel over."

But he understood that reality had hit her. She'd

let him kiss her. More, she'd kissed him back. Kissed the first man who was not her husband.

"It was only a kiss, Jess," he reminded her gently. "An amazing kiss. But that's all it was."

She didn't make an attempt to move again, but she didn't say anything, either. So he gave her something else to think about.

"I have to fly back to Florida tomorrow."

He sensed a slight tensing of her shoulders.

"I didn't know what to plan for. You could have sent me away. We could have 'remembered big' and realized there was nothing here to hang on to." He chuckled softly. "I don't know about you, but I think we put *that* notion to bed."

He finally pulled back, cupped her shoulders in his palms, and flexed his knees so they were at eye level. "And as much as I'd like to take *you* to bed, right now, I'm not going to. I want you to think about it, though. I want you to think about us."

Oh, he could see she was doing a lot of thinking.

"I need to go back. I need to take care of some things at work so I can clear my schedule. That is, if you want me to clear my schedule. Tell me it's all right for me to come back."

He didn't know who was more surprised when she moved back in to him, kissed him softly, and whispered against his lips. "If you don't come back and finish this, I might have to hunt you down and hurt you."

Chapter

9

Afghanistan, August

Tortured moans woke Rabia, jerking her straight up in bed. She should be prepared for them by now, yet she never was.

Heart pounding, she rushed out of the small room that was her sleeping place and into the room that by day was a gathering area and by night was a sleeping space for her father and now this American soldier. As she had done many nights since she'd brought him down from the cave, she knelt beside the pallet on the floor, where he thrashed in his sleep. She dipped a cloth in a bowl of water she'd left nearby, quickly wrung it out, then placed it over his forehead. The coolness sometimes soothed and settled him.

But nothing stopped the nightmares. They grew stronger and more frequent. They also held the answers, she suspected, to the past he could not remember.

She glanced over her shoulder to where her father still slept soundly. His old ears no longer heard as sharply. Tonight that was a good thing. Relieved that he had not awakened, she sat quietly, alone with her thoughts, waiting for the worst to pass, conflicted over the unexpected things she felt for the man she had found by the side of the road more than a month ago.

In the beginning, she had been determined to be unaffected by his suffering. He represented a liability and an obligation, no more. She had resented having to care for him. Determination, however, was no match for human suffering. Time had passed, and she had weakened . . . and eventually grown to pity him.

Even more, she found herself wondering about him, as she wondered while she sat with him tonight. Where had he come from? What horrors had he endured? His body told part of the story. His flesh was colored and marred by old scars and new. His mind had also been abused. And he had been nearly starved to death when she found him.

She gently held the cloth to his forehead. Extremists would condemn her for the reluctant compassion she now showed this American soldier. This infidel who stood for things the Taliban warlords proclaimed Islam did not tolerate. This man and men like him who professed to be saviors yet dropped bombs on her country.

Weary, she leaned back against the wall. She was a Muslim, and the Koran was the primary source of her faith. The Koran dealt with the subjects that concerned all human beings: wisdom, beliefs, worship, and law. It focused on the relationship between Allah and his creatures, provided guidelines for a just society, for proper human relationships and equal divisions of power.

The Taliban preached the Koran and twisted the intent for its own purpose. Under Taliban rule, women were powerless. Under the Taliban, there was only pain. Since its fall from power almost a decade ago, women now held seats in parliament. Girls went to school in many provinces without fear of having acid thrown in their faces, or worse, of death. Women had rights. Women had jobs.

All, in part, because of the Americans. And yet the Americans had brought more war to a country that had seen too much destruction and dying.

She rewet the cloth and applied it again to his brow, reminding herself of a truth she had taken a long time to see. This was but one man, not an army of men. This was a lost man. Lost and in pain. Physical, emotional, spiritual.

"Perhaps you should pray to your God," she had suggested one day when she had found him in the cave huddled and weeping and beyond his endurance.

"My God?" Wild, angry eyes had met hers. "There is no God."

She had been so shocked her breath had caught. "You must not say that."

"For fear of bringing down his wrath? What else could he do to me? Strike me dead? Bring it. I'm past ready. It would solve both of our problems."

"Your injuries have darkened your spirit."

Bitter laughter degraded to tears. "My spirit left with my memory. I am not a man. I don't exist. Why can't you let me die?"

She thought of the despair on his face and in his voice that day as she watched him now. Thought of how the next time she had come to him, he had found the inner strength to pull himself together. To endure. As he endured these nightmares. How could she not admire him for that?

She had learned not to wake him. Once she had tried and ended up ducking his wild, swinging fists and covering her ears against his animal-like screams. Those screams could awaken the village. Or, worse, attract a Taliban patrol and create a bigger nightmare for all of them.

Always, she lived with the fear of Taliban discovery.

So she waited in the dark with him, hoping to keep him quiet, and wrestled with both compassion and resentment for the danger he had placed her and her father in.

His eyes moved rapidly behind his lids, his legs jerking restlessly. Yet the weight of his despair held him to the bed. He might not have believed it, but he was a creation of God. They all were. The Koran said so. It also encouraged kindness to others . . . while the Taliban killed and tortured in the name of Islam. Stoned women for showing their faces to the sun, beheaded them for seeking an education, tortured them on a mere suspicion that they did not obey sharia law.

She bathed his forehead and temples, wondering how her faith could be so divergent in interpretation. These were the things she struggled with every day. But in one thing, she was certain: it was right to honor her father's wishes. And her father's wishes had been to honor this man's request for Pashtunwali.

"He asked for refuge, daughter. Pashtun law demands that if a person asks for asylum, it must be given."

If she had picked any other day to come home from Kabul, she would not be in this position. She would not have found him by the side of the road. Bleeding, dazed, clearly sentenced to death if he were found by whoever hunted him.

Dressed as he had been—in tattered clothes traditional of her tribe, his long hair and beard matted with blood and grime, his skin darkened by the sun—she had not immediately recognized him for what he was. She saw only a man in distress. A man who had whispered, "Pashtunwali," and begged her in Pashto to help him. To hide him.

For all she'd known at the time, he was Taliban.

But Pashtunwali demanded that she give him aid regardless of whether he was friend or enemy.

She had quickly taken him to the mountains. To the secret, concealed caves where she had played as a child. There she had hidden him until she could consult her father. It was only after she had removed his bloody garments to treat his wounds that his pale skin had alerted her. He was not Afghan. And it was only after hearing the whispers of fear spread through the local villages that she realized Taliban forces were in search of an escaped American soldier.

Her heart felt heavy as she watched his fingers claw at the bedding. Even at risk to her own life, how could she not care for him through fever and pain and these horrible nightmares and not feel something?

Last week, she had to move him from the mountain cave when the Taliban patrols had increased there. The risk of discovery had become too great. Now the risk, if he was discovered in her father's home, was even greater for her. And for her father. No matter what he said.

"I am an old man, daughter. I am unwell. I do not fear for myself. Allah will take me home soon. For you, though—I regret you have been placed in this position."

She watched the soldier's face contort in agony and regretted it, too. This man was a danger to them. As soon as he was well enough, she had to find a way to get him away from here and to someone who could help get him home. But that time, she feared, was still in the far distance. While there had been some improvement in his overall condition, often all it took was the wrong movement of his head, and the vertigo overtook him and brought him to his knees. The headaches still attacked with piercing pain. The vision in his right eye had faded. And the leg he so heavily favored made mobility difficult.

He flung his arm out wildly, then covered his face. "Fisher! Oh, God . . . Fisher."

Fisher. She was not familiar with that word in English. Was it a curse? Was it a prayer? A command? A name? He yelled it often. She had asked him one day what it meant.

He had looked puzzled. "It's a name . . . but I don't know what it means."

Perhaps she should cut back on the opium. Perhaps the drug triggered the nightmares and had become more detrimental than the pain relief it provided. She feared he was now addicted. If so, that was her doing, because she had been unable to bear watching him suffer.

"What happened to you?" she wondered aloud, as a groan rumbled from deep in his chest and his breathing quickened. The scars on his body told of a long history of torture. The more recent wounds told of his fight to escape. Only a strong man could have survived.

Only a warrior.

Who now depended on her for strength.

✳

His GMV—ground mobility vehicle, which was basically a souped-up humvee—lined up third in the convoy of four vehicles bouncing slowly down a mountain goat path that the locals called a road. Right. Without rappelling gear, on this ice and snow, even the goats would have to be suicidal to take it.

But here they were. Freezing their asses, their toes, their fingers, and anything else the Afghan winter choose to freeze.

He wiped his gloved hand over his jaw, scratching at the stubble and grime. Bone-tired, his ass sore from the long, rough ride, and his reserves depleted from the grueling op, he was more than ready to get back to the post and relieve his weary feet of the boots he'd been wearing for more than seventy-two hours.

"What time is it, Fisher?" he asked his buddy over the grind and whine of the GMV's engine as it crab-crawled over another pile of fallen rocks and deep drifts of snow.

"Zero dark thirty, Sarge," Fisher drawled from behind the wheel.

Pat was the team's weapons specialist, comedic relief, and for a proud Oklahoman who rarely saw snow, he did a damn fine job plowing through the stuff. He slowed the vehicle to maneuver around yet another cluster of white-covered rocks—no easy task wearing night-vision goggles.

"What day is it, Fisher?" he asked around a yawn, then shook his head to wake himself up.

"It's either Monday, Tuesday, or Wednesday. Possibly Thursday—that is, if it ain't Friday, Saturday, or Sunday, Sarge."

He grunted. "Thanks for pinning that down."

"Anything to make your life more pleasant."

They took small pleasures when they could—even tolerated Fisher's stupid jokes—because patrol in and around the Paktia Province, specifically Chamkani, had pitifully few pleasures. The prospect of returning to the post after a cross-border op into Pakistan—bad U.S. Army, shame, shame—was at the top of the pleasure scale tonight. Thoughts of a hot shower—crude as it may be— outranked even the success of their mission to interdict the Taliban supply lines that, of course, the Pakistanis denied even existed.

And there were no poppy fields in Kandahar.

In the bitter cold, the cloudless night sky was a shower of green dots through the frost-coated windshield and the night-vision goggles that every man in the small convoy wore. As team medic, he was happy as hell not to have had to treat any casualties on this mission. Just because they'd survived the op without so much as a paper cut, however, didn't mean they could let down now. Like the Travelocity gnome, Mr. Taliban was everywhere. Until they reached the remote old Soviet base serving as their temporary home sweet home, he wasn't going to breathe easy. None of them would.

Every inch of terrain held potential traps. This road in particular. He didn't like it. Not one bit. Only one way in, only one way out of their target area. It was a target-rich environment for the Taliban, who loved their IEDs and ambushes. That they were about to cross over from Pakistan into Afghanistan meant diddly-squat. The Taliban knew that Special Forces patrols regularly scooted across the very loosely defined border to hunt.

Beside him, Fisher felt uneasy, too. "Don't mind tellin' ya, Sarge, I'll be happy as a pig in slop when we get off this freakin' stretch of ro—"

BOOM!

A monster blast shocked the air, sucked the breath from his lungs, and sent the GMV airborne.

A cloud of flying snow and rock projectiles enveloped them. The GMV rocketed back to earth, crashed with a bone-jarring thud, rocked and then started to roll. Holding on to anything he could grab, he rode with it, trying to recover his breath from the shock of the explosion. When the rocking stopped, the vehicle had flipped upside down, and so had he. Snow and frigid cold blew in through the broken windshield.

"Fisher!" he yelled, barely hearing his own voice above the ringing in his ears.

The one thing he should have heard above the din he didn't. The sound of heavy weapons. Which meant no one was able to man them. Which meant they were all in a world of hurt.

"My arm!" Pat roared in pain over the zipping of bullets flying around them. His goggles had been knocked off, but he could see Pat moving around beside him in the dark. He'd clamped his hand over Pat's upper arm. Blood spurted between his fingers.

More explosions and gunfire echoed around them.

He needed to triage Pat's arm. He needed to radio for help. The mike dangled over his head. He reached around his rifle sling and grabbed it. "Red Striker Two is hit! Red Striker Two has been IEDed!"

No answer. The radios were probably screwed up in the blast.

Or there was no one left in the convoy to answer.

He craned his neck around to look at the back of the GMV. Simmons and Blanco were crumpled on their heads at odd angles and eerily still. He clawed his way halfway over the seat, tugged his glove off with his teeth, and checked their carotid arteries. Nothing. They were dead.

"Can you move?" he yelled to Fisher.

"Like . . . Jagger," Fisher managed, a smart-ass to the end.

He quickly applied a tourniquet to Fisher's arm.

"Then let's get the hell out of here!"

Pain screamed through his leg as he dragged himself out of the half-open GMV door into a night lit with tracers, burning vehicles, and thick black smoke. Gunfire echoed around him. Gunfire and the screams of men hurt and dying.

"Go. Go. Go. I'll cover!"

With his M-4 in hand, he fired from the cover of the vehicle, giving Fisher a chance to run for an outcropping ten yards away. He dropped one AK-wielding thug. Then another. But not before they nailed Fisher.

Oh, Christ. Oh, Christ. *Fisher was down.* The guys in the back were dead. He swallowed back rage and overwhelming sorrow.

Bullets pounded the snowdrifts around him. Muscle memory, training, and instinct kicked in, and he became what he'd been trained to be. A soldier. A soldier who had been marked.

He had to move. He grabbed the door and hauled himself to his feet. His right leg gave out, and he collapsed in the snow as knife-like pain screamed through his shin.

He swore through a groan when he caught his breath then fought from the ground. He laid down a burst of fire, then started dragging himself toward Fisher, cutting a path in the snow with his body. Then he roared in anger and horror when he realized that half of Fisher's head was blown off. Red blood stained white snow and bled to black in the dark.

Fighting tears, using his buddy's body for cover, and running on rage and adrenaline, he fired off several more bursts, then dragged himself to the rock outcropping and hunkered down behind it, nailing another two bad guys on the way.

Winded, reeling with pain, he chanced a peek around the rock and assessed his situation. When he saw what was left of the convoy, he knew he would die here.

All the vehicles but his were burning. One lay on its roof. Two teetered on their sides. Lifeless bodies hung out of doors, lay sprawled on the snow.

A masked figure ran toward him, brandishing an AK-47. "Allahu Akbar!"

More attackers followed with RPGs.

"Allahu Akbar! Allahu Akbar! Allahu Akbar!"

He dropped them all, then lay back fighting for breath in the brittle air. Finally, something gave him hope. The sporadic sound of M-4s returning fire. Horrah! Some of the guys were still out there; they'd found defensive positions. And they were giving those Tangos what for.

He quickly took stock of his weapons and ammo. He had a handful of frag grenades, his M-4 and a hundred rounds, his Beretta and three full mags, and the knife his brother had given him before his last deployment.

He pulled the pin on a grenade and lobbed it toward the AK fire. When it exploded, he nosed around the rock and nailed two bad guys who had survived the blast. They weren't going to take him alive.

Another M-4 popped in the distance. "Go get 'em, boys," he cheered, then double-tapped a charging figure that fell in a crumpled heap.

Winded, hands shaking from adrenaline and cold, he propped himself up against a boulder, then, on a deep breath, peeked around again and started taking out targets with single and double shots to conserve ammo.

Bullets slapped into the rocks around him. He knew

he needed to move again. Moving targets were more difficult to shoot. But he had a bad feeling his tibia was broken. Which meant he was stuck until reinforcements arrived. If they arrived. He held out a small hope that someone had reached the post on the radio.

Another group of fighters charged him. Their muzzle flashes almost blinded him as they sprayed his position. He emptied the M-4's magazine, then pulled his Beretta, killing the last Tango who'd gotten so close he fell at the base of the rock.

He belly-crawled around to the other side of the boulder, reloaded, then returned a new barrage of fire, his shell casings bouncing off the rocks, the hot metal burning his face and neck.

A streak of light registered out of the corner of his eye. He turned in time to see an RPG light up his GMV.

The ground shuddered; the air exploded around him. He covered his head, felt a blast like an inferno, then mind-blowing pain, and lost the fight to blackness . . .

Chapter

10

He awoke gasping, his heart hammering so hard his chest felt as if it would explode from the pressure. Visions of fire and blood and bullets flew through his mind like a cyclone, all mayhem and madness and speed. Too fast for him to decipher. Too horrifying for him to want to.

Then soft hands covered his, held tight in a night that was warm and dark but for a pale light burning nearby in the cave.

"You are safe, *askar*," a woman whispered in Pashto.

You are safe, soldier.

"You are safe," she repeated, her voice soothing and sleepy, as though she had recently awakened.

Rabia.

His heartbeat slowed fractionally, then started to settle when he realized it was her. She'd come to him again in the cave. *No. Wait.* He opened his eyes. Not the cave. The ceiling above him was whitewashed plaster, not dingy, dripping rock.

Slowly, so as not to wake the vertigo, he looked around. Walls. Structural walls, not made of rock. A window was covered with fabric. A soft light burned from a small wooden table. An intricately patterned rug hung on the wall.

He remembered now. She had moved him out of the cave. She'd brought him to her father's home in the village.

"How long?" he asked through a scratchy throat as his breathing stabilized.

"One hour. No more." She offered him water. He drank gratefully as she held his head, then carefully resettled him on the pallet.

"No. Not how long was I asleep. How long have I been here?"

"Four days only."

Painstakingly slow, he turned his head so he could look at her. And felt his heartbeat quicken again.

The burqa was gone. She didn't wear it in the house. It wasn't the first time he'd seen her face, but each time he did, it was a fascinating revelation. One that held him in thrall and incapable of looking away, even though he saw that his scrutiny made her uncomfortable.

"I will leave you now." She moved to go.

"No." He reached for her hand. Held on with as much strength as he could muster. "Please . . . please stay. Just a little while."

With reluctance, she stopped resisting as he continued to stare unapologetically at the woman who represented the sum total of his life.

She was incredibly beautiful. Night-black hair, long and loose and falling over slim shoulders. Most Afghan women were easy on the eyes—God only knew how he knew that—and she was no exception. Clear olive complexion, delicately arched brows over dark, intelligent eyes that had once been angry and cold but now offered compassion. Her reaction to him made her uncomfortable, though. Clearly, she struggled with what she felt.

"I'm sorry. I don't mean to stare. It's . . . it's just that I wondered what you looked like for so long. It's still new to me every time I see you."

She looked away, then rose to her knees, her soft white gown falling over her bare feet. "I must go back to my bed now."

She looked tired, so he let her go. She needed sleep, even if he wasn't going to get any. After one of his nightmares, he never slept. He was afraid to.

"Why do you do this, Rabia?" he whispered, aware of her father sleeping across the small room. "Why do you take care of me?"

She looked from the hands she'd clasped at her lap

to his face, then back to her hands again. A heartbeat passed while she decided what to say. "Because you invoked Pashtunwali."

"Yeah, so you told me." She'd explained how she'd found him and he'd asked for refuge. He didn't remember. Had no idea why he even knew that word. Another mystery. Like the mystery of why both English and Pashto words mixed together in his head. So much muddled together that when they spoke now, it was in an odd blend of English and Pashto that somehow worked.

The bigger mystery was that he didn't think it was only Pashtunwali that compelled her to help him. There was more to it now. When she had first come to him, she'd been hostile. Hell, she'd hated him. Barely tolerated him and clearly felt burdened by his presence.

That had changed over time. What he sensed from her now felt very much like concern and caring—and God, he needed to believe that, because without it, he was completely alone.

He needed it so much that he didn't trust the feeling completely. Maybe there were ulterior motives. Did she and her father plan to ransom him? If so, to whom? The U.S. government? Hell, if someone from the military knew he was alive, they would have already moved heaven and earth to find him. *No man left behind.* It was the Special Forces credo.

The thought hit him like a tank.

Was he Special Forces? If not, why would that particular spec-ops credo step front and center? Why not Navy SEAL or Marine Force Recon or Army Ranger or Delta?

Special Forces. Army. It felt right that he'd worn a green beret.

Or maybe it was wishful thinking because he'd like to believe he'd been so much more than the weak, useless excuse for a man that he'd become.

A familiar pain knifed through his head, reminding him that isolation was not a small house made of mud bricks and straw plaster in the middle of a war-torn country. Isolation was crippling vertigo, fading eyesight, and not knowing your own damn name. Not knowing if you had a family, if you had a life worth going back to, or if you even had a dog.

He forced a deep breath. Then another. He couldn't go there. He had to deal with now. Only now was as unknown as his past.

"I must go," she whispered again, and this time, he stopped her with a request.

"Tea. Please?"

While they never spoken of it, he knew she mixed opiates in a concoction of tea and honey that did little to disguise the bitter taste of the poppy.

She glanced toward the cooking room, then back to him. "Do you need it?"

Yeah. He needed it. He needed the haze of nothingness the drug spread through his mind and body.

The need made him a weak man. He knew that. He knew he needed to resist.

Would tonight finally be the night? Could he do it?

With remnants of the nightmare hovering just out of his grasp, he knew he should at least try. If his head cleared, maybe he would remember something. Maybe tonight he didn't want to.

"Yes, please," he said, ashamed to be so deep into the drug that he craved it more than his strength or the life he'd lost.

Tomorrow, he resolved, as she rose on quiet feet and walked out of the room to make his tea. Tomorrow he would try. Tonight he wanted only relief.

✳

FOUR MORE TOMORROWS passed before he finally found the courage to let go of the opium.

"You are sure, *askar*?" Rabia asked with concern in her eyes.

"I'm sure."

She didn't ask again. She understood. She knew he had to do this.

Once he'd said no more, the tea had become sweeter.

Life had not.

He'd thought he'd known pain. But the withdrawal was beyond anything he could have imagined. Cold sweats, tremors, vomiting, anxiety, and his old friend insomnia. And then there was the pain—muscle, bone, hair, teeth, everything hurt with unconditional torture.

All in a day's work, if you were a junkie kicking the habit.

Through it all, Rabia stayed by his side.

She bathed him.

She cleaned up after him.

She held him while he shook until his bones ached.

She soothed his brow through the night terrors.

And when he finally slept, the nightmares shot at him like bullets. Fragmented images cut into his mind like daggers, waking him to his own screams as he faced fire and smoke and IED blasts until exhaustion sucked him under again.

✱

"HOW ARE YOU this morning, *askar*?"

He opened his eyes slowly. Sunlight slanted in beneath the meager drape of fabric covering the small window. "I don't know. How long has it been?"

"Since the tea became sweet?"

He tried to swallow, but his mouth was too dry. Immediately, she knelt beside him and tipped a cup of water to his lips.

"Yes," he croaked after taking a small sip. "Since the tea became sweet."

"Seven days."

Seven days of hell. But he was alive. "Let's not do that again real soon."

"On that, we agree."

Because he heard a soft smile in her voice, he smiled, too, something that he realized he hadn't done since he'd come to, chained by his ankle in that cave.

Suddenly overwhelmed with gratitude for all she had done for him, for all she had been to him, he reached for her hand. "Thank you."

She wove her fingers through his, squeezed, and inexplicably, the darkness in his heart lifted. He didn't think about it. He brought their linked hands to his mouth and kissed the back of her knuckles.

The action was spontaneous and achingly intimate.

Just as suddenly, it was over.

She tugged her hand out of his. "I must prepare the morning meal."

Then she was gone, leaving him wondering what the hell he'd been thinking. Well, that was pretty damn clear. He hadn't. He hadn't thought at all. For an instant, neither had she. For once, she'd responded in a way that wasn't an offer of comfort or aid. She'd touched him out of affection. He'd reacted in kind.

And it had scared the hell out of her.

Hell, it scared him, too. And, unexpectedly, aroused him.

He stared at the ceiling, experiencing what it felt like to be a man responding physically to a woman and instinctively knowing he had not lived his life in a sexual vacuum. There had been women. Possibly one special woman. Was one waiting for him even now?

Would he ever remember her if there was? And what would it matter if he never got out of this damn country and reclaimed his life?

Frustrated, fighting defeat, he willed his thoughts away from the softness of Rabia's body and the fullness of her lips. Thinking of her that way was one-hundred-percent out of line. Thinking of her that way would not happen again.

But the house was small, the walls thin. There was no way to distance himself physically or mentally. For long moments, he listened to her speak softly to her father in the cooking room. For the first time in seven days, the smells coming from her kitchen didn't nauseate him.

And for the first time since he'd come to in that cave, he decided that it was time to see his own face.

He stared at the wall beside his pallet and the small mirror that hung above the wooden table. Flat-out, unadulterated fear accelerated his heart rate. What if he didn't recognize his own face?

What if he did?

What if seeing his image triggered his memory and he didn't like the man he'd been? What if who he'd been was so horrible that his mind had been protecting him with the amnesia?

There was only one way to find out.

He lay there a little longer, gathering his courage, then, moving slowly and carefully, struggled to sit up. Winded and weak, he gripped the table for support and eventually made it to his knees. Several steadying breaths later, when the vertigo hadn't reared its ugly head, he managed to get one foot under his weight, then the other, while constantly repeating his mantra.

No sudden movements.

Do not dip your head.

Do not turn your head.

Do not look down.

Still, the room started spinning wildly. He gripped the table for several seconds before the world righted itself again.

Heart slamming, knees threatening to buckle, he drew several bracing breaths, then faced his nemesis in the wavy, mottled mirror—and experienced another loss so acute that it trumped all others.

The eyes of a stranger stared back at him from a face half covered by beard and skin stained dark by the henna dye Rabia had applied to help disguise him in the event that he was spotted through a window.

He'd been certain he'd at least recognize his own face, and in truth, he had put off looking for fear that he wouldn't . . . and still he wasn't prepared for the tears that suddenly clouded his vision at yet one more blow fate had seen fit to deal him.

Shock and curiosity finally beat out despair, and he studied this man who was him and whom he didn't know. The eyes looking back at him were brown, the skin drawn, the cheeks sunken; streaks of gray were threaded through the tangle of dark hair and beard.

Despite the weakness, he had, for some reason, decided he was not an old man. He'd been certain he was in his thirties. Now he wasn't so sure. The emaciated man staring back looked much older. Maybe it was his eyes. The eyes looked a hundred years old. Eerily empty. Because of his injuries? The opium? The absence of self? Had he lost his soul when he'd lost his memories and been sent into a time continuum where he'd aged by decades? Or was his soul merely as damaged as his body?

Somewhere in the back of his mind, a thought persisted. This was not who he was or had been. He was not all about darkness and despair. As much as he feared he'd be disappointed, he believed deep down that he had not been a bad man. This pitiful, weak man had not been a part of his life before he'd lost himself. He'd been someone. He'd been some*thing*. He'd been vital and driven and real.

The man he saw in the mirror was none of those things. This man was a ghost. A shell. A man without a future because he had no past.

The familiar taste of fear, sharp and sour and overwhelming, pooled in his mouth. Would he ever find himself? Would he ever remember? Or was he stuck here in a hellish limbo for the rest of his life? Like he was stuck in this hostile country with no hope of rescue.

Shaken and defeated, he drew several more deep breaths and settled himself down. If he gave in to the fear, the darkness would eat him alive, and he'd be begging Rabia for opium again.

Composed but still unsteady, he turned his attention to the pitcher of water on the small table. A bar of coarse soap and a clean rag sat beside it. He used both to wash his face, a small task that felt monumental.

It felt both strange and good to be on his feet, but he knew he didn't dare test his strength for too long. He didn't dare count on the vertigo to leave him alone, either, or for the pain in his leg to allow him to walk without a limp.

Or for the sight to return miraculously in his right eye.

The vision problems had come on gradually. At first, he'd thought it was a side effect of the vertigo and the opium. At least, he'd hoped. He couldn't hold that hope any longer. Looking in the mirror had confirmed his worst fears. Like his memory, the vision in his right eye was gone.

Rabia had done her best for him. But he knew he needed medical attention. He suspected he'd sustained a traumatic brain injury—a recently healed wound at the base of his skull supported that idea. A TBI could account for the loss of vision and the vertigo. And more. Another sign of TBI was the fact that his amnesia had lasted this long, suggesting that it was extremely severe.

Retrograde amnesia, possibly?

RA commonly results from damage to the region

of the brain most closely associated with episodic and declarative memory, including autobiographical information. In extreme cases, individuals completely forget who they are. Memory loss, however, can also be selective or categorical, manifested by a person's inability to remember events related to a specific incident or topic.

Whoa.

He gripped the table when he felt himself reeling. Where had *that* textbook analysis come from?

The same place as the short frantic bursts of information that flew at him out of the blue since he'd started weaning himself off the opium. Most of the time, it came at him like bullets—rushing by so fast he couldn't capture it all. He'd see fire and smell burning rubber, hear blasts, feel pain. The next time, he'd see blue skies, glimmering water, winter snow, summer sun.

This was the first time anything had manifested with such clarity. So much clarity it almost set him on his ass.

He circled back to the medical terminology. Was he a doctor? A doctor who was a soldier? That didn't feel right. A medic, maybe? *Yeah, maybe.*

"Congratulations," he muttered. "You've just solved exactly nothing."

He still didn't know who he was or how he'd gotten here or, more important, how he was going to get out.

And go where?

Yeah. Go where?

Very carefully, he eased back down onto the pallet. Winded and shaky, he leaned back against the wall and recovered what little strength he had. When he felt steadier, he reached for the stack of clean clothes Rabia had folded neatly on the edge of his pallet.

If anyone visiting accidentally saw him in the house, they would see a man in traditional Pashtun dress, with a loose-fitting shirt that reached his knees, called a *qmis*, and a vest that covered the shirt and pants, a *shalwar*. He tied the trousers with a string and then, with the rest of his energy, slipped his bare feet into the *chaplay*, or thick leather shoes. Then he rested again.

Several minutes later, he'd regained enough strength to deal with the *pagray*—a turban—and the long strip of cotton cloth that Rabia had taught him to wind around his head and leave one end dangling.

Finally, he reached for a long, wide piece of cloth and draped the *chadar* over his shoulders. Then he lay back down, angered by his weakness and pumping heart but looking like a proper Pashtun man.

Like a man, he thought grimly, lost between a world he had forgotten and a world where he didn't belong.

Like a man confused about a woman who was a part of that world.

Then he drifted into another fitful sleep.

Chapter

11

*R*abia startled and slapped a hand to her breast when she realized the *askar* had joined her in the cooking room.

"You are up and walking," she said when she had regained her composure.

"Barely. I feel like a toddler taking his first steps."

"Toddler? I do not know this word."

He made his way to a low bench in the corner of the room and eased down onto it. "A baby. Learning to walk."

"You are no baby," she said, then immediately regretted it when his gaze held hers for a long moment.

She quickly turned back to her stove and the meal she was in the middle of preparing. But she could not stop the thoughts of that moment by his bed several days ago, when he had kissed her hand. Or thoughts of the way she had held him during the withdrawal tremors, the way she had bathed his face and cooled his brow when it felt as though he were burning up with fever.

Memories of her hands on his feverish skin, of his warm body pressed against hers, of his face pressed against her breasts as she had held him in the dark and willed him through the worst of it would not leave her alone.

Her face flushed hot, and not from the heat of the summer day or the cookstove. It was not acceptable to be thinking of him that way. She had already broken many Pashtun laws because of him. Every time she was alone with him or touched him, she went against her tribal customs. Every time he met her eyes and she did not look away or spoke to him without being spoken to, she violated another law.

Now was not the time to be reminded that she was a woman who had once lain with a man. This was not the man who should remind her.

Her hands trembled as she reached for her special and treasured blend of spices to season the small piece of lamb she had managed to barter for. To even think such things was a sin. To act on those thoughts would bring shame to her and her father and her people.

That was why she had worked hard to keep her distance from him when possible. She did not attend to him as she once had. She let him bathe and dress himself. She allowed him to test his physical limits, even as she knew his struggle was difficult.

It had taken him a full week after the opium was out of his system to be able to walk from one end of the small social/sleeping room to the other. Another few days before he ventured out of the room.

Now, today, he sought her out in the cooking room.

From now on, it would become more difficult to avoid him.

She wondered if he had been thinking about the same things she had. Then she realized he had become very quiet, and she could not resist looking back over her shoulder at him.

His dark eyes studied her with a heat and intensity that had her spinning quickly back to her cooking and praying for forgiveness and strength.

✳

HE MADE HER nervous. He was sorry about that, but he was also tired of avoiding her. No easy task, given the size of the little house that consisted of this kitchen, the sleeping/social room, Rabia's sleeping room, and little else. They generally took their meager meals outside in the back, in a courtyard shaded by fruit trees and surrounded by the same type of brick and straw walls that had been used in the construction of the house. The head was a separate building out back and very primitive.

He thought of all of this and tried not to think about the soft body hidden beneath her long dark blouse and skirt or about the hair she had covered with a white scarf as she worked over the stove.

So he took some time to get his head back together and study the room. A heavy black iron stove with three cooking tops had been pushed against a wall. A stove pipe extended outside. A worn and dented bucket sat on the floor beside it. A dwindling supply of coal and wood chips lined the bottom.

The room was summer-hot, but the aromas actually had his stomach growling. He thought he might have gained a little weight during the past week. He knew he'd gained some strength. Their belongings were meager, as were the meals Rabia prepared, and he felt guilty for taking food from her mouth and her father's.

"What are you cooking?" he asked, to break the tension that felt as uncomfortable as it felt edgy.

For past meals, she'd made thin barley and rice soup, the occasional serving of fresh yogurt, and small loaves of bread she baked in her oven. Fruits, nuts, tomatoes, and potatoes filled in at every meal.

"Tonight we will have *yakhni pilau*, mutton steamed in rice. And *oabili—pilau* again but with raisins and shredded carrots. Perhaps also some almond and pistachio nuts if I have them."

"What's the occasion?" This he knew was a special meal, one that must have cost her a fortune.

"I exchanged favors for the meat and the raisins," she said simply.

"What kind of favors?"

"Only some sewing."

So that's what she'd been doing in the night when he'd awakened and seen a light on in her room.

"Is that what smells so good?"

"Perhaps it is the bread. It is almost done baking."

It seemed odd, suddenly, that she represented his entire life and he knew very little about her. "Did your mother teach you to cook?"

She shook her head and continued stirring her pot. "My aunt. My mother died giving birth to me. I was my father and mother's only child."

Which explained why there was no extended family living with them, which was the Pashtun way— another tidbit he hadn't known that he knew.

While there was no self-pity in her tone, he felt her sorrow and her loss. "I'm sorry."

"As am I. She was my father's second wife. His first wife bore him no children. I am told she died of a sudden illness. Like my mother, she was very young," she said softly. "I am told my mother was a beautiful woman. I miss not knowing her."

"I didn't know my mother, either."

The world inside the small room skidded to a screeching halt. Rabia froze at her stove, then slowly turned to look at him.

"I don't know where that came from," he said, his

eyes wide, his heart pounding. "I don't know why I know that."

"This is a good thing. Do you remember any more?"

He resisted the knee-jerk urge to shake his head, catching himself at the last second. He'd had an actual memory, not a piece of information that he couldn't attach to anything. It was short and incomplete, but it was real, and he didn't want to cloud it by launching a vertigo attack. "No. That's it. I just know that I didn't know my mother."

"Then I, too, am sorry."

He closed his eyes and tried to will the thought to flesh out, to develop, to do something more than lie there like a lead weight to compound the other weights pressing down on his shoulders.

So. He didn't know his mother. Why? Was she dead, too, like Rabia's mother? Or had she left? What about his father? Did he have a sister? A brother? A wife? He'd wondered all of this often, but today a tangible piece of his past was within reach, and he felt the need for answers much more urgently.

His head started to hurt again, so he thrashed around for another diversion.

"Do you mind if I ask how old you are?"

She moved to her work space beside the stove and started chopping vegetables. "I am twenty-eight years."

Despite her hard life, she looked younger. "Why aren't you married?" The question had been rumbling around in the back of his mind for a long time now.

She hesitated with her back to him, then let out a breath. "I was."

Was.

Divorce was uncommon in Afghanistan because of the social stigmas. Marriages were also generally arranged social and economic contracts between families. More nuggets of intel he had no idea that he'd known.

He wanted to ask what had happened, but he'd infringed on her privacy so much already that he let it go.

As it turned out, she volunteered the information.

"Rahim was a policeman in Kabul. He was killed by a Taliban fighter posing as a fellow officer."

What a world. What a country. "Again. I'm sorry. How long ago?"

"Four years. We had passed our second year as husband and wife."

He felt very tired suddenly. And didn't think he could bear to ask her any more questions. He wasn't the only one who had lost. This war had cost her dearly.

Without another word, he slowly rose to his feet and left her alone with her thoughts.

★

HE DIDN'T TURN his head when Rabia joined him on the flat roof of her father's house. He lay still on his back and stared into a sky that was obsidian-black and sprayed with stars shining over a land as foreign to him as his own face.

"You should not be up here, *askar*. You could be spotted."

"And what would they see? A crippled-up old Pashtun scarecrow of a man with threads of gray in his hair. Even if I was spotted, no one would give me a second look."

She sat down beside him, folding her feet beneath her hips. "The village is small. You are a stranger."

"I'm your long-lost uncle visiting from the big city, remember?"

She didn't think much of that, even though the cover story had been her idea, but she didn't say anything, at least not for a while.

"How did you get up here?"

"Same way you did." He'd painstakingly climbed the wooden ladder propped up against the back of the house.

"I meant, how did you get up here by yourself? You could have fallen."

"I didn't."

"But you could have. The dizziness still comes and goes."

That it did. The vertigo and piercing headaches crippled him more than his bad leg and the loss of vision ever could. Earlier this morning, he had moved too fast, and it had taken him down. He'd needed more than an hour before the room stopped spinning and the nausea had backed off to tolerable. So, yeah, climbing up here was probably a stupid risk. But he still couldn't tolerate bright sunlight and couldn't risk being seen in the daylight, anyway. This was the second night he'd ventured out on his own—but it was the first night she'd come looking for him.

"The house is warm. I felt caged in." More than caged. He'd felt restless and edgy. He'd needed space. He'd needed distance from where she slept in her bed on the floor in a room not five feet away from him.

He never should have touched her that day. He never should have kissed her hand. Everything had changed between them in that moment. He was aware of her now. She was aware of him, and she kept her distance because of it, which was just as well, because there wasn't a damn thing he could or should do about it, anyway.

He needed to get out of here. And there was the rub. Go where? Go how?

"Perhaps you wish you were back in the cave," she said, breaking into his thoughts.

He laughed bitterly. "Or maybe you wish you had me chained up again so you could keep better track of me." He didn't know why he was angry with her.

"The chain was for your own protection. I could not be with you all the time. You were often disoriented. You could have wandered off. Fallen off the side of the mountain. Walked into a Taliban patrol."

"Careful. I'll start thinking you care."

He turned his head slowly, chancing a glance at her then . . . intrigued by what he saw in the moonlit night.

She did care. She didn't want to, but she did.

"I would care if you were caught and led the Taliban to us," she said grumpily. "My father is old. I do not wish him to die at the hands of those barbarians."

Yeah, there was that.

"Does your father know you're up here?"

"He is asleep."

The old man slept a lot. During the day, he napped quietly either in the back courtyard or in the shade of his front stoop, occasionally waking up to hold court with villagers who stopped to speak with him. He seemed oblivious to what went on inside his own house. It made him wonder if the old man might be ill.

Her father's name was Wakdar Kahn Kakar. Kakar, she had told him one day when he'd asked, was their tribe's name.

"Wakdar means 'man of authority,'" she'd said, then added, "Do not speak to him unless he speaks to you first. Then you should address him as Shaghalai Kakar, to show respect."

"So what is he? Some sort of tribal elder?"

"He is the *malik*, the village representative, and speaks for the people at the *shura*, the village council."

"So everyone brings him their problems."

"And he takes them to the *mullah*—the religious leader—who decides if they will be presented to the council."

"How would the *mullah* like it if he knew an American *askar* was hiding in the *malik*'s house?"

She'd had nothing to say to that. But he suspected she thought about it a lot. Most likely, she thought about it tonight up on the roof.

"Maybe I should run and save you both a lot of trouble."

It was her turn to look at the sky. "Where would you go? How far would you get?"

"That was a joke." He could barely walk, let alone run. Even if his leg wasn't a problem, the vertigo would take him down before he got ten yards. "Joke? A funny statement?" he clarified when she said nothing.

"I know what a joke is."

"Yet clearly, it's a concept you don't understand." He crossed his arms and made a pillow for his head.

He realized now that he could easily start living for the night when he could come up here and see the sky and not breathe air that smelled of strong spices and her father's tobacco smoke. Up here, it smelled of living things instead of the bat shit and the must of the cave where he'd been for so long. Other foul smells hovered at the edge of his memory. Smells that he associated with pain but couldn't pinpoint.

She started to get up. "We should go back inside. Come. I will help you down."

"Not yet. Relax, OK? Even the bad guys snuggle up to their RPGs and sleep sometimes. They're not looking for me tonight."

She did not find his sense of humor remotely funny. He found it ironic that he had one.

The truth was, Rabia found nothing funny. Then again, how the hell would he know? It had only been a couple of weeks since he hadn't been blitzed on opium.

"So if you're not worried I'll run, then why are you up here?" Unaccompanied women did not venture out after dark in this land of sharia law and public stoning. "Or are we back to the possibility that you were worried about me?"

The biggest joke of all. She might not know how to handle the sexual undertones rattling around between them, but she knew how to erect distance. When she again said nothing, he decided it was time to find out more about his reluctant nurse and host. That was the thing about opium. He had pretty much not given a damn about anything while he was on it. Now he had questions. Now his head was clear—empty but clear.

"What do you do, Rabia *jana*?" he asked, surprising her by adding the formality used when addressing young women. "When you aren't risking your neck hiding American soldiers? You speak English. You're educated. That's clear." It was also unusual. Ninety percent of Afghan women were illiterate.

There went another one. A random piece of information he hadn't known that he knew.

"I am a teacher of girls. My school is in Kabul."

"Kabul?" This village was in the Kandahar Province, south of Kabul and west of the Pakistan border. Another mysterious nugget of information.

"You don't normally live here?"

"I was born here. My father sent me to live with his brother in Kabul when I was sixteen. Right after the Taliban were removed from power."

"In 2001, when the U.S. and Coalition forces launched an offensive."

She looked at him sharply. "Do you realize what you said?"

Not until it had come out of his mouth. "Yeah. I do. Like I said, that's been happening on and off lately."

"Since you've been off the opium."

"Yes. And it seems to happen when we talk. That day in the kitchen. Now. Conversation seems to trigger these . . . memories. Keep talking to me." He worked to contain his excitement. This felt like a breakthrough. If he could remember things about Afghanistan, maybe he could remember something about who he was.

"You are right," she said, and he could hear a barely contained excitement in her voice, too. "The American and Coalition forces defeated the Taliban in 2001. Radical sharia law was thrown out. Girls returned to school. Women went to work. At least, in some provinces."

"But not in Kandahar?"

"No. Not in Kandahar."

"No wonder you prefer Kabul."

"What I prefer are basic human rights. The Taliban have been ousted from political power, but they still rule by terror here in Kandahar Province. Women here are expected to follow sharia law. We have no rights. We are chattel. Only because of my father, only because he is a *malik*, was he able to send me to Kabul, where I went to school."

"To become a teacher."

"Yes. And to become active in the Afghan women's movement. Because of us, there are women in parliament now. Some of us even drive."

Her statement triggered another memory. "You were driving when you found me."

"Yes." Pride filled her tone. He understood why. She was a trailblazer.

"Isn't it dangerous for you to drive in this part of Afghanistan?"

"Because of the heavy Taliban presence, yes. But I studied hard to pass the test and earn the right to drive as any man does."

"That doesn't explain why you risked driving through Taliban territory."

"My father called me home. I drove during daylight hours to avoid the night patrols."

She was not only beautiful, she was also smart and brave, and she honored her father. Here a daughter obeyed her father with no questions asked.

"Your father is ill, isn't he?"

She drew a long breath. "He is old. And yes, he is not as well as he once was."

He had noticed that the old man barely picked at his food. And then there was the excessive sleeping. "He should see a doctor."

"He refuses. He is a stubborn man, my father. Like you, I believe, are a stubborn man." She stood then and held out her hand. "Do not tell me no again. We must go inside. And you will accept my help." Sheer determination filled her eyes.

"And if I say no?" Because she looked so stern, he couldn't resist baiting her.

"Then you will be responsible for me not getting any sleep this night."

She'd known exactly how to get to him. "That's not playing fair."

"What about life is fair?"

Didn't he know it? And yet this exchange made him smile.

He took her hand and slowly rose to a sitting position. Standing had gotten easier, but he always had to take extreme care with sudden movements, or he'd land on his ass, sweating like a marathon runner in the last mile, swallowing back his dinner, and hanging on to the world while it spun out of control.

"Wait until you are steady," she said when he finally had his feet beneath him.

They stood side-by-side in the moonlight, his weight on his good leg, his world fairly level. It struck him then that for a woman of such strength, she was neither tall nor heavily built.

"How tall are you?"

She told him in Pashto.

That calculated in English to five feet four inches, which made him around five-foot-eight or -nine since the top of her head was level with his nose.

"Ready?" she asked uncertainly.

Ten feet separated them from the edge of the flat roof. "I can do this."

Only the first step out of the gate proved he couldn't. His bad leg promptly cramped, and he started to go down. Rabia moved in fast. She tucked herself under his shoulder and wrapped an arm around his waist, steadying him.

"That went well," he gritted out as he rode through the burning ache in his shin.

"I suspect your leg was once broken and did not heal well," she said as he leaned on her for support.

"Bastards wouldn't set it. They dumped me in that hole and——"

He stopped, felt his gut tighten, as a wrenching memory of a hole in sand-colored soil crystallized through a murky fog.

Four feet deep, four feet wide, six feet long.

Covered with a crude lattice hatch of rough wood that only opened once a day when they threw starvation rations of food and water at him. If he was quick enough, he tossed out the contents of his waste bucket.

Snow and ice covered him.

Rain washed in.

Sun burned and baked.

He carved lines into the dirt wall with his knuckle to mark the time that crawled like the snakes that sometimes slithered into the hole with him.

Two hundred fifty-five lines that he counted over and over again so he wouldn't ever forget, wouldn't ever forgive.

A cold fear gripped him. A cold sweat enveloped him.

Two hundred fifty-five lines? Two hundred fifty-five *days*?

It couldn't be. He wasn't thinking straight. And yet he knew the number was significant.

"*Askar?*" Rabia. Her voice sounded far away and full of concern.

"My God." He dropped to his knees, dragging her down with him. Horrible, excruciating memories shot across his mind's eye like tracer rounds in a sky lit up with RPGs.

Two hundred fifty-five lines.

Not twenty-three lines in a cave.

Not another twenty-eight days in Rabia's father's home.

Somewhere, somehow, had he really survived two hundred fifty-five days in a hole in the ground where he'd been caged like an animal?

No. He wouldn't believe it. It couldn't be true.

He wouldn't *let* it be true. He *couldn't* let it be true, because that meant he hadn't merely survived a month or two before Rabia found him. It meant he'd been lost for nearly a year.

Or was it even more than a year?

"My God, my God." He started shaking uncontrollably.

How much of his life had he lost? And how many *more* lines had he made in other holes that he didn't remember?

Chapter

12

Northern Minnesota, August

If you don't come back and finish this, I might have to hunt you down and hurt you.

Jess still didn't know if she should be mortified or proud that she'd issued Ty that ultimatum three weeks ago. Either way, she'd said it. And she'd meant it. Now, twenty-one long days later, she was going to have to make good on her words. Good sense or bad, she could hardly wait.

"What are you looking for?" Kayla asked as Jess rummaged around behind the counter for Bear's leash.

"Before it gets any darker, I want to take Bear for a quick W-A-L-K." Since the Lab understood the word *walk* and went wild with excitement when she said it, Jess spelled it out for Kayla.

"How will you ever be able to tear your eyes away from the clock for that long?" Kayla teased.

"You're a laugh a minute, you know that?"

"I do, yes." Kayla counted back change to a customer.

Kayla was right, Jess thought as she got sidetracked by another last-minute sale and stopped to scoop up two ice cream cones and ring up a bag of marshmallows and a bottle of peppermint schnapps. She'd been watching the clock for the better part of an hour, like a teenager waiting for her prom date. The fact that it was almost nine P.M., closing time, was secondary. Ty's plane had been due to land in International Falls at eight, and she expected him to show up anytime now.

She shouldn't have missed him this much. She shouldn't have gone to bed every night and awakened every morning thinking about him. She should have been more mature. And sane. Apparently, however, she wasn't either. And the deal was, she no longer cared.

Ty Brown made her feel alive and desirable and special. So after the first few days of being mortified by the way she'd all but melted in his arms, she'd decided not to fight it. She'd decided to enjoy it—whatever *it* was. She was way too wary to call it anything more than chemistry and infatuation, regardless of what it felt like. She only knew that every time her phone rang or her text alert sounded, her heart went a little haywire. He'd called every day. Sometimes twice a day. He sent her silly e-mails and sexy text messages.

More than once in the past three weeks, Kayla had caught her grinning at her phone and called her on it.

"Commando Cutie's getting frisky, is he?"

"Don't you have shelves to stock?" was her standard reply, even though Jess knew she wasn't fooling Kayla.

"When's he coming back?" was Kayla's stock retort.

"Who said anything about him coming back?"

"You know, you can go to hell for lying."

"Oh, for the days when the younguns respected their elders."

And so it went. But tonight was the night. Ty was coming back, and she felt like one electric, twitchy nerve because of it.

She'd finally found Bear's leash when the hose at the gas pump dinged, alerting her that she had yet another customer outside.

"You act like you're looking for someone." Kayla again. Too astute.

"I'm ready for the day to be over is all," Jess lied. What she was ready for was for the night to begin.

That was the other decision she'd made. She was an adult. With needs . . . needs that she'd stored in dry dock too long. Everything would change between her and Ty tonight. It was going to get physical . . . and she could hardly draw a deep breath thinking about it.

Hearing him talk about Maya that day on the lake, about how he'd loved her, how he would always love her, had somehow made her accept that she could do that, too. She could always love J.R. But it was OK for her to open up to her own feelings now. It made it all right. Ty was moving on with his life. It was time she moved on, too, regardless of what happened between them in the long term, because the long term was something she wasn't looking for—not with Ty.

She knew where that path led. What she was looking for was a fling with a nice guy, a gorgeous guy, and she wasn't going to sabotage her chances by over-thinking things like repercussions and expectations and guilt. She'd lived in the past for too long. The time had come to live in the moment.

"You know," Kayla said as she stepped over Bear to get out from behind the cash register, "I'm not stupid, and I'm not blind. Something's up. The makeup looks good, by the way. Hair, too."

Nothing got past that girl. If Kayla suspected that some of the packages she'd brought home from Duluth last week were filled with loot from Victoria's Secret, she'd never hear the end of it. Jess had made the two-and-a-half-hour trip on the pretense of checking out a craft show. Since one section of her store was devoted to touristy-type knickknacks, she was always looking to replenish her inventory with something unique. And since her underwear drawer was just that, a utilitarian underwear drawer, she'd been in dire need of a little silk and lace.

"I like seeing you this happy," Kayla announced, looking smug.

Kayla's statement gave her pause. "Have I really been such a sad sack?"

"No," Kayla assured her quickly. "You weren't ever a sad sack. But you weren't ever . . . what's the word? This *bubbly* before."

"Bubbly? Oh, please, God, save me."

Kayla laughed. "What? It looks good on you."

If her personality change was that obvious, then Kayla couldn't have been the only one who noticed. And Jess knew it for a fact.

"Something's amiss. Do you have a secret lover, my little lotus blossom?" Boots teased her every day.

"All right. I confess," she'd finally told him this morning. "You found me out. I'm having a torrid affair with the bait man."

Boots slapped a spread palm to his chest, faking a heart attack. "Cooter? You'd choose him over me? Me who buys your coffee and sings your praises daily? That man smells like a fish and looks like a bear. Besides, he's a grampa."

"So are you, you old flirt."

She knew others were also speculating. And she knew her brother-in-law was not happy. Brad had made that clear the morning Ty had flown back to Florida.

"Your life. Your business," he'd said when he stopped by on the pretense of filling his travel coffee mug, his tone implying that he very much thought it was his business, too. "But you need to remember that you're a target, Jess."

"What are you talking about?"

"I know about your date with the pilot. And I know you spent a day with him on the lake."

Even knowing this was coming, she hadn't been prepared for the flat-out hostility in Brad's eyes. Or for her own anger as she suddenly realized that Brad's attitude had been part of the reason she hadn't been able to move on. "Look, Brad—"

He'd cut her off with a dark look. "You're a target," he reminded her. "A widow with an income. Men will take advantage."

She'd wanted to laugh but contained herself. Brad clearly hadn't been in a joking mood. In fact, when he was like that, he reminded her very much of J.R. Brad was taller and heavier than J.R., and his complexion and hair were lighter, but there was an intensity about him that was J.R. through and through.

"Brad," she'd said reasonably, making herself settle down, "I barely make ends meet here, you know that. I think we can safely rule out the possibility of some golddigger targeting me for my money."

"Any man who takes advantage of another man's wife isn't much of a man in my book. And any woman who forgets where she came from . . . well, just don't forget where you came from."

She'd been so stunned by his vitriol she could only watch him stalk out the door.

Any man who takes advantage of another man's wife.

She was no longer anyone's wife. She was a widow,

and she was entitled to a life. Brad would never see it that way. Maybe if he met Ty, he'd see what a good man he was.

And maybe fish would fly.

The bell above the door rang and drew her out of her worrisome thoughts. She recognized the ball cap first. Then she recognized the smile and the hitch in her breath that she should be used to by now but always caught her off-guard.

He looked good. He looked so very, very good.

"Well, well." Kayla's grin stretched a mile wide. "Look who found his way back north."

"Hey, Kayla." Ty's gaze never left Jess's face. "How's it going?"

"Why, it's going just fine, thanks for asking." She darted an amused look from Ty to Jess. "Go ahead and take Bear for that walk, boss. I'll close up."

At the word *walk*, Bear bolted out from behind the counter with a happy yelp and barreled past Ty to get to the door.

"Whoa, big fella." Ty laughed and grabbed the excited pup's collar as Jess rushed out and clipped on the leash.

"He's starting to grow into his feet." Ty squatted down and scratched the dog's ears, then looked up at Jess. "Mind if I tag along? I could use a stretch after my flight."

Jess didn't understand how he could look so cool and collected and in control when she was melting by slow, hot degrees.

"We'll be right back," she told Kayla, and headed out the door, feeling happier and more vital than she had since the night Ty had kissed her and left her wanting more.

"Take your time." Kayla's voice floated out after them, sounding annoyingly pleased and far too amused.

✱

"I TAKE IT no one knew I was coming back today?"

The dog sniffed happily at the grass along the shoulder as they walked down the blacktop road.

"I didn't figure it was anyone's business but mine."

Ty liked being her private business. He liked the way her eyes had lit up when she'd seen him walk in the door. He'd had hopes. When they'd talked or texted or exchanged e-mails, there'd been a quality in her voice or her tone that suggested she was ready to open herself up to this. That she was ready for them. But until he'd seen her face, he hadn't been counting on anything. Now he was counting on a lot.

She looked good. While he loved the wholesome look of her without makeup, he liked it that she'd made a special effort to look nice for him.

"I thought this day would never come," he confessed, and reached for her hand.

Warmth spread through his chest when she eagerly entwined her fingers with his. "I'd started to think it wouldn't."

Better and better. "I'm sorry it took me so long. Everywhere I turned, I ran into red lights that slowed me down. But it's all good now. My deck's cleared."

"For how long?"

"Two weeks, at least. Longer if you want it to be."

He'd hoped he'd see that pleased look in her eyes, but until it was a certainty, he'd been holding his breath. It made his next move so easy.

He stopped and pulled her toward him. "No cars ahead of us. No cars behind."

"My powers of deductive reasoning lead me to conclude that we must be alone, then."

He loved this carefree, playful side, too. Apparently, absence not only made the heart grow fonder, it also made it grow braver. "Reason to celebrate."

She looped her arms around his neck. "What'd you have in mind?"

"The same thing that's been on my mind since the last time I saw you."

"Then why are you wasting so much time talking about it?"

He laughed and pulled her snugly against him, letting her feel exactly what she did to him. "Oh, what a difference three weeks and a handful of suggestive text messages can make."

She laughed, too. "There you go. Talking again."

"There you go. Reminding me."

"Ty. Shut up and kiss me."

"Yes, ma'am."

Chapter

13

*M*idnight had been lonely for so long. Midnight had become an hour Jess dreaded and that she spent awake and alone too many nights.

That she wasn't alone tonight felt like a small miracle. She didn't want to remember how lost she had been. She wanted only to think about the touch of this man's hands, alternately rough and gentle and oh so skilled. She wanted to be swallowed up in the solid, hot bulk of his body. The feel of him deep inside her. The suction of his mouth on her breast as she came with an involuntary convulsion of muscle and a gasp of wonder.

When she could take a breath that wasn't a shudder, she lightly bit his shoulder, steeping herself in the maleness of him, his strength, the way his mouth cruised over her body and brought life where life had been gone for so, so long.

"You OK?"

She stretched in contentment and framed his face in her hands. "You really have to ask?"

He'd brought her there twice tonight. Eased her up the first time and taken her over. Then he'd turned on the lights and taken her fast and hard and desperately.

Now, in the aftermath, his heart slammed hard and true against her breasts. She loved the vital maleness of him. The heat and the scent of his skin, the bulk of muscle pressing her into the mattress as he rose up on his elbows and scattered kisses along her throat.

"You're so beautiful."

She needed that. He must know she needed that. She'd been shy when the first moment came. She'd led him to her bedroom and turned off the lights. Undressed in the dark. Met him on the bed where she'd never lain with a man, trembling, vulnerable, and more alive than she ever remembered feeling.

It had been so long. So long since the press of flesh on flesh had electrified her. So long since she'd lain beside a man whose caresses and low groans told her that yes, she was enough, and yes, she excited him, and yes, this was what magic felt like.

There had never been any question where this night would end. She'd wanted him in her bed since the moment he'd left her—probably even before that, if she were being honest. She'd wanted him so badly that it should have frightened her. It might have, if the deep, aching need hadn't outdistanced any thought of caution and consequences.

There'd be time enough to sort it all out. To-night . . . tonight she wanted to indulge.

She caressed his shoulders, explored the play of muscle over bone, and wondered how she had lived without this.

"Too heavy?" he murmured against her jaw.

"Too confined. I want to touch you. All of you."

He groaned low and deep and with effort rolled off her and onto his back. Spread-eagle. Totally male. Utterly remarkable.

"Be gentle with me."

She pressed up on an elbow and grinned down at him. "I'll try to restrain myself."

"So you know . . . I need a little recovery time."

She kissed the center of his chest. "Not a problem. All you have to do is lie there."

"I can do that."

She didn't want thoughts of J.R. in this bed. Not fair to him. Not fair to Ty. But the differences were too huge to ignore. With J.R., it had been all about the intensity. With Ty, it was that and more. It was fun. There was laughter. She liked the laughter. She liked the heat. So she ignored the scars—the ones on his back and the one she'd discovered on his shoulder—because she didn't want more reminders of war in this bed tonight, either.

She took her time, then, took her pleasure exploring and engaging her power over him with each light finger stroke, with the press of her lips against flesh that was tender and sensitive and so responsive.

"You're killing me." His hands knotted in her hair, gently tugged.

She smiled against that sensitive spot where groin met thigh, fascinated by the thrum of his pulse beneath her lips, the depth of his ragged breaths, the fact that her brazen exploration delivered the sweetest kind of torment.

"And oh, what's this?" He swelled in her hand as she surrounded him. "Not so much recovery time, after all?"

He laughed. "Remember . . . you started this."

She rose to her knees and straddled him, slowly guided him home. "I did. Now I'm going to finish it."

And then she moved. Taking him in. Taking him deep, until his hips rose to meet hers, and his hands covered her breasts, finessing her nipples into aching, hard peaks, and she became as caught up as he was.

"Jess." Her name eased out on a whisper, a curse, and finally a plea as he gripped her hips and slammed her down over him one final time, coming on a low, throaty groan and tipping her over the edge with him.

✱

IT WAS BARELY daylight when Ty eased out from under the sheet so as not to wake Jess. On the floor by the bed, the pup raised his head, his tail thumping softly on the rug.

"Shh." He scratched the dog's ears and lightly tapped his thigh so Bear would follow him.

"You're a good dog, aren't you?" he murmured.

The Lab padded out of the bedroom with him, toenails clicking softly on polished hardwood as he followed Ty down the hall to the kitchen.

He hadn't seen much of her apartment last night. The minute they'd returned to the store and double-checked the locks, she'd led him upstairs. She'd flicked on an end-table lamp that had bathed the living room in a soft glow. He'd gotten quick impressions of lived-in leather, old wood, and splashes of vibrant color. But he'd had eyes for nothing but Jess as she'd led him to her bedroom and, in the shadows, welcomed him to her bed.

"Do you know where she keeps the coffee?" he asked the pup, who sat in the middle of the kitchen with an expectant look on his doggie face. "No? Bet you know where she keeps the dog biscuits."

Bear's tail swished softly across the floor.

With the first cupboard door he opened, he hit pay dirt—for him and the dog.

He opened a box of dog biscuits and tossed one to the pup. Bear caught it like a pro.

"Somebody's been practicing."

He'd figured out how to load the coffee pot and had turned it on when he heard Jess behind him.

He turned around and thought, *wow*. She looked exactly the way a woman should after a night of amazing sex. Her lips looked bee-stung, her hair was beautifully tousled, and her eyes were sooty and sleepy. The only thing out of place was the tentative smile.

"We woke you."

She shook her head. "No. It was time to get up."

Wearing only the jeans he'd found on the floor by her bed, he walked barefoot over to where she stood wearing a short, silky blue robe and, he hoped, nothing else.

She moved in to him on a sigh, and he drew her against him, gathered fistfuls of silk, and moved it out of his way so he could fill his palms with her bare cheeks.

"Last night was amazing, Jess."

She tipped her head back, and he saw the smile he wanted. A confident woman's smile that negated the hint of uncertainty he never wanted to see in her eyes again.

"It was," she agreed, and lifted her face to his. Then she kissed him the way a man liked to be kissed.

"Now, that's the way to tell a man good morning."

"It is a good morning."

She kissed him again, and he toyed with the belt of her robe. "Maybe we should take this back to the bedroom."

"I wish. But I've got to get moving."

He liked the disappointed look on her face. And he'd known she needed to get ready for work but couldn't help being disappointed himself. "How much time do you have?"

She stretched up on her toes and looked over his shoulder to the clock that hung on the wall above the sink. "Less than an hour. And I've got to take Bear for a run, shower, set up the cash registers—"

"Enough said," he said reluctantly. "You're a working woman. Go. Take Bear for his run. I'll have breakfast ready when you get back."

She regarded him from beneath knit brows. "Seriously?"

"Sure. Why not?"

"Because you don't have to do that."

"Cook for you? I want to."

When she still looked skeptical, it dawned on him that maybe it wasn't the cooking that was hanging her up. This was a small, tightly knit community. His presence here so early in the morning would be cause for much speculation and gossip. Something she wouldn't be comfortable with.

"Do you want me to go? To not be here . . . as in *here*, here when you open up?" He lifted a hand to encompass her apartment. "It's not a problem. I can head over to Whispering Pines and rent a cabin from Shelley."

"No. I want you here. I just feel bad. Two of my regulars asked to have their hours cut because they've started football practice. I won't be able to take as much time off to be with you as I'd hoped."

He touched a hand to her soft curls. "Jess. I didn't expect you to drop everything to entertain me—well, except maybe in there." He hitched his chin toward the bedroom and gave her a lecherous sneer.

He loved the sound of her laugh as she pulled away and headed for the bedroom. "You're going to be bored."

"Not if last night was any barometer."

"I'm talking about during the day."

"Let me worry about that. Go walk your dog. He's standing by the door with his legs crossed."

When she came out of the bedroom in shorts, a tank top, and running shoes, her face was sober. "You need to know. J.R.'s brother, Brad. He'll show up once word spreads. He won't be happy about you being here. In fact, there's a good chance he'll be looking for a fight."

He walked across the room and cupped her shoulders. "I understand about brothers. It'll be OK." Then he gave her a squeeze. "Now, go. Bear's about to spring a leak."

✳

"MORNING, JESS," KAYLA said. "Interesting to note that the rental pickup Ty drove up in yesterday is parked in exactly the same spot that it was in when I locked up last night."

"Interesting to a snoop, maybe." Jess smiled to take the bite out of her warning to Kayla.

Of course, it didn't faze the nineteen-year-old, who found Ty's return and the fact that he'd obviously spent the night way too interesting. "So . . . is he as good as he looks?"

Jess expelled a deep sigh. "When do classes start for you?"

Kayla giggled. "Ready to get rid of me?"

"Ready to strangle you, but since there's a law against it, I guess I'll have to come up with something else."

"Don't worry, boss. Your secret's safe with me."

About that time, her "secret" opened the door that led to the stairs to her apartment and walked into the store, looking absolutely edible in faded jeans and a white T-shirt.

He glanced from Kayla with her Cheshire Cat grin to Jess and lifted his brows. "Did I interrupt something?"

"Kayla was about to straighten up the shelves holding the sweatshirts and T-shirts. We had a crowd in here yesterday, and I swear they dragged every single shirt out of its cubby and stuffed it back in a wad."

"Guess I'll be folding shirts if anyone needs me." Kayla gave Ty a thumbs-up and headed for the shelves.

"What's that about?" Ty met Jess on the other side of the counter.

"She thinks we're cute."

"I think *you're* cute." He leaned in close. "And very, very hot."

She hated that heat flushed her cheeks. The fact that it made him laugh didn't take much of the sting out of her involuntary physical reaction.

"Why don't you put me to work today?" he said, still grinning.

"What? No. I don't want to do that."

"I want you to. If you don't have anything for me to do in the store, give me something to do outside. I'm not a thumb twiddler."

"I seem to recall you bought a fishing pole and some tackle last time you were here. You should go fishing. Or hike one of the trails. Or explore the shoreline. Shelley and Darrin would loan you a kayak. Just don't go too far out in open water, or you might get lost."

"You sure you're not trying to get rid of me?"

"After that breakfast? Are you kidding?" He'd fried bacon, made French toast, and squeezed oranges for juice.

"Ah, so it's my cooking skills that won you over?"

She glanced over to the shirt section to make sure Kayla was out of earshot. "Among other things."

Her cheeks were still stained bright red when the bell above the door rang and the first customer of the day walked inside.

Chapter

14

I approve of your new handyman."

It was almost noon when Jess closed the lid on the ice cream cooler to see Boots walk in.

She looked up at him. "Handyman?"

"Good-lookin' fella. Struck me as a nice guy. Knows what he's doing, too. Had a little talk with him outside while he worked on your shed roof."

She scowled, wiped her hands on a paper towel, and headed outside. "Kayla. Ring up these cones, will you? I'll be right back."

Ty had made himself scarce, and it had been a busy morning, so Jess hadn't had time to give him more than a passing thought. OK, a lot of passing thoughts, most of them having to do with the way they'd spent last night in her bed and how eager she was for tonight to get here so they could start all over again.

In the meantime, she'd hoped he'd gone fishing or kayaking as she'd suggested, but as Boots promised, she found Ty on his knees on the slanted roof of her storage shed, a hammer in one hand, a nail apron tied around his waist, and a square of shingles on the roof beside him. He'd already torn off all the old shingles, laid tar paper, and nailed the new shingles over three-fourths of the roof.

She shielded her eyes against the sun and glared up at him. "What are you doing?"

"A damn fine job, according to your watchdog." He slammed the hammer down, then dug into the apron. "Boots, right? Now, there's a character."

"Get down from there right now."

"Save that tone for tonight. I love it when you go all boss lady on me."

"Ty!"

He hammered another nail. "I'm almost done."

"You *are* done. I'm serious. I don't want you working like that."

He finally looked down at her, then glanced around the parking lot to make certain no one was within earshot. "Afraid I'll be worn out tonight?"

That grin, she'd learned, could be as infuriating as it was infectious. And the way he looked . . . his hair and shirt damp with sweat, the veins in his forearms bulging with pumping blood, his worn jeans hugging his hips and thighs and showing a hint of pale, smooth skin where his T-shirt had ridden up . . . well, as upset as she was, if she managed to haul him down off that roof, she might not stop hauling until she'd led him up the stairs, straight to the shower, and joined him there.

"I don't want you working," she insisted, dragging her gaze back to his face. "Period. I especially don't want you shingling my roof."

"You're saying it didn't need it? Look . . . I was digging around for a hammer to fix the back door, and I found the shingles inside the shed. Figured you planned on hiring someone to do the job."

"What I planned was to do it myself when business slows down in the fall."

"Then that's all the better reason for me to do it. Gives me a chance to feel all studly on your behalf."

She grunted. "Spoken like a manly man."

He laughed. "Consider it payment for room and board."

As if she was going to charge him. "You're going to hurt your back."

"You let me worry about my back. I'll have this finished by mid-afternoon. Easy peasy. Tomorrow I'll put that roll of window screen to use."

She wanted to be mad. But how could she? He'd saved her a ton of work and had probably done a better job than she would have. As for the window screen, she'd bought it two years ago with the intent of replacing the ratty screens on both the store and her apartment windows. Various other projects had always taken priority.

Then again, everything about the store was a project. The building was more than eighty years old. It required constant maintenance, most of which she tried to do herself to save money. Besides, doing things herself was important to her. She didn't want to be dependent. She particularly didn't want to depend on Ty, who was not about to become a permanent fixture in her life. And she didn't him want him to be.

She didn't want to find it endearing, either, that he liked her dog, was fascinated by the lake, and made her breakfast. And she didn't want to get used to him "fixing" things for her. Before she knew it, she'd become reliant on him. She'd already, in this very short time, come to count on him to make her smile, to make her feel pretty, to remind her what it was like to be a woman who was attracted to a man—a man who made it clear, without pushing, that he was very attracted to her.

But none of this was about the long term, and if she wasn't careful, she could end up wishing that it was.

"Did you know that those gorgeous brown eyes of yours actually snap when you're mad? Hey," he added softly when she didn't smile. "Don't look so mean. I told you. I'm not good at twiddling my thumbs. I like to work. And as Boots and you can both attest, I'm pretty good with my hands."

That teasing grin again. And oh, she knew exactly how good he was with those hands.

"Jess?"

"What?" She crossed her arms belligerently around her midriff and scowled up at him.

"As long as you're out here, I could use another bottle of water. It's warm up here."

"Ya think?" Anger seemed her only option. "It's August. It's noon. It's at least ninety degrees outside."

Her mini-tirade didn't daunt him. "You forget. I live in Florida. This is jogging weather."

"You're going to learn not to tease me, flyboy." She spun around and headed back to the store for his water. "There will be retaliation."

"If I said, 'Oh, goody,' would I lose my stud card?"

She didn't turn around, but she knew he was having a good chuckle at her expense as she jerked open the store's back door. In spite of her determination not to be charmed by everything about him—even his teasing—she smiled as she reached into the cooler and pulled out a bottle of water.

✳

"I'M THINKING YOU made a great nurse. You have healing hands. Very healing hands," Ty murmured into the pillow as he lay on his stomach on the bed, enjoying Jess's back and shoulder massage.

It had become a nightly event this past week. One he looked forward to—among other things—at the end of each day. Currently, she straddled his thighs, and even without seeing her, he knew that the straps on her short black silk and lace nightgown were giving her trouble. The thought of that soft, tan skin made it difficult to stay on his stomach. The massage, however, proved great enticement to stay put. She really did have magic hands.

On the second day after he'd returned, she'd finally quit hassling him about fixing things for her. Not that she'd given in easily. They'd more or less agreed to disagree when she'd finally accepted that he was as stubborn as she was. There were so many things that needed to be done that he never ran out of projects. Today he'd found a gallon of paint in her hall closet marked "Kitchen," so he'd painted the room for her. The woman had too much on her plate. He liked lightening her load.

And she liked pampering him because of it. A win-win any way you sliced it.

"I saw a float plane buzz the store on the way to the lake today," he said sleepily. "What's the story there?"

She squirted more lotion on her hands and went to work on his lower back. "That would be Wade Cummings. He flies charters into fishing camps on Crane and Rainy Lakes. Keeps him busy most of the summer and even into the winter. Some of these guys can't get enough, so he switches out the pontoons with sleds and flies in groups for ice fishing."

"He the only game in town?"

"He is now. A guy out of Vermillion, about forty miles south of here, ran his own charter, but he retired last year."

He didn't say anything else, but he was thinking. A lot. Maybe someone ought to start another charter business. Maybe that someone should be him. Key West Air Cargo might need to diversify. But it was still early in this game. He and Jess were still getting to know each other—at least, she was getting to know him. He knew all that he needed to know about her.

He also knew that he was falling for her. Falling hard and fast, growing more enamored by the day with this independent, hardworking woman who had taken so much on her slim shoulders and bore the weight without complaint or a hint of self-pity over the hits life had given her. She was a survivor. She was a siren. And he hoped like hell that one day soon, she'd acknowledge and accept that there was no need for barriers between them.

The problem was, they seemed to be going backward in that area. She'd let him into her bed, yes, let him into her home, but she'd made it clear—more in deed than in words—that she was determined not to let him into her heart.

In bed, she was adventurous, exciting, and surprisingly trusting. Out of bed was a different story. Instead of opening up to him, she'd started holding back. It was almost as if she'd realized she was letting herself get involved with him and put on the skids.

OK. Fine. If she needed more time, he had time to give. He wasn't going anywhere. Not even after he'd accidentally discovered what must have been her husband's truck lovingly covered and stored in the large shed behind the store. He'd looked beneath the tarp. It was a newer-model Chevy, all tricked out, not even two thousand miles on the odometer. Yet she drove a ten-year-old Taurus with more than a hundred thousand miles on it.

Letting go was not something she did easily. Loyalty was not something she took lightly.

"Tell me about these," she said softly, as her fingers gently massaged the surgical scar tissue on his lower spine. "And this." She touched his bicep and the scar there.

He'd felt the softness of her fingertips on his scars often during the night. Had known these questions wouldn't hold much longer. Actually, he'd been surprised she hadn't asked before now. A month ago, the day they'd gone kayaking, she'd asked, but he'd avoided answering. He hadn't wanted to rehash the injuries. But now she'd asked again. He didn't miss the significance. If she really wanted to erect barriers to avoid emotional intimacy, she wouldn't have brought it up again. Which meant he needed to bite the bullet and spill it if there was any hope she'd eventually do the same.

It wouldn't be easy. Recounting the way a man earned a Purple Heart and a Silver Star never was.

"The short of it is, I was flying away from a combat zone with casualties onboard. We were clear, so our air cover had left. Then we weren't clear anymore."

Her hands stilled. "You got shot down?"

"Job hazard. An RPG blew the chopper's tail rotor off. Not the preferred method of meeting the ground from too damn many feet above it."

"You crash-landed?" She sounded horrified.

"Pretty much, yeah." With a little maneuvering on both of their parts, he managed to turn onto his back so he could see her face. Her beautiful, troubled face.

He stroked her arms and met her eyes in the dim bedroom light. "Hey. Don't look like that. I'm here. I'm OK."

Her hands rested on his chest. "You were hurt."

"Me and a lot of others. Some more than hurt."

He'd lost his copilot and his gunner. Wives had lost husbands. Children had lost fathers. She didn't need to hear that. She'd already lived that.

"Anyway, we had a bit of a hard landing, and the welcome wagon didn't exactly greet us."

"And your air support was gone. You had no weapons."

"We had rifles. And handguns." Rocks. Pieces of the bird. They'd used everything they could gather to defend their position.

"The scar on your arm. It's a gunshot wound, isn't it?"

He felt torn between loving that she felt such

empathy for him and concern that she gave too much importance to something that had happened a long time ago. But when a woman had lost a husband to war, there were questions that would always remain unanswered.

"You go to war. You get shot at," he said, shrugging it off.

Only none of it was as casual as he wanted to sound. He'd survived the crash, but it hadn't ended there. They'd been sitting ducks. The only reason he was alive today was that the radio hadn't gone the way of the tail rotor. He'd been slammed through the windshield on impact and thrown out of the chopper. Walking hadn't been an option—exquisite pain from several herniated discs and a couple of cracked vertebrae made it impossible. So he'd dragged himself back into the cockpit and called in air support. Directed them "danger close"—within two hundred meters with smart weapons and three hundred meters with unguided weapons.

For a while there, he'd been more afraid of friendly fire taking them out than of Saddam's Royal Guard—although one of the bastards had nailed his arm.

"End result, I herniated a few discs. No biggie. Surgery fixed them, and now I'm good as new."

More like good as it was going to get, even after two surgeries and months of grueling physical therapy, but she didn't need to know that, either.

"No biggie? You could have been paralyzed. You could have died."

"But I didn't." He touched a palm to her cheek. "I didn't die, Jess."

"No. But your naval career did. The injuries are the reason your career was cut short, aren't they?"

He breathed deep. He didn't like thinking about this. "A grounded pilot isn't much good to the military, and the Navy docs wouldn't clear me to fly." Another crash or even a hard landing might cause permanent paralysis. His CO had put the paperwork for a medical discharge in the works before he'd even gotten out of the hospital.

Flying for the military and flying for himself, however, were two entirely different things. He'd had no difficulty passing the physical to get his civilian flight license.

"I'm sorry." She leaned down and pressed a kiss to the center of his chest.

"For everything there is a season . . . For every rhyme there is a reason."

She smiled against his skin. "Making up your own verses, I see."

Her smile was his cue. Time to lighten things up. For both of them.

"I like making things up as I go. For instance, how about we get rid of this?" He tugged the straps of her gown down her arms. The soft fabric caught on her nipples before spilling around her hips. She was so stunningly beautiful. "Let's see what else we can make up as we go along."

Chapter

15

*W*hat would you think about moving the display holding your souvenir items against the wall, then sliding the cubbies full of T-shirts and sweatshirts into a central aisle in their place?"

Ty had been after Jess all morning to take a break from her book work and walk this idea through with him.

"The truth is, I've been wanting to do that, but—"

"You never had the time." He finished the well-used phrase for her.

"Don't look so smug."

"Permission to proceed?"

"If you're looking for an 'Aye-aye, sailor,' you're not going to get it from me."

He laughed. "And if you don't want me to do it,

speak now, or forever hold your peace. Some of this stuff is so small it's easy to slip into a pocket, and these shelves are out of view of your mirrors."

He'd given her more than a hard time over her less than state-of-the-art surveillance system this past week. Jess knew it was lacking, but then, this wasn't exactly the city, where shoplifting was a major problem. This was the north woods. People came here with relaxation, not petty larceny, on their minds.

"You're going to do what you want to do anyway, so what difference does it make if I say no?"

"Hey." He gripped her arm and gently turned her to face him. "This is your business. You make the calls. Period. I'm not trying to intrude, you know that. Right? I'm not trying to run your show, Jess. You say the word, and I leave things as is. I'll find something that needs to be fixed. Lord knows, that's a never-ending list."

Because he looked and sounded so concerned that she would think he was interfering, she smiled at him. "As if I'd ever let you get by with messing in my business. Knock yourself out. If you need an extra hand, give me a yell."

"I need an extra hand," he said, all low and sexy. Then he guided said hand to his heart. "Here." Then to his lips. "Here. Wanna know where else?"

She was laughing at the suggestive gleam in his eyes when the bell above the door rang—and then she wasn't laughing anymore.

Brad. J.R.'s brother had made himself scarce ever

since Ty had returned. Jess had been intending to call him or even go see him. Give him a heads-up about Ty so he wouldn't be blindsided. But she'd known it would be ugly, so she'd put it off. The anger in Brad's eyes was the main reason.

She'd been dreading this—and she'd known he'd show up, because the grapevine had to be working overtime with news of the stranger staying with J.R.'s wife in the apartment above the store.

She had hoped that when this time came, Ty would be off on an errand. She had desperately hoped that when Brad did show up, he wouldn't see them in a compromising position.

So far, she was batting zero for two.

She slowly pulled her hand away from Ty's and walked across the store to meet her brother-in-law.

"You've been a stranger," she said, hoping to avoid a confrontation between the two men by heading Brad off at the proverbial pass. "Everything OK with you?"

Brad had not looked at her since he'd walked through the door. His angry gaze had fixed on Ty like a laser-guided missile with one intent: destroy the man in its path.

Judging from the silence in Ty's general direction, he was very much aware that something significant was about to happen.

"Let me get you a cup of coffee." She stepped in front of Brad, determined to distract him from something that could come to no good.

"I don't want your coffee. I don't want anything from you."

Brad shouldered around her and walked directly toward Ty.

"Brad—"

"It's OK, Jess." Ty held out a hand. "You must be J.R.'s brother."

Brad stopped, shoulders square, feet spread wide, directly in front of Ty. He ignored Ty's extended hand. "And you must be the lowlife shacking up with my brother's wife."

"Brad!" Jess rushed to step between them. "If you came here looking for a fight, turn around and go right back out the door."

"It's OK, Jess," Ty said again softly. "I've got this. Go finish what you were doing."

"Yeah, Jess," Brad said bitterly. "Do what the man says. The way I hear it, he's pretty much running the show around here. Taking care of this. Taking care of that. Taking care of you."

"That's enough." Ty got right in Brad's face. "You got a bone to pick with me? Fine. But you're not going to disrespect Jess."

"I don't have to. She took care of that when she opened her door and her legs to you."

Jess gasped at the insult and anger in Brad's voice. And she could see in Ty's eyes that he was mad as hell at Brad's goading.

"This is how your brother would want you to treat

her?" Ty challenged with a calm that stunned her. Before Brad could counter, Ty leveled another verbal blow. "I didn't know your brother. But I was deployed to Iraq the same time he was. I knew of him. Knew of his unit. Knew what a stand-up group of soldiers they were. Hell, they were legends. Every last one of them.

"So let's get something clear. Your brother and I fought the same fight. I'm not here to disrespect him. I would never do that. And he would never disrespect Jess. Neither will you. Now, if you can't man up and apologize to her, then walk out the door, and don't come back until you figure out how to do the right thing."

For several long moments, the men faced off. Hands clenched in fists. Legs spring-loaded and ready to pounce.

Jess watched with her heart in her throat.

Finally, Brad turned away. His face burned red with anger as he shouldered past her and stomped out the door.

She hadn't even realized her heartbeat had accelerated until the speed of it made her lightheaded.

"I'm so sorry," she said, horrified and mortified by Brad's behavior. "I should have talked to him a week ago. Explained."

"You've got nothing to explain. It's your life, Jess. And you've got nothing to be sorry for. He, however, does. And he knows it. That's why he's so pissed."

"That could have gotten so much uglier."

He shook his head. "No. That wasn't going to happen. We'd have taken it outside long before it ever came to blows."

She hugged her arms around herself and shivered. "He loved his brother."

"And seeing you move on with your life . . . it's a grim reminder that J.R. is gone and he's not coming back. I'm sorry, Jess," he added softly. "I'm sorry he's gone. But I'm so glad that I'm here."

★

THAT NIGHT, AFTER they'd made love, Jess sat in a chair in the corner of her bedroom, her knees tucked under her chin, and watched Ty sleep.

The worst possible thing had happened. What they had . . . it had become so much more than a fling. But then, she suspected she'd been fooling herself on that count from the beginning. Fooling herself into believing that she wasn't going to fall in love with him.

But how could she not? How could she not love a man who shared her grief over losing her husband, who empathized and understood his brother's anger, and who defended her honor without humiliating her attacker?

How could she not love a man who made her laugh and shingled her roof and made love to her as though she was the end and the beginning of everything he wanted in his life?

She could no longer cling to her argument that he

was just like J.R. That had been a weak prop from the get-go. J.R. had eaten, breathed, and drunk Army from the moment he'd put on the uniform. If he'd lived, he'd have been career. And he'd have been putting himself in harm's way for as long as his CO would let him. Ty, while every bit as heroic, had clearly left that part of his life behind. She wasn't going to lose him to combat—although the memory of the night she'd first met him, with his warrior face on, ready to lay it all on the line, was not something she'd soon forget.

So here she was. Falling in love. Trying not to regret it. Wondering where it would lead. Stunned to find herself in this position.

Quietly, so she wouldn't wake him, she eased off the chair and back into bed. He stirred and turned and pulled her snugly against him, whispering her name in his sleep.

He'd lost as much as she had. Yet he had so much to give. So much life. So much joy. And although he hadn't said the word, it was clear that if she gave him the right signal, he'd give her all the love she could possibly need.

✱

A WEEK LATER. Jess watched Ty drive off to the airport to return to Florida long enough to take care of some pressing business. She missed him already.

"You know, that's what I got you for, Bear." She dropped down onto one knee and cuddled the dog close as Ty's truck faded from sight. "To keep me company and make me laugh and keep my bed warm in the middle of winter. Look how well that worked out."

But as she'd often realized during the past two months, a puppy wasn't a man. And there weren't many men like Tyler Brown.

Later that night, she slowly removed her wedding ring and tucked it inside her jewelry box.

Chapter

16

Afghanistan, September

*T*he cooking room stayed relatively cool, the thick exterior walls blunting the effect of the afternoon sun. Rabia stood back in the shadows near the window, watching the walled courtyard and worrying that the *askar* pushed himself beyond what was wise.

He was still so thin and not yet well, but there was no getting him to stop the grueling exercises he called a workout. Such a stubborn man. A determined man. A man she could not help but admire for the stoic way he endured his injuries and the way he had willed himself off the poppy. She did not know many men who, once mired in the drug, had the strength to fight their way free. And she knew of no man who had suffered as he had during withdrawal and not begged for the relief a dose would bring.

He was also a kind man. Like her husband had been kind. But something had changed inside him the night on the roof when they had talked of his leg.

"I suspect your leg was once broken and did not heal well," she said as he leaned on her for support.

"Bastards wouldn't set it. They dumped me in that hole and . . ."

He had not said anything more. But she knew he had remembered something. When she had asked, he had insisted it was nothing. That the thought had made no sense.

He had not been truthful. Whatever memory had come to him had caused him much anguish, and he did not wish to share.

For many days after that, he had been sullen and silent. Now he was restless and driven to fight his way home.

She did not know how this would be possible, no matter how much of his strength he regained. The village was cut off from Internet and telephone lines, so they all relied on foot messengers passing from village to village. The latest report had arrived yesterday. Taliban patrols had doubled in the two months since the *askar* had escaped.

Find his way home? How? How did he plan to do that? She had no idea if there were any American forces left in the country. Before she had left Kabul, she had heard of the American draw-down and knew it was about to take place. The Americans had decided the ground had been washed with enough American blood.

She watched her *askar* as he sweated and strained. This ground had been washed with *his* blood. She did not want any more of it spilled.

"What American forces?" she had demanded when he had said he would find a way to reconnect with them. "There was once an American military post at the halfway point between here and Kabul. Even if it is still there, you could not get to it. Messengers report that all roads in the province have Taliban checkpoints stationed every half-mile or so or over the next hill or bend in the road."

She had told him all of this, and still he was determined to find a way.

The thought frightened her. Only because she had much time and care invested in him, she told herself. And because if he were captured, he would be tortured, and if he broke, the Taliban would then come after her and her father.

But this was only part of the truth. She had come to care too much. He reminded her with his presence what it was like to share a life, share a bed, and sometimes, foolishly, she wished he could be content to stay here.

Foolish. Impossible. But the thought came, unbidden, especially when she let herself look at him.

He was still so very thin. The meager meals she made for him and her father had added little weight to his bones. His eyes, however, no longer looked empty. He no longer seemed only a victim of the brutality and torture his scars suggested.

Today his chest was bare and slick with perspiration. His head and feet were also bare. He wore only the trousers she had given him. And looking at him like this, in secret, where neither he nor her father could watch her, she felt an ache low in her core that neither guilt nor prayer could deny.

His skin was burned brown from the many days he had spent in the courtyard, testing his strength until his limbs trembled and he could hardly hold his head up.

"What is that you do?" she asked one day as he had lain on a mat on the ground.

"Leg lifts. I'm up to ten sets of five. Slow, tedious." He grunted and pushed himself to do yet one more. "Baby steps."

"And what does this do for you except cause you to grunt and swear and make horrible faces?"

Her grumpiness had made him smile. "You don't like my horrible faces?"

She had crossed her arms at her waist. And said nothing.

"It builds core muscle strength," he'd explained. "I can't do sit-ups, so this will have to do."

She had watched him try to do his sit-ups. The dizziness had hit hard and fast. He had vomited violently, then lain very still for a very long time until the dizziness left him.

"Can't do squats, either." Because of his leg, she knew. "So I have to modify."

He had asked for heavy rocks from the street, which he lifted over and over again above his head. At his request, she had found him a heavy iron bar that he had propped between the forks of two apple trees in the courtyard. Every day, he painfully and slowly chinned himself over and over again.

Ten nights ago, she had awakened to a noise outside and found him climbing the ladder to the roof.

"Why are you not sleeping?" she had whispered from the ground.

"Got to build my lung capacity. Can't do this in daylight. And it's the closest I can come to running stairs."

Then he had proceeded to climb up and down and up and down, his leg clearly giving him pain. Finally, she could not stand watching anymore and had gone back to her bed.

Now here he was again. Pushing himself beyond his limits. She could not bear it any longer and stepped out into the courtyard. "I will not drag your carcass inside if you burn like meat on a spit out there in the heat."

He stopped chinning and looked at her. Sweat ran down his temples, slid down his neck, then trickled down his chest. "I promise it won't come to that."

"You are right. Because you must stop now. Evening meal will soon be ready. You must bathe. You cannot sit at my table covered in dust and sweat and smelling like a goat."

He laughed out loud—a sound that, judging by the look on his face, surprised him. It surprised her, too. She had never heard him laugh. That she had been the cause for such a rich, deep expression of joy made her own heart swell with happiness.

"Yes, ma'am." He touched his fingers to his forehead in salute. "I learned long ago, never piss off the cook."

"Piss off? What does this mean?"

He laughed again, and she could tell it felt good to him, too. "It means I'm going to go clean up so you don't hit me over the head with one of your cooking pots."

This time, she smiled. "You are stubborn but wise. My pots are very big and very hard and very heavy."

He was still smiling when she spun around and headed back inside.

And later, when he appeared again in the courtyard, smelling of soap and dressed in clean clothes like a proper Pashtun man, she could not help but wish it were so.

She had become accustomed to seeing him at her table, which was a cloth laid outside on the ground surrounded by cushions. Because of his bad leg, he could not sit cross-legged. Instead, he'd gotten as comfortable as he could, and as she had taught him, he had left his shoes at the front door and made certain he did not sit with his legs outstretched or his feet facing either her or her father—to do so would be an insult.

He spoke softly in Pashto, inquired about her father's health as was considered polite, and complimented him for having such a good cook as his daughter. He held the acceptable amount of eye contact with her father and avoided looking at her altogether, again, to honor her father and respect Pashtun law.

He had listened and learned her lessons and waited respectfully for her father to eat first from the communal dishes she had prepared. Because his left hand was his dominant hand but was considered unclean in her culture, she could see him concentrate to remember to use his right hand to pass food and to eat. He had become quite accomplished at scooping his food up into a ball at the tip of his fingers and then eating it.

Yes, she had turned him into a proper Pashtun man—who would leave her like a bird in flight if he could but find his way home.

✶

HE HAD STEPPED out into the courtyard to start his workout the next morning when Rabia's father lifted a frail hand and beckoned him over.

Rabia had left for the market, so the two of them were alone, as they were every day when she left to shop. This was the first time, however, the old man had shown any interest in him. He often made himself scarce, respecting their prayer time and staying out of the old man's space. Consequently, they had exchanged few words in the month or more he'd been here, so Shaghalai Kakar's summons surprised him.

So did the first words out of the old man's mouth when he sat down beside him.

"My daughter is a precious jewel. I regret that I called her back here."

The old man sat on the ground, his legs crossed in a yoga position, his back pressed against the outside wall of the house. A grape arbor of sorts shaded them from the summer sun. Smoke curled up from the hand-rolled cigarette the old man held between fingers stained by tobacco. His face was a wrinkled road map carved by time, loss, war, and worry.

"Had you not called her back, I would be dead. For that, I am grateful," he said, also in Pashto, giving the elder tribesman the respect he deserved. "I regret, however, that my presence here has put you and her in peril."

"Life is peril. Life is regret. Only Rabia proves the latter wrong."

"Rabia *jana* is a fine woman," he agreed respectfully.

"She is a fine Muslim woman." The squinty eyes staring at him were yellowed and filmy with cataracts. "She is Pashtun. When you look at her, your eyes often say that you forget."

Ah. So Wakdar wasn't as out of touch as his silence and constant sleeping suggested. His eyesight was also better than he had thought. He was also right.

"I do not wish to dishonor you or her."

"Wishes mean little. Only actions speak."

Right again. "As soon as I figure out a way to leave here, I will be gone."

"You are welcome to take refuge as long as you have need."

Even Pashtunwali, it seemed, trumped a father's concern for his daughter's virtue.

"I thank you for that."

"Make certain when you go that you will not be captured. They will torture you. You will tell them that we harbored you."

"There is little I remember about my life. But this I know. I would not betray you or Rabia *jana*. I will die first."

"You will pray for death, but they will not let you die until they find out who protected you."

With that, the old man closed his eyes. The discussion was over.

Everything he'd said was spot-on right. He watched Rabia far too much. Watched her work, watched her gentle way with her father, watched her as she hummed softly while she cooked. Watched the door where she slept in the room only a few feet away from him. Watched and wanted her.

He had to get out of here. But the old man was

right about that, too. Until he was stronger and came up with a plan that would minimize the risk of capture, he also risked their lives if he tried to leave.

Deep in thought, he limped over to his chin-up bar. He'd finished five lifts when he heard the front door open and close. Rabia had returned from the market. A bee buzzed by his head as the back door flew open and she ran outside.

"Come. Quickly!" She ran to him, out of breath. "Taliban patrol. They are searching houses. Hurry!"

He followed her as fast as his leg would let him as she ran back inside.

She didn't have to ask him to help her move her work table in the kitchen. Shortly after he'd become ambulatory, they had gone over the plan to hide him should something like this happen.

Together, they moved the table aside. She tossed back the rug to reveal the trap door in the middle of the floor.

"Hurry!" she pleaded as she jerked it open.

He took one look at the small hole dug into the earth and got broadsided by a wave of nausea and fear so great he froze like a statue.

He was back in that four-by-four-by-six-foot hole, with the snakes and the ice and the snow and the heat.

Two hundred fifty-five lines.

"Please, *askar*. You must hurry!" Rabia entreated again.

His throat closed up, and his lungs seized as he

stared at the damp, dark hole. And he couldn't do it. He couldn't make himself crawl inside.

Yet if he didn't, he would sign Rabia's and Wakdar's death sentences.

Swallowing back stark, consuming terror, he lowered himself down, closed his eyes, and prayed to a God he thought he had stopped believing in to give him strength.

The last thing he saw as Rabia lowered the trap door over him like the seal of a tomb was her face, awash with fear, backlit by the sunlight streaming in through the window.

The last thing he thought as absolute darkness closed in and his pulse spiked and his breath clutched at his throat was that he had to keep it together.

Then the claustrophobia set in. And the panic doubled.

This was bad. He knew this was bad. Raw terror quickened his heart rate. Increased his respiration. Blood rushed from his head, and the vertigo hit him with a vengeance.

He clamped a hand over his mouth to keep from screaming.

Willed himself to concentrate on regulating his breathing.

Slow.

Deep.

Steady.

Again.

Slow.

Deep.

Steady.

Over and over and over, until, amazingly, the panic began to subside, and he felt transported to another place. A familiar place. A place he remembered. A place that had gotten him through endless days of pain and starvation and despair.

And there he stayed. Aware of every measured breath. Aware of every single heartbeat.

Aware that if he didn't keep it together, Rabia would die a horrible death.

★

AFRAID AND OUT of breath, Rabia hurriedly replaced the rug and, fueled by adrenaline, moved the heavy wooden table back into place. She quickly scanned the kitchen to see if there was anything that would give away that a third person shared their space.

Then she ran to the sleeping room the *askar* shared with her father, quickly gathered up his bedding, and laid it on top of her father's. Knowing that time was short, she rushed to her bureau, pulled out her burqa and donned it, covering her face and hands so as not to provoke the Taliban fighters.

Satisfied that nothing in the house would give his presence away, she rushed back to the cooking room, hesitated briefly, and resisted the urge to get down on her knees and ask the *askar* if he was all right. He had to be all right. None of them would live through this if he wasn't.

She rushed to the back door and almost knocked her father over as he stepped inside.

"Is all in order?"

"Yes, Father."

"Then calm yourself. They will not find him."

It was in that moment that she realized she feared as much for the *askar*'s life as she did for her father's.

She flinched when a loud knock sounded at the front door.

Her father placed his hand on her shoulder. "Calm," he said again. "All will be well."

The door crashed open before she could open it. Seven Taliban fighters burst inside, wielding AK-47s pointed directly at them.

Terrified, she kept her head down and said nothing, as was the expected behavior for an Afghan woman.

"Why do you disrespect me by entering my house pointing guns?" The anger in her father's voice horrified her, and she feared he would be shot outright.

But the leader of the group ignored him and nodded to his men. "Go. Search."

The fighters split up and began searching the house and the courtyard, even climbing up to the roof.

"You dishonor yourself, and you dishonor me with your intrusion. You could but have asked, and I would have welcomed you to my home."

"A man harboring an enemy of Islam is already dishonored."

"What enemy of Islam?"

"An escaped American prisoner," the warlord said, insulting her father even more by not apologizing for this disrespectful breech of etiquette.

"It is common knowledge that you have been searching for this man for some time," her father said calmly. "I assure you, you will not find such a man here. As I assure you, you are not an honorable man."

Rabia flinched, silently willing her father to stop baiting the warlord. Honor to a Pashtun was the defining characteristic of his self-worth and reputation. Honor to her father was courage and responsibility to his family. This type of insult—forcefully entering the home of a village leader—represented the most grave display of disrespect.

The Taliban warlord considered her father and, for whatever reason, chose not to take offense. "You will understand if we look for ourselves."

"It appears I have no need to understand. I have only to tolerate this invasion."

Again, instead of becoming angry, he laughed. "Such bravery for an old man. You would have made a good warrior in your day, I think. Do you have a son?"

"I have no son. I am no warrior. I was a farmer until my bones became old and brittle and would not let me work the fields any longer."

"This is your wife?"

Rabia stood with her head down, not daring to look up.

"My daughter," her father said. "My wife is dead."

"Your daughter? Does she have a husband?"

"Also dead. She takes care of my house."

The fighter moved so fast Rabia didn't see it coming. He ripped off her burqa.

She stood frozen, willing herself to keep her head down and her gaze on the floor. If she dared to meet his eyes, he could order her stoned to death.

After a long, terrifying moment, he shoved the burqa at her.

"Many a cowardly infidel has hidden beneath women's clothes," he explained, as if that excused his actions. "Cover yourself."

With trembling hands, she pulled the burqa over her head as the fighters started trickling back into the room, all reporting that they had found nothing.

Beside her, Rabia's father seethed with anger. "You will leave my home." His hand shook as he lifted it and pointed a finger toward the door. "You will disrespect me and my daughter no longer."

"Do you know anything of this infidel?" The warlord ignored him and pushed past them into the cooking room.

Rabia held her breath as renewed fear shot through her.

"Only that you are looking for him." Her father followed. "And that he is but one man who eludes an army."

Knowing he was attempting to hold the warlord's attention but afraid he'd pushed too hard this time, Rabia threw herself in front of her father to protect him from a bullet or a blow.

When none came, her father set her gently away.

"Unfortunate she was not a son," the warlord said thoughtfully. "She has the spirit of a warrior."

He walked around the cooking room. All was in order, Rabia reminded herself. Then she saw the corner of the rug covering the trap door. It was turned under. And the table was not quite square on top of it.

Praying he would not notice or, if he did, he would think nothing of it, she held her silence, her heart hammering, perspiration trickling down her back.

The warlord took his time looking around. Insolently helped himself to a handful of currants sitting out on her work space. When he peered out into the courtyard, a wave of light-headedness hit her. What if he noticed the chin-up bar? What if he—

"You will leave now." Her father's stern command interrupted her fearful thoughts.

The Taliban leader turned around, took three steps forward, and spoke an inch from her father's face. "The entire village will be searched and warned before we leave. If anyone knows anything, they must report or expect Taliban justice. Neighbors may turn on neighbors. No one will be safe. Do you understand what I am saying, old man?"

"Do you understand that perhaps you do not find this infidel because he is dead?"

"He will be dead," the leader said angrily, "when we find his body or when we execute him. Until then, we search."

With a final quelling look, he stormed out of their house, his men following.

Chapter

17

When Rabia awoke in the middle of the night and her *askar* was not in his bed, she knew where she would find him. Bothered that she too often thought of him as her soldier but unable to think of him any other way, she walked quietly outside on bare feet and climbed the ladder to the roof.

As he often did, he lay on his back, a blanket beneath him, the stars overhead. His eyes were open, his thoughts as far away as the moon.

Two days had passed since the Taliban had invaded their home and he had hidden in the dark under the floor. He had not come out of the hole the same man who had gone in. He had become sullen and quiet. And she worried for him.

"Is this what Americans call the silent treatment?" She hoped to provoke him into talking to her.

He didn't look at her. "Go back to bed, Rabia. You don't want to be around me right now."

If he were an Afghan man, she would have done as he had told her. But he was not. He was unlike any man she had ever known.

She sat down beside him. "Because you are troubled?"

When he said nothing, she gathered her courage and pushed again.

"Do you think the pain in your mind is more difficult to confront than the pain your body has endured? Do you think that the woman who cared for you through it all, who has survived years of war, is not strong enough to deal with what happened to you while you hid in that hole?" Concern for him made her bold. "Do you think I do not understand that it changed you?"

He closed his eyes. He looked so very weary. "What I think is that you almost died that day because of me. What I think is that I have to get out of here before they come back and do something worse than search your house."

"This is not news. There has been risk from the beginning. Something else troubles you."

He remained quiet for a long time. This time, she waited. She was good at waiting.

"I remembered," he said, after what felt like an entire phase of the moon had passed. "I lay in that hole, in the dark, under the floor . . . and I remembered what happened to me. I remembered my name."

Her heartbeat quickened. He blinked slowly, his gaze still on the sky. "Jeff. Jeffery Robert Albert."

Jeffery. She rolled the name around in her mind. Then whispered it softly. "Jeffery."

He reached for her hand. She entwined her fingers with his. "Say it again. Make it real."

"Jeffery. Your name is Jeffery."

The muscles in his throat constricted. "Eighteen-Delta, Special Operations Medical Sergeant, Albert, Jeffery Robert," he said, as though he needed to hear it again and again and again. "Operational Detachment Alpha 364, 3rd Special Forces Group, C Company, 8th Battalion, 1st Special Forces Regiment."

"I do not know what this means." She only knew it was of major significance.

He pinched his eyes with his thumb and forefinger, and when he spoke again, he sounded very weary. "It means I'm Special Forces, Airborne. I'm a medical sergeant. It means my unit was deployed to Afghanistan four years ago. It means my convoy was attacked six months after we arrived. It means," he said, finally looking at her, his eyes glassy with moisture, his voice gritty with anguish and anger, "that I've been missing in action for three and a half years."

He looked away then, covered his eyes with his free hand, and roughly wiped away his tears. "Three and a half—" His voice broke, and he started again. "Three and a half years of my life are gone."

She stared at their clasped hands, giving him his privacy and time to grieve and time to regain face. Giving herself time to digest this news.

She had thought, when she had found him, that perhaps he'd been captive for several months. She knew he had thought it, too. But this . . . three and a half years . . . this had to be devastating for him to accept.

Her heart felt as though it had started to bleed. For what he had endured. For what he had lost. War was loss on a grand scale. An abomination. Unending suffering. But one man's loss in the midst of war was larger than life itself.

Below, the village slept, at peace in the night. Here on the roof, there was no peace, only troubled quiet and troubled hearts.

"Tell me, *aska*—" She stopped, corrected herself. "Tell me, Jeffery. Tell me what else you remember."

He swallowed back emotions that she could not fathom enduring, and then, in a controlled voice, he started talking.

"We were on our way back from a patrol. We'd pulled off a major mission that put a roadblock in the supply lines running between Afghanistan and Pakistan. We'd confiscated a ton of documents, cell phones, and laptops and destroyed a huge supply depot. We were about to cross the border back into Afghanistan and home base when they hit us."

He paused, and she knew that the horrors of his nightmares had finally broken free. "Our GMV rolled over an IED. Exploded before we could bail. The rig rolled." He stopped. Squeezed her hand harder. "Simmons, Blanco—they were in the back. Dead. Their necks broken. Fisher was driving. He'd been hit. I told him to run. I'd cover him. They blew his head off."

She clasped her other hand over his, enfolding it between both of hers.

"I don't know how many came at us. Seemed like hundreds. My leg was broken in the rollover, so I couldn't walk, let alone run. I took a bullet in the arm. Another in my body armor."

He stopped. Drew a steadying breath. "So many dead. The vehicles all in flames. I knew I was going to die there. But I was going to kill as many as I could before they got me. I . . . I finally managed to crawl away from the GMV just before an RPG hit it. I don't know." He pressed the heel of his hand against his temple and rubbed. "The rest is still a little fuzzy. I must have gotten a hit in the head, knocked out. When I woke up, two of them were dragging me across the snow in the dark, my leg screaming in pain. I think I passed out again. The next thing I remember, I came to when they threw me in that hole."

"The Taliban," she said softly, hurting for him.

"No." He finally looked at her. "Not the Taliban. The ISI."

She shifted so she could see his face more clearly,

wondered if his memory, so long in returning, was playing tricks. This could not be. "The Pakistan Intelligence Service? Why would they attack you? Pakistan is not at war with America."

He made a bitter sound. "Aren't they? Hell, we all know that Pakistan is in bed with the Taliban and Al-Qaeda. We tiptoe around it, keep it under wraps to maintain what little cooperation we get from our supposed ally. The truth is, there's so much weapons commerce crossing over the border between the Pakis and Al-Qaeda, it'd make a Walmart look like a mom-and-pop store. That's why the ISI attacked us," he said, as if something had clicked into place. "We were putting a major crimp in their operations. They needed to stop us, or the Taliban would go to some other supplier for their guns. The Pakis were losing revenue because of us. So they dressed like Taliban to make certain no one could pin the attack on the ISI and let the Taliban take the blame."

"Did they take you to Pakistan?"

"Yes. They kept me in a special place."

A hole. A freaking black hole.

"Tell me," she said urgently, and only then did he realize he was shaking.

"Most of the time, I was in isolation." She didn't need to know about the hole. About the two hundred fifty-five days he'd spent there in between the repeated interrogations, the beatings, the starvation.

"Sometimes I was in a cell." Those were the good

times. Often there was heat. Occasionally, he'd get meat. But any perk came with a price. "For two years, I was in the same encampment. Like a prison. Once they moved me south, I think. It's still a blur." For good reason. He was often unconscious from the beatings.

"How did you get away?"

There was the irony. "I don't think they knew I'd picked up Pashto, which is what they mostly spoke. I overheard the guards talking one night about making a prisoner trade with the Taliban. The next morning, they loaded me and several Taliban prisoners into the back of a troop-transport truck. I knew then that this was my chance. It was the first time I was out of a cell or—" He stopped short of saying *the hole*.

"We didn't travel far. They set up tents in the mountains—right where the foothills met the peaks. They kept me separate from the Taliban prisoners. Wasn't long before the Taliban contingency arrived. I could hear through the tent walls that it was not a friendly meeting. There was a lot of tension. A lot. And a lot of heated negotiation. It finally got dark, and they were still talking. I knew it would be my only chance.

"It was surprisingly easy to take out the one guard they'd placed at the door of my tent. Guess they figured I was too weak and broken to be any threat. I dragged him inside, grabbed his gun, and snuck off. And I hobbled away as fast as I could go. After about an hour, I heard shouting and gunshots. I knew they were behind me. I tried to run faster. My leg gave out.

I remember stumbling, falling, sliding down a cliff face—and that's it.

"That must be when I hit my head . . . when I fell. I woke up totally disoriented, alone, not remembering anything. Dizzy as hell. I couldn't move without throwing up or keeling over. But I started walking, stumbling, crawling . . . and that's when you found me."

He stopped again, wiped a hand over his face. "How can I remember this? How can I finally remember it so clearly, when—" He trailed off abruptly.

"When what, Jeffery?"

"When I don't remember one thing about my life before the attack."

The suffering for this man seemed to have no end. She did not know that she was crying until a tear dropped onto their bound hands.

Allah, help me. She had not meant to let it happen, had not even known it was happening, but she had come to feel too much for this brave, broken man whose ways she did not always understand but whose heart had touched her like no other.

She must leave him now before she brought dishonor to her father and her religion. She wanted too badly to offer him more comfort than was wise. She wanted to look too long upon his face, press her lips to his, and touch him in ways only a wife should touch her husband.

But then he whispered her name. And the need and the yearning in his eyes sent her heart beating wildly. They drowned out the voices of caution and conscience and constraint.

She lay down beside him on the roof below the stars and let him wrap her in his arms.

✳

SHE WAS WARMTH and softness and a desperately needed constant in a world that felt like crumbling shale beneath his feet. He'd wanted his memory back. Now he had it—at least, part of it—and he'd been clinging to sanity ever since.

He buried his hands in her hair and kissed the top of her head when she laid her cheek against his chest. She was the one thing that held him together. She was the one thing that mattered in a moment that now seemed inevitable. She, who had given up so much for him, now offered the most selfless gift of all. And damn him for a selfish bastard, he was going to take it.

He knew what that made him, and still he took it. Couldn't not take it as he ran his hand over the gentle curve of her hip, gripped the soft cloth of her nightgown, and slid it up to her waist—and died a little for the exquisite tactile sensation of his rough fingers stroking warm, pliant flesh.

For long, indulgent moments, he lost himself in the feel of her skin. In the tender kisses she pressed to his jaw. In the promise of her gentle hands that finally touched him as a lover.

Right, wrong, he couldn't make himself care. He

could only feel. For the first time since he'd climbed
out of that hole in her kitchen, he quit thinking of the
months of isolation in another hole—two hundred
fifty-five days in that other hole—that had been both
horror and haven because it provided sanctuary from
the beatings and the mind games that had him begging them to do it. To just shoot him. Or hang him.
Or poison him. Just do it, instead of standing him
before a firing squad, or slipping a noose over his neck,
or holding his head under water until he was all but
drowned . . . day after day after day.

No more, no more, no more.

He would not think of that now. He was here now.
He was with her now. He was safe now. And she, *oh,
God . . .* she was a sweet, giving sanctuary that eclipsed
egregious suffering, obliterated pain and despair, and,
in this moment, made him feel new and relevant and
whole.

Whispering his name like a prayer, knowing he
needed to hear it, she knelt over him and lifted her
gown over her head. Starlight and black night framed
her slim shoulders and narrow waist, shadowed the
lush flare of her hips. Moonlight kissed her breasts,
and she shivered, her abdominal muscles clenching,
her perfect dark nipples peaking. Her hair fell over her
shoulders, silken and sweet-smelling and seductive.

She made him breathless, weightless in body and
mind. She made him believe that in this moment, life
was beautiful and good, as he crushed handfuls of her

hair in his hands, then filled his palms with her breasts and indulged in the sweet mercy of such incredible softness.

"I need you in my mouth," he whispered on a low groan, and pulled her slowly toward him. With his thumb and index finger framing her breast, he guided her nipple to his mouth and suckled.

Nothing tasted this good. Nothing responded so completely. Velvet-smooth, then diamond-hard. He groaned again and feasted, aware of another level of pleasure as she untied his trousers, opened them, and took him into her hands.

He arched his hips on a gasp and pressed his erection deeper into her touch, awash in her tremulous smile, her soft eyes, and the boldness with which she caressed him.

Too much. Too good. And still he needed more. He fit his hands around her waist and eased her on top of him. She melted over him like sacred oil, fragrant and priceless and healing, as she guided him inside her.

Chapter
18

Northern Minnesota, September

*J*ess had never been a clock watcher until Ty appeared in her life. When J.R. had deployed, orders came without warning, and he'd pack a go bag and be gone. Six or nine months later, he'd show up again. Exhausted, ten to fifteen pounds lighter, still revved from a mission he couldn't discuss. On either end, she'd never had any heads-up or warning. And there'd been no point in marking time.

But after a three-week absence, Ty had called from Minneapolis to tell her his plane was due in the Falls in less than an hour. She hadn't been able to keep her attention from the store clock since, as if willing it to move faster would make it do so.

"How much do you want me to mark down these shirts, boss?"

By mid-September, kids were back in school, and the families who bought store merchandise were back home settling down to normal life. Only the diehard fishermen braved the cold weather that sometimes set in in the fall, so business had slowed. Fall markdowns were status quo.

"Go ahead and make them thirty percent off," she told Kayla, who had also gone back to college in Duluth but came home on weekends to see her folks and to help Jess with the heavier weekend business. "Let's move as much as we can to make room for the spring shipment."

She went back to figuring her quarterly taxes—which seemed to come around a lot more often than quarterly, especially since revenues would be lean until spring—when her phone rang.

"How's my favorite shopkeeper?"

Ty! Her heart skipped. "Where are you?"

He laughed. "At Whispering Pines. Drive down. I want to show you something."

"What are you doing at Whispering Pines?"

"Drive down," he repeated. "I know Kayla's there, because I already talked to her." He hung up.

"What do you know that I don't?" she accused Kayla.

"Loose lips sink ships. That's all you're going to get out of me."

"I could fire you, you know."

"Yeah, sure, fine. Now, get going. Only a fool would keep that man waiting."

And only a fool would feel this giddy.

"I'm taking Bear," she told Kayla.

"You're going to want to leave him, OK? And don't ask," Kayla reminded her.

"You are so close to being out of here."

"As if," Kayla shot back with a grin that had Jess shaking her head.

"I'll be back in a few."

"Wouldn't count on it."

She'd had enough goading and teasing, so she grabbed her jacket and headed out the door.

A bowl of brilliant blue sky greeted her, along with an afternoon sun that warmed the crisp September air. Fall was Jess's favorite time of year. She didn't have to run her legs off taking care of business, the leaves were turning, and the temps hovered in the high sixties. They'd already had one unexpected killing frost, so the bugs were gone, which made jogging with Bear every morning that much more pleasant.

As she drove down Gamma Road toward Whispering Pines, she passed Brad's guide business. A few days after Ty had left for Florida, Brad had stopped by the store and apologized. That first visit had been brief and strained. No gentle reconciliation, but he'd made the effort, and for that she gave him credit. A week later, she'd invited him to dinner, fully expecting him to turn her down. To her surprise, he'd accepted.

They'd had a good talk, both cried over J.R. and admitted that they'd been enabling each other by not letting go. It wasn't easy for Brad, but he was finally making an effort to move on, and he'd accepted that she had a right to move on, too.

Moving on was what she was all about these days. It had taken her long enough. It had taken Ty Brown.

For every season, turn turn.

This seemed to be her season.

When she pulled into the resort five minutes later, Ty, looking like everything good and vital in the world, waited for her on the deck of the main lodge. Like her, he wore worn jeans and a lightweight flannel shirt and a jacket to accommodate the cooler weather.

"I thought your flight wasn't due for another hour," she said as she stepped out of her car and headed up the deck steps.

"I may have fudged a little on the time. But let's back up. Is that any way to greet a man who had a whole different scenario in mind—especially after that phone, um, *conversation* we had late last night?"

Despite the fact that he'd managed to make her blush, she walked into his arms and kissed him. Long and deep and thorough. "That more like what you had in mind?"

"Makes me wish I'd come straight to your apartment instead of instigating this little outing."

"Outing?"

He draped an arm over her shoulders and walked her down the steps toward the shore. A light breeze made a rustling sound through the ash and maple leaves that had started to turn but had not yet fallen. The foliage hid all but glimpses of the water in the bay until they were almost down the hill, so the yellow float plane moored by the dock took her by surprise.

"Whose plane?" she asked when she spotted it.

"Remember when you told me about the guy in Vermillion? The one who retired? I looked him up. This is his plane." He grinned at her.

She walked down for a closer look. "What are you doing with his plane?"

"Thinking about buying it."

That whipped her head around toward him. "Buying it? Why would you buy it?"

"Because it's for sale?" When that feeble reason earned a scowl, he laughed. "Planes are my thing. Come on. I want to take you up in her."

"Oh, no. I'm not going up in that thing."

He laughed again. "Why not?"

"For one thing, it's a wreck. For another . . . commercial is more my style."

"OK. The body needs a little work, I'll give you that. But the engine's sound. I wouldn't suggest you go up with me unless she was perfectly safe. Heck, I flew her up here from Vermillion."

She gave the plane another once-over. "I'll take your word for it."

"You aren't seriously afraid?"

What she was was horrified. Planes might be his thing, but heights had never been hers. "In a word, yes."

"We're going to fix that right now. Come on. Sit in her with me."

"And you won't take off?"

"Not unless you say it's OK."

Because she didn't want to disappoint him and because she trusted him, she let him help her out onto the float, grabbed the wing strut, and climbed up into what could loosely be called a cockpit. She slid under the yoke in the pilot's seat and into the shotgun seat.

He climbed in after her, shut the door, and settled in.

"What do you think?"

"I think it's a relic." The leather in the two front seats was worn and split. The instrument panel looked like something out of World War I, and the four passenger seats in the back practically sat on the floor. "I see a lot of duct tape."

"She's nicely broken in." He grinned at her horrified look. "OK. So she's a fixer-upper. But it's all about the engine, and the guy who owns her has kept it in excellent shape. She's got a lot of hours, but with a bird like this, that's a good thing."

"Um, Ty." She craned her neck to her left, then her right. "We seem to be floating away from the dock."

"That's because I cast off before I got in. Don't worry. I'm only going to scoot around on the water, let you get a feel for how she moves."

"And then you're going to try to talk me into taking off."

"That would be the plan, yeah. Relax. You're in good hands. But you might want to buckle up."

She was about to spout a comeback when he cranked the engine. It hiccupped and coughed, then engaged and revved like a rubber band on a bicycle spoke, before really kicking in and negating any chance of talking.

He reached above him, grabbed a pair of headsets, and handed one to her. Following his lead, she put one on, fastened the seat belt, then groped for something to hang on to as he maneuvered away from the dock and out into open water.

For several long moments, they did exactly as he'd promised. Jess couldn't shake a mental image of a damaged dragonfly skimming along the water's surface.

"How ya doing?" he asked into the headset.

"We'd better go back. I think I left something cooking on the stove."

"Come on, Jess." He reached over and squeezed her thigh. "Have a little faith. It'll be fun."

She pinched her eyes shut and, because it was so important to him, gave him a quick nod.

"That's my girl!"

He didn't give her any opportunity to change her mind. He throttled back, and the plane responded, picking up speed, and finally, with a dip in her stomach, they were airborne.

"Don't pay any attention to the vibration," he told her. "It's only wind resistance. It's all good."

"What about the groaning?"

She heard him laugh. "I thought that was you."

"It *is* me. Oh, my God, I can't believe I let you talk me into this."

"Open your eyes. Look at this view."

On a deep breath, she forced herself to look. And while the sight of the lake with its many fingers, bays, and islands a few hundred feet below them had her gripping her handholds tighter, she had to admit, it was stunning.

Gradually, she relinquished her white-knuckle grip and, to her amazement, started enjoying the flight, even pointing out landmarks to him and discovering bays she hadn't realized existed. That didn't mean that every time the plane hit a little air pocket and they dropped a few feet, the butterflies didn't take flight again.

"Do you love it?" Ty crowed through the headset.

What she loved was his excitement. "*Love* is a strong word. But yes, it's growing on me."

"What about me? Am I growing on you?"

Oh, yeah. He was not only growing, he'd taken root and was flourishing.

"Depends on if you get me down from here safely."

"I can do that," he promised, and fifteen minutes later, after one last buzz of the lake, he did.

The pontoons kissed the surface of the lake with a swoosh of parting water in a soft-as-silk landing.

She couldn't help but grin as he expertly taxied the little plane back to the dock and gently beached it.

"You did great, Jess." Ty beamed at her after they'd unbuckled and stowed the headsets. "Sit tight. I want to tie up before our wake washes in and lifts her off the sand."

He stepped out onto a pontoon, grabbed the wing strut for balance, and expertly plucked a tie line out of the water. After securing it to the strut, he walked to the back of the pontoon and did the same.

He helped her out and up onto the dock, then followed. "So what do you think?"

"It was fun. I admit it. But I still don't understand why you'd want to buy it."

He took her hand and led her to a log bench that faced the water. "What if I said I wanted to start a fishing charter business up here?"

She hadn't fully processed the implication of his words when her heartbeat spiked, her hands started to tremble, and a light-headedness hit her hard enough to make her dizzy.

He was talking about much more than purchasing a rickety six-seater float plane. He was talking about a commitment. He was talking about a future.

"Whoa. I recognize that look. Take a deep breath. Let's back up a second."

Now she was confused. He *wasn't* talking about a commitment?

"Look. I've blindsided you twice. Once in the dead of winter. Once in July when I showed up again unannounced. It's not my intention to do it again."

"Too late."

He smiled and pressed a kiss to her forehead. "OK. So I have a little trouble in that area. But there's no pressure here, Jess. I want you to know what's on my mind. And I want you to think about how you feel about it." He gave her hand a gentle squeeze. "I want to make a life up here. With you."

Heart racing, she looked up at him.

"I want to marry you, Jess. I love you. I think I fell a little bit in love with you the first time I saw you."

Her voice got trapped somewhere in the wellspring of emotions knocking around inside her. Elation. Fear. Excitement. Fear. Joy. *Fear.*

She didn't want to be afraid. Not of him. Not of them. And yet . . . was she ready for this? Was she capable of this?

"Like I said, I didn't want this to be another blindside, but sweetie, I've tried to make it clear that I'm crazy about you."

He tipped her face up to his, and she could tell he was doing his best not to laugh at her.

"Not talking, huh? That's OK. I know you need some time to process the idea."

She needed more than time. She needed oxygen.

"So . . . I'm going to fly the plane back to Vermillion, OK? I need to get her back before sundown, and it's about a thirty-minute flight. How long is it going to take me to drive back to Kabby? Hold up your fingers if you can't talk."

"Thirty-five . . . forty minutes," she said numbly.

"OK, then. I'll see you in a little more than an hour. I'll stop and pick up something for dinner, so don't cook. Jess?" he added when she stared at him. "See you in an hour?"

She nodded, leaned in to him as he pressed another kiss to her forehead, then watched him walk to the plane.

She was still watching the sunlight glint off the wings in the far, far distance when Shelley walked up beside her.

"Hey," Shelley said in that quiet way she had of hinting that she knew something was up.

"Hey."

"You OK?"

She breathed deeply and looked at her hands clasped together on her lap. "I'm not sure."

Shelley sat down beside her. "Is that a *good* not sure or a *bad* not sure?"

She looked at her friend. "Not sure about that, either."

Chapter

19

"No talking." Ty grabbed her hand when he finally arrived at the store shortly after closing time and led her straight up the stairs.

It had taken him more like two hours to make the drive from Vermillion to the store. Judging by the look on his face, she suspected he'd timed it that way.

He wanted to be alone with her. He wanted her in bed.

"No talking," he growled again, dropping their takeout dinner onto an end table and walking her to the bedroom, where he stripped off his clothes and hurriedly helped her out of hers.

"Only this," he murmured, lowering her onto the bed and covering her naked body with his. "Only this."

Only, however, did not belong in the same breath

with the *this* he had in mind. Because he didn't *only* make love to her. He didn't *only* drive her to the brink of madness, then shove her over the edge into free fall. He didn't *only* do anything.

He destroyed. He possessed. With his hands. With his mouth. With the strength and the fire of a man who would do anything to please his woman.

When he knelt between her thighs and ran his hungry hands from her breasts to her belly and finally to the heat of her, he demanded, "Open for me."

A thrill shot through her, and she opened her legs and let him pull her to the edge of the bed, let him drape her thighs over his shoulders as he knelt down to the floor. Let him devour her with his mouth and his passion as he brought her to a lush and powerful climax that both shattered and restored her and had her screaming his name as pleasure so exquisite it scared her fired through her body.

She was still coming down when he dragged her to the floor with him, positioned her over his heat, and took her there again, only then giving in to his own release.

✳

WHEN THEY'D RECOVERED enough strength to move, they crawled back into bed and burrowed under the covers, wrapped in each other's arms.

Several long, luxuriant moments passed while their breathing settled and their heartbeats slowed.

"OK," he whispered against her hair. "You can talk now."

"Easy for you to say."

She felt his smile before he tipped her face back so he could look into her eyes. "Hello."

"Hello."

"So. How are things?"

She laughed. "*Things* may never be the same again."

"Can't tell if that's a complaint or—"

"We'll go with *or*." She lifted a hand that felt like lead and caressed his cheek. "We will definitely go with *or*."

He tucked her head back beneath his chin and held her close.

How she felt lying here with him, naked and spent and steeped in the wonder of his strength and heat, was something she treasured. Nothing else mattered but these moments. Nothing else counted but this feeling. She didn't want to catalogue or define it. She didn't want to think outside this little pocket of intimacy. She wanted to live it, breathe it, be lost in it. For a long time, that's what she did. Until it occurred to her that he was probably starving.

"Are you hungry?" she whispered into the silence.

"You think I'm lying around like a slug because you wore me out? Hell, no, woman. I'm weak from starvation."

"Anyone ever tell you that you have a teensy-weensy theatrical streak?"

"Minored in musical theater in college."

That brought her up onto an elbow. "Seriously?"

"I'm liable to break out in show tunes at a moment's notice."

Now she knew he was kidding. "I've heard you sing in the shower. I was not impressed."

"You were impressed a minute ago."

She laughed. "Yes, I was. And I hope to be impressed again after I feed you."

"Count on it."

She leaned in and kissed him, then got out of bed and reached for her robe.

By the time he joined her in the kitchen, she had the food on the table.

"Looks good," she said.

"Kentucky Fried. Nothing but the best for my lady."

He'd pulled on his jeans and shirt but hadn't bothered to button it. His hair was mussed, his eyes were sleepy, and his lips were swollen from kissing her—and other things.

And he really was hungry. He dug in as if he hadn't eaten in a week.

Soon, however, the elephant in the room refused to take a backseat to polite table talk.

"You know, you're killing me here, Jess. Say something."

Suddenly, they were back on the bench by the lake, and he was wanting to make a life with her.

"Yes," she said, feeling and sounding breathless, as if she'd just stepped off a cliff.

"Yes . . . what?"

A nervous laugh burst out. "Well, I may be a little slow on the uptake, but wasn't there a proposal mixed in somewhere with wanting to buy a plane?"

A slow, pleased smile spread across his face. "No. That wasn't a proposal. That was a preamble."

He shot up from the table, disappeared into the bedroom, and came back with a small blue box in his hand.

He got down on one knee in front of her, opened the box, and held it out to her.

She pressed a hand to her chest, stunned by the extravagant emerald-cut diamond that winked at her from inside the Tiffany box.

"This is the proposal. Although, I've got to tell you, I didn't imagine myself half-naked when I made it."

She lifted the ring out of its satin mooring with trembling fingers. Met his eyes.

"I love you, Jess. Will you marry me?"

"You're really sure about this?"

"Never been so sure of anything in my life."

"Then yes." She threw herself into his arms. "Yes, I love you, too. And yes, I'll marry you."

★

"DID YOU EVER think about having kids?" Ty asked later, after they'd made love again. "You and J.R.?"

It was a fair question. "J.R., well, he'd seen a lot of ugly things. A lot of troubling things. He didn't want to bring a child into the world he knew."

"What about you? What did you want?"

"I tried not to think about it."

He was quiet for a moment. "You want to know what I think? I think you'd make a great mom."

She turned her head on the pillow so she could see his face. The expression she saw there told her what she wanted to know. "And I think you'd make a great daddy."

He grinned. "I hope so."

So easy. Again, everything was so easy with him.

"I want to tell you something," she said. "And I don't want you to think that I'm speaking badly of J.R."

"I know you'd never do that."

"I loved him. I did. As best as I could, at least. But I never really understood him. You know, growing up here, it's pretty confining. You'd be amazed how many married couples started out as high school sweethearts. You might say it's a tradition.

"Anyway, that's how it was with J.R. and me. We fell in love as kids and never really got to know each other as adults. It seemed like he was deployed all the time. And when he wasn't, he was still all about the Army. It took me a while to realize that no matter what, I'd always come second with him. I'd reached a point before he died where it wasn't enough."

He remained silent, giving her time to get this off her chest.

"We fought before his last deployment. I wanted him to resign after his hitch was up. I told him I wanted us to be a couple, that I was tired of leading two separate lives and that if he didn't resign, I was leaving him. I don't even know if I meant it, but when he made it clear that wasn't going to happen, I started seriously thinking about leaving. We went to bed angry. In the morning, he was gone. I never saw him again."

"I'm so sorry."

"Yeah. Me, too. I did love him. And in his own way, I know he loved me. But it was never easy. He was a good man. I want to make that clear. A good provider. A good soldier. A good friend . . . to everyone but me."

The truth was, he had often shut her out, and the deep connection she'd always thought they would make in time had never come. She'd tried. She'd followed him from post to post, but when his deployments became more frequent, his emotional distance became more pronounced.

"It won't be like that with us, Jess."

She turned in his arms so they were nose-to-nose. "I know. Promise me. Promise me that you won't ever leave me to fight someone else's war."

"Try to get rid of me, see what happens."

"You'll sing show tunes?"

He squeezed her hard. "Worse. I'll do my Elvis impersonation. Thang ya. Thang ya verra mush."

He could joke all he wanted, but he needed to understand something. "It takes a special kind of person to live up here. Especially in the winter. Winters are long and cold and isolating."

"You forget, I grew up in Colorado. I know about winter. And I know something else that's far more important: I have never loved anyone the way I love you."

She believed him. Just as she was starting to believe that she might finally get her happily ever after.

Chapter

20

Afghanistan, October

The roof at night had become his refuge. The stronger and more complete his memories of his time in captivity became, the more he needed the wide-open sky above him, the absence of walls and bars. The illusion of being free.

And then there was Rabia.

Each night for more than a month, she came to him here. Each night, he lost himself in her soft, giving body, her sweet, tender mouth, and for the moments they were together, he forgot he was a man trapped in a hostile country and hunted by the Taliban. He forgot, even, that he had no idea how he was going to get home. Forgot that he still didn't know where home was.

The nights had grown cool. She brought blankets

with her when she came to him now. They lay wrapped in one tonight, while a sky free of light pollution exploded with magnificent starlight. Her naked flesh warmed him like a furnace, pressed to his side as she slept.

He ran his hand absently up and down her arm, spent in the aftermath of their lovemaking, grounded again in the reality of his situation and the wrongness of what they did together in the night. The futility of it. The cultural and political impossibility of it for her. He knew that being with her this way made him complacent. He had to beef up his physical conditioning routine. He had to somehow overcome the vertigo and blinding headaches and the physical limitations of his bad leg. He had to get away from here and somehow hook up with Coalition troops.

She stirred, and he pulled her closer, tugging the blanket higher over her bare shoulders. The thought of leaving her, however, weighed on him the way the holes in his memory weighed on his psyche. He'd come to care for her. Too much. Too, too much.

She had become his escape. And while he still had difficulty piecing together his past, he had no problem drawing on lessons from a psychology class he must have taken at some point in time. He understood the psychology of dependency. He understood about Stockholm syndrome. Rabia had been both captor and healer. She had been his lifeline—the giver of food, the provider of relief in the form of opiates during the worst of his physical pain. She'd been his savior during withdrawal. And now she was his lover.

Even more than that, he had grown to respect her. The longer they were together, the more they talked. Not only about him but also about her.

He'd discovered that she was a rebel, that she'd risked her life for more than his sake. She'd downplayed her role in the Afghan women's movement. She didn't merely belong. She was a leader, responsible for bringing an underground movement out in the open and operating in defiance of the Taliban, who would have them back in chains and stoned for minor infractions of sharia law.

She stirred in her sleep, and again, he pulled her closer, missing her before he'd even left her but knowing that he would leave her. He would leave this woman who had saved him on more levels than he could count.

"Why do you not sleep, Jeffery?"

He should have known. Even in her sleep, she sensed his unrest, and it had awakened her.

"I have to leave, Rabia. You know I have to leave here."

She was quiet for a long moment. "I know. But you do not have to leave this night."

She rose up on an elbow then, her long hair falling over her shoulder, her lush breasts bare under the starlight. And he agreed as she moved over him, blanketing him in the warmth and vitality of her body, that no, he did not have to leave her this night.

✷

THE NEXT AFTERNOON, Rabia rushed into the cooking room and set her small parcel on the table.

"What surprises have you brought home from the market today?"

She spun around, startled to see Jeffery standing in the doorway. She was not yet ready to face him. She had not yet processed the news she had heard at the market. She had not yet decided what to do about it.

"Hey." He limped over to her, touched his hand to her arm. "What's wrong?"

She shook her head and turned back to the fresh vegetables she had purchased. "All is well. You . . . surprised me. I did not know you were behind me."

"Well, you know it now. Yet your hands are still shaking. What's going on?"

She had hoped to delay telling him. If she were truthful with herself, she had hoped to conceal the news completely. But she could not. He had to know.

"There was a runner in the market. I overheard him tell of an American Army patrol near Emarat."

When she finally met his eyes, she saw both excitement and unbearable hope. "An American patrol? How many? When were they there?"

"He said twenty-five or thirty men. They have been coming through the village every five days for the past three weeks, offering aid, searching for Taliban, making camp overnight before moving on."

His gaze left her face, and he stared at the far wall. He was in shock, she realized. He was searching, planning, seeking a way to make contact.

"How far is Emarat from here?" he asked abruptly.

"Farther than you can travel on a road heavily patrolled by Taliban." She did not want him to go. She did not want to lose him.

But she knew what must be done.

"I will go," she said, swallowing back the pain. "I will make contact."

He didn't hesitate. "No. It's too dangerous."

"I am Pashtun," she said defiantly. "This is my country. My land. I am free to travel. They have no reason to suspect me."

"It doesn't matter. Even if you go, how are you going to make contact without being seen? No, Rabia, it's too risky. I can't let you do this for me."

"And what would you do?" she countered angrily. "You cannot walk that far on your leg. You cannot run. You still have vertigo attacks that make you violently ill and unable to stand. You cannot drive because of it. So how do you plan to get there, let alone make contact? And if you are caught, how long do you think it will take them to connect you back to my father's house?"

She could read his frustration and sense of helplessness through his eyes. She understood that his disabilities made him feel like less of a man. She knew it pained him to be so ruled by his injuries.

Several long, tension-filled moments passed before he looked back at her. "How can I let you go?"

She knew then that he understood she was his only hope.

"We will develop a plan together. We will make certain it is safe." She touched a hand to his arm. "You will go home soon."

He searched her eyes for an eternity, then drew her tightly against him. "If I could stay, I would. I would stay with you."

She buried her face in his chest and pinched her eyes against the threat of tears. "I know this. I know this very well."

Just as she knew this was the beginning of good-bye.

✳

THE NEXT MORNING, his chest tightly knotted, he watched Rabia drive away from the cave where she had first hidden him. They had agreed that he couldn't stay in the house alone. There would be too much opportunity for a chance encounter with one of the villagers—or a return visit from the Taliban.

So here he was, where it all began, hiding in a cave like a coward. An even bigger coward for sending her to save him.

He had bedding, food, and water enough to last him several days.

Several days alone.

The panic knotted in his chest shamed him. Rabia

had been his lifeline. There was not a day in his memory that she had not been in his life.

Now she was in danger because of him.

He ducked into the cave, olfactory memories of the month he'd spent here calling forward reminders of pain and opiate hazes and the shackle around his leg. Of Rabia coming to him every day.

Now she was gone.

If all went well, she would soon be back, and he would be gone from here.

The thought of leaving her drilled a hole in his heart.

And he was left feeling more alone than he'd thought humanly possible.

✸

"WHAT IS YOUR business on this road?"

Rabia had expected the Taliban patrol to stop them. For that reason, she was covered in her burqa. Four fighters manned the checkpoint. Two approached the car.

Her father rolled down the rear window of her older-model Toyota and addressed them. "I am Wakdar Kahn Kakar, *malik* of the village of Salawat. I am traveling to Emarat to consult with the *malik* there."

"Why does this woman drive?"

"This woman is my daughter. I am an old man. I have no sons. I am in need of her to drive me where I wish to go."

The fighter walked around to the driver's side. Rabia had hidden her hands in her lap to avoid breaking Taliban law. She kept her head down.

"Show your hands," the fighter ordered.

She waited for her father's consent. "Show your hands, daughter, so that they will know you are not a man in hiding."

She did as she was told, apparently to their satisfaction, then quickly covered her hands again.

"Give me the keys."

She did as he said, then waited while the guard opened the trunk and checked their luggage.

Finally, he returned the keys and motioned her to drive forward.

Grateful for once for the confining burqa that concealed how nervous she was, she started the car and drove on.

They encountered many more checkpoints on the three-hour trip, each one as nerve-wracking as the other, before finally reaching Emarat right before the noontime meal.

While they were not expected, they were welcomed with great generosity, as was the Pashtun custom.

Because her father was eager for the American *askar* to leave, he had consented to participate in the plan she and Jeffery had carefully worked out. Once inside the Emarat *malik*'s house, they would dine and socialize with the family, who would be eager to share news of the region. As soon as Rabia found out when the American patrol was due back through, she would attempt to make contact.

She didn't have to wait long. The patrol was due the next day.

✳

DRESSED AS A boy, her hair pulled up on top of her head and tucked under a cap, Rabia sneaked out of the house, careful not to wake the other women sleeping in the room with her. Heart pounding, she double-checked her pocket for the letter Jeffery had written and the blood and hair samples he had insisted she take.

"Since I can't go myself," he had said, handing her a knife, "they will need physical evidence as proof that I'm alive. The letter won't be enough."

The village was small, no more than three thousand people. It did not take her long to reach the outskirts of town, where the Americans were said to be camping. The land was flat here. Tonight a thick layer of clouds covered a sky that was usually lit with stars. She was glad for the absence of light, which made it easier for her to slip through the village undetected.

For long moments, she stood at the town's edge and searched the terrain beyond. It took only moments for her eyes to acclimate and spot the shadows of several tents about a quarter of a mile away.

On a deep breath, she stepped out of the concealment of a row of dwellings and started walking through the dark toward the encampment. With each step, she prayed that there would not be Taliban fighters hiding in the dark. And as she grew closer and could make out the silhouette of an American soldier carrying a rifle, she prayed to Allah that he would not shoot her before she had an opportunity to tell them about Jeffery.

Chapter

21

*P*rivate First Class Danny Gleason hated freaking night watch. Fact was, he hated everything about everything that had to do with the U.S. freaking Army. He was nineteen years old. He'd joined up because it was either that or get sent to juvie for a little run-in with the Georgia State Police. Hell, he'd just been having some fun. He hadn't known that asshole Dale Feckers was going to boost some beer from an all-night liquor store on the other side of the state line and expect him to be his wheel man.

Some friend he'd been. And now, because of Feckers, Danny was in Af-freakin'-ghanistan, eating sand and watching his back for fear some Tali-freakin'-ban jihadists decided they wanted to kill themselves an American infidel.

They could have this country. And Uncle Sam could have his Army. He had twenty-three months left on his hitch, then he was out of here. Back home to some sweet Georgia peach who would think he was some kind of a hero because he'd worn a uniform and toted a gun.

He didn't say a thing about that to any of these other yahoos in his unit. Hell, they were all gung-ho, God-and-country soldiers. The kind of men people back home looked up to. The kind who made him feel like maybe he had something missing inside him because he couldn't swallow that line of patriotic BS. There was one in every crowd, right? In this crowd, he was the one.

He stubbed his cigarette out in the dirt and resumed his walk of the camp perimeter. He had another hour, then Winters would relieve him. Talk about gung-ho. Winters was Captain freakin' America wearing sergeant's stripes.

He yawned heavily, then stopped short when he saw a shadow move in the darkness about twenty yards away.

Heart slamming, he shouldered his weapon so fast he hit himself in the jaw with the rifle butt. "Who's out there?"

"I am not armed."

What the hell? That sounded like a woman. Yeah, and everyone knew Afghan women liked to hide bombs in their big tent dresses—or in this case, those baggy pajama pants.

"Show yourself. Hands in the air," Danny barked, exactly as he'd been instructed.

A figure materialized out of the dark. With his free hand, he found his Maglite and switched it on, shining it directly in her face.

Now he wasn't so sure. Was it a woman or a boy?

"May I please speak to the soldier in charge?"

Definitely a woman. Who spoke English. "No, you may not. Get down on the ground. Face in the dirt. Now! Keep them hands above your head when you're down there."

Satisfied that she couldn't do him any damage and with his rifle still trained on her, he clumsily pressed the button on his shoulder mike. "Lieutenant Court, PFC Gleason. I've got a situation on the perimeter, sir. Need assistance quadrant seven ASAP. Sir," he added for good measure.

He'd never had occasion to speak directly to the lieutenant, let alone wake him up in the middle of the night. He hoped to hell he hadn't committed some major freaking infraction, but damn, this was big.

After a brief silence, Court responded, sounding pissed. "Say again."

"An Afghan woman approached the perimeter, sir. Says she wants to talk to the man in charge. Request instructions on how to proceed, sir."

Court replied that he would dispatch two men to assist and after completing a full body search to bring her to his tent.

"Roger that."

Danny heaved a deep breath, glad there was help on the way. The woman hadn't moved. And damn, he was glad for that. He didn't want to shoot her. But he would, he told himself, if she even looked as if she was going to blow herself up and take him with him. He'd shoot her dead. He wasn't dying on account of some Afghan, no, sir.

And as he stood there waiting for reinforcements, it occurred to him that he'd just acted like a real soldier. That, in fact, he might be a real freaking soldier. For the first time since he'd enlisted, it struck him that maybe he understood what all this gung-ho crap was about.

★

LIEUTENANT ALEX COURT was accustomed to interaction with the local Afghan population, specifically the Pashtun. He was not accustomed to being approached in the middle of the night by a woman dressed as a boy and telling a story like this woman had told him.

"Why didn't he come himself?" he asked, after she'd told him a wild story about a Special Forces soldier who had been held captive by the ISI for over three years but had escaped during a prisoner exchange with the Taliban.

It made no sense at all. ISI? Seriously? Still, he listened because she was here for a reason, and he could possibly find out what it was.

"He is unwell," the woman said. "I believe his leg

was once broken and never set. Walking is difficult. He has also had head injuries. This has caused him problems with memory, headaches, and vertigo. He is unable to travel alone, and it is unsafe to attempt to transport him with the many Taliban checkpoints on the roads. The Taliban are actively searching for him. They have already searched our house once."

"Why didn't they find him?"

"He was hidden under the floor."

If this was a story, it was a well-crafted and imaginative one.

He could not get a good read on her. She was soft-spoken and intelligent. And her English was perfect, which was a point of interest to him.

"You're educated."

"At my father's insistence. My father has also aided in harboring this man. We wish to help him connect with the U.S. military so that he can return home."

This was absolutely bizarre. Court wasn't aware of any MIA troops in Afghanistan. And the U.S. presence in the Kandahar Province specifically had been minimal.

"You'll understand if I'm not convinced. This is a pretty wild story."

Almost as an afterthought, she reached into the pocket of her loose trousers.

"Stop right there," he commanded, drawing his pistol.

She held her hands up. "I wish only to give you a letter he has written. May I?"

Because his men had searched her, he nodded.

"The letter provides Jeffery's full name, rank, and serial number, his unit, battalion—more. He also explains how he was captured and when. Also, there is a recent blood sample and live hair follicles. His fingerprint is also on the letter." She handed it to him.

"Put it on the table." He didn't want to touch it and compromise the evidence, if there was, in fact, evidence.

"What's in this for you?" he asked, because he was not only cautious but also curious.

"We wish only for Jeffery to return home."

He stared at her, trying again to get a read. She seemed sincere enough, but there were a million sincere faces in Afghanistan. Some of them had led U.S. troops into ambushes.

"We also wish to make the exchange in such a way that there is no possibility of my father and myself being linked to him. As I said, the Taliban are searching for him. If they find out we harbored him for these several months, we will be killed."

He stared at her long and hard, compelled to believe her yet wary. "OK. Once more. Start from the beginning, and don't leave anything out."

✴

THE AMERICAN LIEUTENANT was a tall, lean man with blue eyes and an air of wariness that made Rabia realize he could, if he chose, decide to hold her as a possible enemy combatant.

She told herself to remain calm, that she spoke the truth, and because it was the truth, he would believe her.

"We're pulling out in the morning," the lieutenant told her after offering her a seat on a camp chair. "When we get back to our forward operating base tomorrow, I'll pass your story and the material you brought with you to the camp commander. He'll have everything run through our computers. If it checks out, it'll go immediately up the chain of command. Once they give the word, we'll be back to get him."

Rabia struggled with both relief and regret. "Then you believe me."

He hesitated a moment. "I believe that if we have a soldier out there in danger, we need to get him home."

"You will promise to do what you said? To check thoroughly?"

"We'll investigate. I can promise that."

While his response gave her a measure of relief, she was not convinced. "How long will this investigation take?"

"It depends on a lot of things. But it will be done as rapidly as possible."

She nodded. "When will you be back in Emarat?"

"You'll understand that's not information I can share."

Clearly, he still did not trust her. And she did understand, as she was still deciding if she could trust this man to do what he said he would do. "It is my understanding your patrol arrives here every five days. We, too, have our ways of gathering information, Lieutenant Court," she added when he gave her a look. "Just as the Taliban will also know of your coming and going, since you are clearly not conducting a secretive mission."

He nodded, conceding the point to her.

"Would it be correct to assume I could make contact five days from now?"

"Possibly sooner if your story checks out."

"There is more Jeffery has done to assure you that he is alive."

"More?"

"Do you have a map of the area?"

He nodded.

"May I see it?"

After a moment's hesitation, he dug a map out of a satchel.

"Here is my village." She pointed it out for him when he spread it out on a small folding table. "It is a three-hour drive by car from here. Jeffery assures me there are surveillance drones in constant flight over the area. Direct them here, to my village. Jeffery left a message on the roof of my father's house to prove he is alive and there."

When he looked up from the map, he was frowning. "What kind of message?"

"This I do not know. He said the American military would understand and recognize it."

The lieutenant, while still skeptical, was clearly interested. "Let's say the blood and hair follicles confirm they're recent samples belonging to Sergeant Albert. How do you propose we extract him without implicating you and your father?"

"Jeffery is now in hiding in a safe place away from my village. When you return here after confirming that I am telling the truth, I will provide directions to where you can find him."

"This could all be an elaborate trap," he said thoughtfully.

"The proof I provided will confirm that Jeffery is alive. He needs medical care, Lieutenant. He needs to return home. I urge you to bear that in mind. I urge you to hurry. We cannot keep his presence a secret much longer. I am also fearful that in an effort to protect my father and me, he will attempt to find his way to you on his own. In his physical condition, he will be captured. And then he will be dead."

✶

RABIA WAITED FIVE days. Each evening, she dressed in black and carefully made her way through the streets to the edge of the village. Heart pounding, she would search the flat, barren landscape for signs of the U.S. patrol.

Lieutenant Court and his men did not return.

She expanded her search of the perimeter of the village then, scouring the entire area every night, thinking they might have set up camp somewhere else. One night, she encountered a Taliban patrol. Thank Allah, she heard them before they saw her.

She dropped to the ground, lay as still as the earth, and listened as they passed within twenty yards of where she hid in the open with only the dark as cover.

As frightened as she had been, she still came back every night for five more nights.

The Americans did not return.

She did not know how that could be. The blood and hair—they had to find a match. Jeffery's letter. The message he had left on the roof.

Finally, her father made her accept the truth. They had not believed her. They were not coming back.

✳

JEFF LAY ON the roof, his refuge, and attempted to deal with the disappointment and despair. Beside him, Rabia lay in troubled silence. It had been more than a week since she'd returned from Emarat, tears in her eyes because she feared she'd failed him.

He stared at the night sky. She didn't understand. He was the one who had failed. He'd let her risk her life for him, and because of his guilt, he'd died a thousand times alone in that cave, waiting, certain something had happened to her. Certain she lay dying or dead somewhere with a Taliban bullet in her head.

He'd been half out of his mind with fear for her when she finally came back to him. That's when he made up his mind. No matter what happened, she had to leave here—or he did.

"You need to go," he said again, as he'd said every day since she'd returned. "How can I convince you? You and your father need to go to Kabul. You have relatives there who will take you in. You have a life there as a teacher. You have rights there that you'll never have if you stay here with me."

"And what of you. Jeffery? If I go, what happens to you?"

How did he tell her that he no longer cared what happened to him? How did he tell her that the patrol had been his last chance?

"They'll come for me," he said, not believing it but wanting to convince her that he did. "They'll put it all together, and they'll come. And they'll come here. That's why you have to leave."

He still couldn't figure out what had happened. Had the lieutenant simply written off her story as fantasy? Had he thought she was trying to lead them into a trap?

In the end, it didn't matter. They hadn't come. They weren't going to come.

And he was done. Done putting her at risk. Done hiding out like a coward.

The Taliban would not give up searching for him, and because of that, Rabia would always be in danger—unless he could persuade her to leave.

"Let us not talk of this tonight," she whispered,

and snuggled closer. "Let us be together. The world and war do not exist in these moments when we are together this way."

When she bared herself to him like this—heart, body, soul—it was so easy to let himself be lulled by her soft words, her soft lips, her giving flesh. But when it was over and she slept, exhausted and sweet beside him, the guilt beat at him like a fist.

One more week. If he couldn't persuade her to leave, he vowed on everything he had once been that he would sneak away and put as much distance between himself and Rabia as he could.

Let the Taliban do what they would to him.

He would not put her in danger any longer.

And he would no longer be less than a man.

Chapter

22

Langley, Virginia, late October

*T*he *International Threat Analysis and Prevention*
unit at Langley was Mike Brown's baby. ITAP
officially fell under the Department of Defense table
of organization as contracted labor. Unofficially, the
ITAP unit was a front for a covert rapid-response tactical team that DOD did not want on anyone's radar,
nationally or abroad.

Mike and his boys operated dark and lean—the
way they all liked it. They also operated with complete
impunity. That was the pro. The con was that with
impunity came deniability. If they screwed up and an
operation went south, DOD would not come storming
in, showing U.S. military muscle and getting them out
of their fix. They swam or sank on their own.

So when Brown got the call from DOD that morning and was told to set up the ITAP briefing room at thirteen hundred hours and to expect company, he'd known something big was about to go down.

"Listen up, gentlemen." Brown addressed his team from behind the podium at the front of the small room. Behind him, a map of Kandahar Province bordering Pakistan was projected on the wall from a laptop. The map had been requested by DOD. "Best behavior, OK? We've got big-leaguers on the way."

"How big?" Peter Davis, ITAP's operations manager, had arrived in his wheelchair, a tablet in his lap and a puzzled look on his face.

"You'll know when I know," Brown said, glancing at his go-to guys, Jamie Cooper and Bobbie Taggart. Both looked alert and curious, as did the team's new recruits, Brett Carlyle, Enrique Santos, and Josh Waldrop, all former independent private securities specialists who had recently been brought into the fold.

"When's this little powwow supposed to start?" Cooper asked, crossing an ankle over a knee, his foot going a hundred miles an hour, relaying that he was both excited and impatient.

Before Brown could respond, the door opened, and six members of DOD's other "off the books" team walked in.

"Holy crap," Taggart muttered when he saw them. "Did the red phone ring in the White House?"

Now that Nate Black and his team had shown up, Brown wondered the same thing. Calling together

DOD's two top covert and highly specialized tactical teams suggested a major development.

Nate Black, former U.S. Marine captain, former CEO of his independent contract firm Black Ops Inc., and now the Black team's CO, was the ranking operator in the room. Nate shook Mike's hand, then joined him at the podium.

"Not sure intros are necessary," Mike said, "but let's dot the Is and cross the Ts, shall we?"

"Oh, by all means, let's." Johnny Reed grinned as he sat and gave the room in general a nod. "Top dog here, in case you didn't remember. You can call me TD."

"Just this one time, dial it down, OK, Reed?" Black nodded to the front row, and the rest of the team introduced themselves. In addition to Reed, Gabe Jones, Rafe Mendoza, Luke Coulter, and Joe Green nodded hellos.

"I'm going to cut right to the chase," Black said, and passed out hard copies of an operations order—called an OPORD—to the members of both teams. "Everyone got a copy? Good. Read along with me, boys. Please hold your questions until I'm finished."

Mike flipped open the document and followed the report while Black started reading aloud.

"Operation Aces High—Background Summary OPORD: In October this year, while conducting a routine patrol in Sperwan Ghundey, Panjwai, Kandahar, Afghanistan, an Air Force patrol operating out of recently established FOB (forward operating base) Shaker was approached by a female Afghan (Pashtun) subject on the outskirts of Emarat. Subject claimed that an American Special Forces sergeant had taken shelter with her family following his escape from enemy forces after being held hostage approximately three years. The subject provided correspondence stating it was written by the SF soldier, as well as physical evidence for verification."

Black stopped and took a sip of water when Mike handed him a glass.

"Operational constraints precluded immediate authentication of said missing SF sergeant's existence. Subsequent analysis of physical evidence, however, confirmed it did, in fact, belong to an American military service member believed to be KIA (killed in action) in February 2011, following hostile action near Chamkani, Paktia Providence, Afghanistan, on the Pakistan side of the border. His body was never recovered.

"Despite repeated attempts to subsequently contact the female Afghan subject at a prearranged meeting place, contact failed. Two weeks ago, however, overflights of the area by drone assets revealed the letters 'DOL' and 'JA' formed on the roof of a dwelling in the village of Salawat as the woman had promised they would be. It could be surmised that 'JA' represents the initials of the missing team member, and 'DOL' could represent 'De Oppresso Liber,'" Army Special

Forces credo. Note: one week later, the letters had been removed."

"Holy crap," Taggart muttered under his breath.

Black continued. "Findings: Probability of said SF sergeant's existence: 85 percent.

"Recommendations: Current political climate in Afghanistan during the draw-down coupled with increased Taliban activity in the area necessitates extreme care in handling this situation. Sanctioned military involvement is not advised. It is therefore recommended to deploy black ops and ITAP teams to conduct a surveillance mission, gather further intel on the existence of KIA/MIA service member and the Afghan subject who contacted the patrol and then report back to DOD for further orders, should an extraction of the SF sergeant, if he actually exists, become necessary."

Black downed another sip of water. "Enemy Forces: Taliban, both foreign and local, are expected to inhabit the area and number fewer than fifty. They have conventional commbloc (Soviet) weapons including RPG-7s, RPDs (machine guns), AK-47s. No evidence of heavy weapons, including DShK 12.7mm heavy machine guns or mortars. Communication with their command staff is limited to radio and cell phones. They utilize a wide variety of vehicles, including small to large pickup-type trucks, passenger vans, small buses, and cars. Their mobility is limited by road conditions, and they are often able to travel only by foot or using animals.

"Assets Available for Mission," Black continued. "Troop assets will be available for a rescue of the SF sergeant, should he be found; however, there will be complete deniability and no participation by U.S. military sources to rescue black teams if it is not also in conjunction with the rescue of the reported KIA. Intelligence assets will be available as required, including drone, satellite, and Elint (electronics intelligence) to monitor enemy radio traffic. Air assets include aerial vehicles ranging from drones to fighter/bomber air strikes, B-52s, B-1s, and AC-130s. Further information on required air assets will be determined at a later date—by us," he added pointedly.

"One Russian-made Mil Mi-17 helicopter with Afghan military markings will be utilized for team insertion and extraction. Utilization of this particular aircraft has two advantages: it adds further deniability that no U.S. forces were directly involved, and the Mi-17 can transport required personnel and equipment to carry out the mission and provide its own air support with conventionally mounted weapons."

Black paused again and, seeing that the men were all engrossed in the OPORD, continued: "A staging area will be provided at the Kandahar airport. Appropriate arms, ammunition, fuel, and other material assets will be made available to the team as specified. Assault and contingency plans will also be developed—again, by us.

"Finally, the subject of the search is Medical

Sergeant Jeffery Robert Albert, U.S. Army Special Forces Group (Airborne), C Company, 8th Battalion, 1st Special Forces Regiment, formerly believed KIA, February 2011."

Black looked up from the report. "I'll take questions now."

Mike couldn't have asked a question if he had a rifle pointed straight at his heart.

Medical Sergeant Jeffery Robert Albert.

It couldn't be. It could *not* be J. R. Albert, the husband of the woman his brother, Ty, had fallen in love with and intended to marry.

But he knew Jess's story. Her husband, J.R., Jeff, had been KIA by an IED in Afghanistan three and a half years ago. This could not be a coincidence.

Jeff Albert might be alive. In all probability, he *was* alive. And while Mike was happy as hell about the prospect of bringing a hero home, he knew what this would do to his brother. It was going to kill him.

He had to talk to Black. In private. He had to get more information.

"Has the family been notified of the possibility that Albert may be alive?" he asked abruptly.

"Negative," Black responded. "That's on hold until we either get eyes on him or confirm that this is a hoax."

"But you don't think it is. You think this guy somehow survived."

"I do," Black said simply.

Before Mike could ask more, the team started firing questions at Black like bullets.

"Where, exactly, are we inserting, sir?" Reed wanted to know.

Black grabbed a laser pointer from a shelf in the podium and made a circle on the wall map in the general area. There were so many small villages scattered throughout the Afghan countryside that many of them weren't even marked on the map.

"Beg your pardon, sir," Bobbie Taggart, former Special Forces himself, spoke up. "But isn't it a bit—how should I put this without mentioning the words *chicken shit*—let's say, *unusual* that Special Forces isn't all the hell over this, draw-down or not? If that was our guy out there, there'd be so many of us jumping out of planes to find him, the sky'd be white with parachutes."

"*Unusual* is the key word, Taggart," Black agreed. "Everything about this situation is unusual, starting with the fact that Sergeant Albert was listed as KIA and ending with the circumstances that brought his existence to DOD's attention."

"Can you expand on that, sir?" This from Gabe Jones, who sat with his arms crossed over his chest, his bad leg outstretched, a sober look on his face.

"February 2011, Sergeant Albert's detachment was headed back to home base after completing a mission in Pakistan. The small convoy was met with overwhelming Taliban forces," Black said, nutshelling the situation. "Two survivors of the attack reported seeing

Albert's GMV get hit by an IED and later by an RPG. The witnesses were fighting for their own lives and barely escaped themselves. Both were one-hundred-percent certain Albert was dead."

"And no one recovered his body?" Green sounded both skeptical and pissed.

"There were extenuating circumstances," Black said. "One, the ambush took place in Pakistan, where 'officially' no U.S. military actions were supposed to take place. Two, before a detail could sneak back across the border to recover the bodies, a monster snowstorm set in. Add to that, beefed-up Pakistani forces on what had been a very porous border precluded the recovery of Albert's body."

"How bad does that suck?" Reed mumbled, and Mike knew every member of both teams agreed.

The room went quiet. It made sense, Mike thought. This mission was not going to be cleared with the Afghanistan government. They would never get permission, so they had to go in black. If things went FUBAR and any of ITAP or Black's team were killed or captured, they could not be linked back to Uncle Sam. The U.S. would disavow their connection and insist that they were a rogue group, possibly mercs or private contractors hired by the sergeant's family to explain away why Americans were running the operation.

"We all onboard so far?" Black asked the room at large.

He got nods all around.

Cooper had a question. "How the hell did Albert survive more than three years held by the Taliban? And why did they keep him alive in the first place?"

"That's where it gets muddy," Black said. "And this was not in the official report—for reasons you'll understand when I'm finished. If we believe that the correspondence the Afghan woman gave the patrol was in fact written by our previously believed-to-be-KIA soldier, he's the one who made the claim. And he states it wasn't the Taliban that attacked the convoy. It was the ISI disguised as Taliban."

"Why the fu—" Coulter cut himself off. "Why the devil would Pakistan's secret service attack an American patrol? We all know that Pakistan only pretends to be our allies, but this makes no sense."

"What about war has ever made sense?" Black pointed out. "In any event, Albert—if it is, in fact, Albert—stated that ISI held him captive. He further stated that it was while they were making a deal with the Taliban to exchange him for some Pakistani prisoners that he escaped. The woman maintained she found him near death and has been hiding him for several months. She also states that he has multiple injuries and medical problems sustained during his imprisonment and escape that have precluded him from making an attempt to contact U.S. forces himself."

"And we're taking her word for it?" Mendoza looked incredulous. "The guy has been listed as KIA for almost four years. Ask me, this screams setup."

Black nodded. "It could be. But the blood sample she provided was a match to that on file for Albert. The hair follicles provided more DNA match. The letter he wrote—if he wrote it—is compelling. Add in the letters on the roof—" Black stopped and shrugged. "Additionally, the woman repeatedly requested that the extraction be made in such a way that she and her father were not implicated in hiding Albert. It was clear she greatly feared retaliation by the Taliban."

"How did she think we could keep her out of it?" Taggart asked.

"She was going to hide him in a location away from her village and reveal the location when she made a second contact with the U.S. patrol. After several days of waiting, she must have decided they weren't coming back and bailed."

"Why didn't the patrol come back?"

"They did, once they decided her claim was legit, but it was more than two weeks later, and like I said, she'd bailed. And to answer the next question, why didn't they come back sooner? That's still under investigation. Either someone dropped the ball, or there was a computer/network glitch at the FOB and they couldn't immediately access their records of MIA and presumed KIA. As I said, it's under investigation."

"If they knew where he was, why didn't they go get him?"

"Believe we covered that earlier. We were no longer looking at a clear-cut extraction in a remote location away from potential local casualties in case the situation goes hot. Now we presume he's still in the village, and that's why we go in stealth. Which means, if Albert is there we'll have two additional extractions: the woman and her father."

The room grew painfully quiet.

"We square?" Black glanced around the room again. "All right, then. Albert is one of ours. If he's alive, we're going to make damn sure he gets back home."

Chapter

23

Northern Minnesota, late October

*H*ey. You're back." Jess walked out of the grocery section of the store and into Ty's arms when he shut the door behind him. "Did their flight take off OK?"

Ty's mom and dad had recently spent a week with them to get to know Jess and to celebrate the engagement and upcoming wedding. He kissed her. "It did. And they both loved you."

"That street goes both ways."

She looked so happy. And she'd handled his family well. Last month, after he'd called his big brother, Mike, to ask him to be his best man, both Mike and his wife, Eva, had dropped everything and made a quick trip to the lake to congratulate them and, as was typical of Mike, to give Jess dire warnings about what she was getting herself into by shackling herself to Ty.

She, of course, had loved Mike and Eva, too. Ty hadn't figured it would go any other way. Jess was vibrant and happy and opening up to him and to life more and more every day. Her parents had even made a trip to the lake, and he'd seen where Jess had gotten her backbone and values.

He couldn't believe it had been more than a month since she'd agreed to marry him, less than a month until their Thanksgiving wedding.

"Let's not wait for Christmas," she'd said two weeks ago, delighting him when he'd suggested they have a holiday wedding. "Let's compromise and make it the Thanksgiving weekend."

That worked fine for him. The sooner she officially became his wife, the better.

Since September, he'd been back to Florida twice. Once to hire an office manager to keep on top of things for him while he was here and a second time to make sure things were going smoothly.

Then he'd bought the float plane. She would be his winter project, but he had every intention of having her painted, spit-polished, and ready for the spring season. Jess had started advertising Kabby Charter Service on her Web site three weeks ago, and that had already generated several inquires.

Everything was coming up roses in the north land, and it was about to get even better. He'd been busting to get her alone to show her his big surprise.

"Come on. Let's take a little ride. I've got something to show you."

"I can't leave the store."

"Thirty minutes. That's all I need. Put a sign on the door. Tell 'em you'll be back at—" He glanced at the wall clock. "Four o'clock. Nothing's happening this time of day, anyway. Come on," he coaxed again when he could see her weakening. "You do not want to miss this."

She gave him a studied look, then expelled a deep breath, and he knew he had her. "This better be good."

He laughed and waited while she made her sign, taped it to the door, and locked up.

✳

"YOU DIDN'T SAY anything about a blindfold," she sputtered, after he'd gotten her into the Jeep and insisted she put on the sleep mask he'd bought for this occasion.

"What kind of a surprise would it be if you saw it coming?"

"I repeat," she sputtered, adjusting the mask. "This had better be good. And it had better not be another junker plane."

"Have a little faith," he said, grinning, and pulled out of the parking lot.

Ten minutes later, after several guesses on her part that had them both laughing, he pulled into a driveway.

"Sit tight. I'll come around and help you out."

"Is this all really necessary?"

Once she was out of the Jeep, he hugged her hard, kept his arm around her shoulders, and guided her down a crushed-rock path.

"I smell the lake," she said when he finally stopped.

"And this would be why." He tugged off the blindfold, then stood back and let her take in the large log house with its wraparound porch, the sloping lawn that led to a wide dock, and the brilliant blue waters of Lake Kabetogama.

She looked at the house, then looked at him. "What are we doing at the Owens house?"

"We're not at the Owens house." He smiled into her eyes. "We're at *our* house."

She blinked at him as if he'd lost his mind. He saw the moment the light began to dawn. And that's exactly the expression that fit. A dawning, glorious light filled her eyes, then spread to a smile both disbelieving and hopeful.

She glanced back at the For Sale sign stuck in the ground by the mailbox, saw the Sold banner covering it. "Seriously? You bought it?"

"I bought it."

She pressed spread fingers of both hands to her breast, looked out over the lake again, back at the house, then back at him. "You *really* bought it?"

He loved that look. Joy, amazement, love. "I really did."

"Oh, my God, Ty. I've always loved this place."

"I know. Shelley told me."

Hers hand flew from her chest to her cheeks as she stared again at the house and the gorgeous view of the lake.

"Want to take a peek inside? I happen to have the keys." He fished them out of his pocket and was about to hold them out to her when she flew into him so hard she almost took them both to the ground.

He laughed as he steadied himself and wrapped his arms around her. "Told you it'd be worth it."

When she pulled back to look at him, tears filled her eyes. "This is the most amazing thing anyone has ever done for me."

He cupped her face in his hands. "And you are the most amazing thing that's ever happened to me." He kissed her then, long and slow and sweet. "We're going to raise some babies here," he said when he pulled away. "And if you keep looking at me like that, we're going to start working on that straight away."

This time, she laughed and grabbed his hand. "Come on. Let's go look inside."

★

LIFE HAD NEVER been sweeter, Ty thought later that night, as they lay in Jess's bed after celebrating the purchase of their new home. He was one contented man. And the woman sleeping beside him was the reason.

A loud pounding on the front door of the store, however, cut into that contentment like a buzz saw. Bear sprang to his feet from the rug by the bed and snarled like his namesake.

Jess jerked straight up in bed. "What? What's happening?"

"Go back to sleep. I'll check it out. Somebody probably ran out of gas."

On a yawn, he threw back the covers and reached for his jeans and shirt.

He was still buttoning up when he hit the bottom step and walked across the store to the door and looked through the glass.

The lights from the pumps backlit the silhouette of a man he'd recognize in pitch dark.

He undid the lock and jerked open the door. "What the hell?"

His brother, Mike, stood on the stoop. He was not smiling. Mike always smiled.

There was only one kind of news his brother would have traveled this far to deliver in person four weeks before he was due back at the lake to be best man at Ty's wedding.

"What happened?" Ty's heart slammed like a piston. "The folks? Oh, God. Did something happen on their flight?"

"No," Mike said quickly. "No. They're fine. Everyone's fine."

"Then what the—" Ty stopped, dragged a hand

through his hair. "What are you doing here? How did you get here?"

"I flew. Rented a car. None of that matters. Ty, let's go inside. I need to talk to you. Both of you."

When Mike looked over Ty's shoulder, Ty knew Jess had come downstairs.

"Mike?"

"Hi, babe," Mike said gently. "How's it going?"

She tightened the belt on her robe and glanced at Ty. "Something tells me it's not going well."

✶

"THERE'S NO WAY to say this but to come out with it."

At Mike's insistence, they'd walked up the stairs to the apartment. Ty and Jess sat on the sofa, their hands entwined. Bear, sensing his mistress's distress, leaned heavily against her leg.

"Jess," Mike sat across from them. "You need to brace yourself."

Ty covered both of her hands with his. He could feel her trembling. Hell, he was shaking himself. "For God's sake, Mike. Spit it out."

Mike let out a heavy breath, then met Jess's eyes. "We've got some pretty solid intel that Jeff is alive."

For long moments, she didn't react. She stared at him.

For long moments, Ty did the same thing, unable to process his brother's words.

Shock and surprise transitioned to anger, which

finally broke the echoing silence. "What the hell are you talking about?" Ty demanded. "Where is this coming from? And how can it be? J.R. was KIA."

Mike lifted a hand. "It's complicated."

"I think we need to hear it," Jess said quietly.

So he told them. "Two weeks ago, an Afghan woman approached a U.S. Army infantry patrol. She said she'd been harboring an injured American Special Forces soldier who had been held prisoner for three and a half years but had recently escaped. She gave Jeff's name, his company, unit, and battalion, and she provided physical evidence. There was also a note, supposedly written by Jeff."

"My God." Jess looked as if she was in shock. Her face had drained to deadly pale, her voice sounded whisper-soft and thready.

"The woman was skittish, and the patrol was not in a position to go with her to her village, which was several kilometers away. She was also afraid of Taliban discovery. They were to meet up again at an appointed time the next week, but the patrol couldn't make it, and when they finally got back, she was gone," Mike continued.

"Why do you think she was telling the truth?" Ty had started to feel a little desperate. This wasn't merely Jess's life hanging in the balance of this discovery. This was his life. This was *their* life.

"The physical evidence. It matches Jeff's military records."

"It could be old. Three and a half years old," Ty insisted.

Mike shook his head. "She had hair samples, complete with live follicles that indicated the samples were taken as recently as a week before testing."

Ty's head hit his chest. He closed his eyes. He could not wish a man dead. Even if that man's existence could mean the end of the best thing that had ever happened to him.

"They never found her again?" Jess asked in a small voice.

"No. But drone surveillance of the general area spotted clear letters formed on a rooftop in a village in the general vicinity."

"What letters?" Ty asked.

Mike told them.

Jess covered her mouth with a hand. "It's him. My God. It's J.R."

Ty pulled her closer against him. "So he's still out there? In some Afghan village?"

Mike lifted a shoulder. "We assume so. Two teams are going in on a recon and possible rescue mission."

When Mike held his gaze for a long, hard moment, Ty knew the rest of the story. "You're on one of those teams."

Mike nodded. "We deploy tomorrow from Virginia at zero six hundred hours. "Look," he said when both Ty and Jess sat speechless. "I hate this, but I've got to head back. As it is, I'm on borrowed time, but I couldn't let you hear about this from anyone but me. And word of the mission can't get out, OK? That's the way it's got to be for now. I wish I knew what to say," Mike added with a helpless lift of his hands.

Ty knew exactly what to say. "I'm going with you."

Beside him, Jess gasped. "No. No, you can't go. My God, Ty. You cannot go. Tell him!" She turned pleading eyes on Mike. "Tell him he can't go."

"Bro," Mike began, preparing to argue.

"You've been trying to recruit me ever since you started your new unit," Ty reminded his brother. "Well, now I'm saying yes."

"This isn't a good idea," Mike insisted.

"What this is, is my life. Jess's life. Our life. I don't merely want to go. I need to go. I need to help bring him home. I want him back. Hell, he's one of ours."

Silent tears streamed down Jess's cheeks. "You promised me. You promised me you wouldn't ever fight anyone else's fight ever again."

"And I'll keep that promise." He gripped her hands in his and brought them to his lips. "But you know this isn't someone else's fight. It's our fight. I have to go, Jess. You know I have to go."

★

NUMB, JESS HUGGED her arms around herself, listening as Ty rifled around in the bedroom, tossing his things into his duffel.

J.R. Alive. Of course, she wanted it to be true.

Wanted it with everything in her. Her mind had been racing, her heart sick, thinking about what he must have endured during his years of captivity. Mike said the Afghan woman told the patrol J.R. was injured. How badly? In what way? What horrible things had they done to him?

And what was she going to do if they brought him back? She loved Ty. But she was married to J.R. He would need support. He would need *her* support. As far as he knew, he had a wife waiting at home for him.

Tears filled her eyes.

What if neither of them came back?

"Jess."

She jerked her head up as Ty walked out of the bedroom, his expression grim, his eyes somber.

"You could die there," she said, unable to stop the tears.

He dropped the duffel and came to her. Wrapped her in his arms. "Nothing's going to happen to me. We'll bring him back. I promise we'll bring him back."

"And then what?" she asked, feeling selfish and conflicted and confused.

"Then we'll figure things out." He touched a hand to her hair. "We'll figure things out," he repeated, but she knew he felt the same disbelief and sense of falling apart that she did.

"I can't lose you, too."

He kissed her hard. "You won't. That's a promise."

She clung to him. "I love you."

"I love you, too." He held her tightly against him. "I've got to go. Mike's waiting."

"Come back to me."

It felt as if a part of her soul was ripped away when he finally let her go, gave the dog a gentle pat, and, without looking back, walked out the door.

Chapter

24

Kandahar Air Force Base, end of October

*S*trapped into the copilot seat, Ty glanced over as Mike lifted the Mi-17 chopper they'd dubbed the "Reaper" off the helo pad. His brother still had the gift. The bird moved effortlessly into the night, seemingly guided by Mike's thoughts alone. Ty had had that kind of connection with his own bird in Iraq. He felt a moment of nostalgia for his Nighthawk and hoped there was a heaven for helicopters, because she had died saving his life.

And now they might die trying to save the life of a man who had, by all accounts, died a long time ago. A man who, if he ended up being alive, would kill any chance Ty had of marrying the woman he'd planned to share his life with . . . and that was the last place he needed to go tonight.

Head back in the game, he sensed that as they spun up higher and headed toward the mountains, the thin, dry air coupled with a full load of weapons on the outboard pods and the weight of the team in the back caused the chopper to handle a little sluggishly. It didn't bother Mike. He flew the bird like the pro he was.

"Piece of cake," Mike had assured him after their brief but intense mission prep minutes before takeoff. "She's not much different from the Mi-8 I flew in Sierra Leone. Nuance, bro. It's all about nuance."

Nuance, hell. Ty had studied the crap out of the Mi-17 in the event he had to fly this Russian-made bird, which was different from any he'd ever flown. Even the rotor spun clockwise rather than counterclockwise like his old Nighthawk. Major difference. If something happened to the aircraft, the direction the rotor spun could make a difference whether they crashed or gently landed. But he was ready. He could take over if he had to—he just hoped he didn't have to.

Ty glanced over his shoulder. Everyone sat quietly, no doubt rerunning the mission plan and their final briefing over and over in their minds.

"Once more for posterity, boys and girls." Nate Black *addressed his fourteen team members, his face somber.*

"Operation Aces High Assault Plan: Zero one hundred hours, we fly the Mi-17 chopper, code name Reaper, from Kandahar en route to the target village of Salawat, Mike Brown at the controls, Ty Brown in the

copilot seat. Waldrop will be your flight engineer for this all-expenses-paid trip to the wild and wacky world of Taliban land."

"Sorry, guys. I'm fresh out of peanuts and soda." Waldrop's ad lib earned him a few snickers and cut the tension in the room.

"Zero three hundred hours," Black continued, "Bravo squad consisting of Reed, Green, Jones, Mendoza, Coulter, and yours truly, along with Alpha squad Cooper, Taggart, Santos, and Carlyle, will fast-rope down to the south edge of the village and make our way to the dwelling identified by drone surveillance as possibly housing Special Forces Medical Sergeant Jeffery Albert.

"From zero three-fifteen to zero three-thirty hours, we conduct a search of the dwelling, attempting to find and ID subject. If found, we will secure him and the two Pashtun civilians who have assisted him, make our way back to the extraction point, and return to base.

"The operation will be monitored and assisted from home base with drone surveillance and operational management by Charlie squad members Crystal Reed and B. J. Mendoza."

"I can promise you more than peanuts and soda if you guys keep your heads down and come back safe and sound." Crystal flashed a smile tempered with concern.

"Just to be clear," Johnny Reed cut in, "that wasn't an all-inclusive you my wife made a promise to. That was an all-inclusive me—and thanks, babe." He *winked at his wife. "Keep your motor running, 'cause Daddy's gonna hold you to that promise when he gets home."*

Black gave Reed a "Seriously?" look. "You done?"

Reed grinned. "Just getting started."

"Zip it," Black ordered, then glanced around the room. "Questions? No? Well, there should be, because we've received updated intel indicating there's increased radio traffic from the Taliban, who have recently upped their numbers in the area as they apparently broaden their search for an escaped prisoner. Guess we know who that might be.

"So look sharp, people. We could run into some heavy resistance, and I don't want to have to explain to Crystal here or anyone else why I brought you home with bloodstains on your tighty whities."

He looked around the room, seemed satisfied that all teams were aware the danger meter had ticked up several clicks, and continued. "Contingency plan: If the extraction helicopter is lost or damaged during the operation and/or the team is engaged by enemy combatants, Charlie squad here at base will assist remotely by calling in necessary air or land support. Ground teams will commandeer local vehicles, then make our way to FOB Shaker to be extracted during normal resupply missions.

"We good?" Black added, to nods all around.

"All right, let's not screw this up. If Albert is out there, let's bring a hero home."

It wasn't ten minutes later that they loaded up and

headed out. And yeah, Ty thought, fully aware of the ten-man ground team in the bird with them, he figured they were all thinking about what lay ahead. Most likely, they were also thinking that they were putting their asses on the line on very sketchy intel. While intel had originally put Taliban numbers at fifty, Black's recent announcement upped it to more in the range of "no idea to a shitload."

One thing was in their favor, though. DOD had come through with the promised assets. The plan was for a drop-in sneak and peek. If Jeff Albert wasn't there, they were on their own getting out again. If Albert was actually on-site, they were to snatch him and get him the hell out of Dodge.

In case things went south, though, they were loaded for bear. Twin pods of twenty unguided 80mm S-8DF missiles hung farthest out on each outboard wing pylon; 23mm gun pods were also mounted on either side, closer to the fuselage. Major odds eveners.

The best weapon, however, was the team itself. Ty had been happy as hell to see Nate Black as team leader, along with Johnny Reed, Gabe Jones, Joe Green, Rafe Mendoza, and Luke Coulter. All were first-class warriors, but Coulter was also a damn fine medic. From Mike's team, Jamie Cooper, Bobbie Taggart, Enrique Santos, Josh Waldrop, and Brett Carlyle were as good as it got. And back at Kandahar AFB, Johnny's wife and Mendoza's wife—Crystal and B.J.—were running the air show. Both women were fearless, steady under pressure, and brilliant strategists.

Ty settled in for what was left of the two-hour ride. Time and miles and mountains rolled by in the dark beneath them, barren and forbidding and hostile. Was Albert alive? Ty wondered. And if so, was he in any shape to survive what could turn into a full-out firefight if things didn't go as planned and they ran into a buzz saw?

Try as he might, he couldn't stop his thoughts from straying back to Jess and the pain in her eyes when he'd left her. This was the right thing to do, he reminded himself. It was the only thing to do. He didn't want to lose her, but he couldn't live a life with her knowing he hadn't done everything he could to help bring Jeff Albert home. What kind of a man would that make him if he'd done nothing? Not one he could live with. Not one Jess could respect. What happened next was anyone's guess. He'd live with Jess's decision either way.

"Five minutes, ladies." Mike's voice was rock-solid steady through his headset, breaking Ty out of his thoughts.

He let out a deep breath as they approached the drop site, knowing questions about his and Jess's future would be answered soon enough.

To his left and behind him, Waldrop held up three fingers, notifying the team that it would be three minutes before the drop.

They all set their goggles, checked their equipment, and made sure the ropes at both the rear and the left door were clear. Mike took the Reaper down fast, swooping low over the hills, then down into the valley that led to the village.

Ty's pulse raced with adrenaline. This was it. Do or die.

"Two minutes." Mike alerted the team.

Ty kept his hands close to the controls, ready to take over if necessary, while the side door opened and a gust of wind sliced through the aircraft. Seconds later, Mike cut speed and hovered the bird near the outside wall of the family compound in the target village. Immediately, Green kicked out the rope coils, and the bird shifted with the weight of the men and their weapons as they fast-roped down.

One by one, Reed, Coulter, Green, Jones, and Mendoza, then Cooper, Taggart, Santos, Carlyle, and finally Nate Black hit the ground, quickly shouldered their M-4s, and disappeared into the shadows.

"All clear," Waldrop reported, and Mike swung the helicopter up and away, barely missing a rooftop antenna as he cut in close.

He flew out and away from the village, hovered, then started to set down about a half-mile away to await word from the ground team.

"Now we wait," Mike said, his voice tinged with tension.

Only they didn't wait long.

"Tracers!" Ty yelled, as flashing lights lit up the

night with glowing balls of green tracers arcing toward them. "We've been made."

Mike swore and abruptly lifted the bird, then veered around the tracer rounds working their way out of the target area. "So much for sneaking in unnoticed. Take out that freaking gun!" he yelled, pedal-turned, and Ty dumped a burst from the 23mm at the gun spewing the tracer rounds and live fire.

The ground gun kept firing, sharpening their aim.

"They're getting closer!" Mike yelled. "Take out the SOB!"

Ty laid off the 23mm and lined up the missiles as glowing green basketballs flew straight at them.

He pulled the trigger, and three missiles shot out of the pods toward the spot where the tracers streamed out of the enemy gun.

"Shit, shit!" Mike yelled when the flash from the missile fire glinted off the fuselage and temporarily blinded him. "Take the controls! I can't see!"

"I've got it." Ty gripped the stick and flipped the weapons selector back to the 23mm guns, then twitched the copter directly toward the machine gun and fired. He walked the rounds right into the throat of the muzzle flashes, then pulled up abruptly before his shells made a direct hit that lit up the ground for twenty feet around the gun.

"That's what I'm talking about!" Waldrop crowed in one breath, then shouted in another, "RPG! Break right! Break right!"

Ty dumped the stick and hit the chaff and flare buttons as he twisted the bird away from a rocket that flashed past the right side of his windscreen.

"Too damn close!" Mike muttered, still rubbing his eyes as more tracers streaked up from the ground. "How many big guns do they freaking have?"

"The correct answer," Ty said as he hopped the aircraft over a hill, "would be too many."

Beside him, Mike grinned. "Nice flying, baby bro."

"You're celebrating a little early, don't you think?"

Something smashed into the tail section of the bird, answering his question. The chopper shuddered, almost stopped, and smoke billowed into the cockpit.

✱

NATE QUICKLY MOVED the team into position. They'd all seen the ground fire aimed at the chopper and knew their position had been given away. This was the exact last thing he'd wanted to happen. Shades of the Bin Laden raid all over, as any hope of an easy in, easy out flew out the proverbial window.

Damn. They'd landed in the middle of Taliban country and he had no desire to have a video of American heads being hacked from their bodies showing up on the Internet.

It wasn't enough that he had to worry about the ground team. He was anxious about Reaper. Mike and the guys had taken a lot of fire. It seemed every idiot with a gun and a grudge was determined to take down the team's only way out. Since the chopper had danced away through the fireworks and out of sight, he put his trust in the guys flying the bird to do their job.

In the meantime, they needed to step it up. Several dwellings surrounded by private walled courtyards stood in the general area of their target building. According to their Predator video feed, which had spotted the letters on the roof, the house was the one next to a storage shed of some sort.

No dogs barked in this section of the village, but it seemed every hound in the surrounding area had set up a ruckus that would wake the dead, much less any bad guys.

With M-4s shouldered, Alpha squad—Cooper, Taggart, Santos, and Carlyle—headed for the courtyard to gain access through the back door. Bravo squad—Coulter, Jones, Reed, and Mendoza—headed to the storage shed to clear it, then scooted around to the front of the house. Back at Kandahar AFB, Charlie squad—Crystal Reed and B. J. Mendoza—monitored their action via drone surveillance and coordinated everything, including contingencies, with U.S. military assets. Nate had a bad feeling they were going to need them.

Hanging back in the shadows, Nate, along with Green, waited during the Alpha and Bravo teams' entry to keep control of any enemy engagement and as lookouts. Nate fingered the trigger of his M-4 as the main building team stacked alongside the doorway, breaching charge already in place. Overkill? No way. They still didn't know for certain if they were dealing with friendlies or hostiles, and he wasn't taking any chances.

Nate looked over his shoulder and saw that the back-door team was in place and ready. "Green light," he said into his radio.

The breaching charges front and back fired with loud cracks, and each team moved into the house via its respective door.

Lights from flashlights slashed through open windows. "First room clear," came over the radio from Alpha team leader Cooper after a long delay.

"Mission clock, three minutes remaining." Crystal Reed's voice broke into the team's commo over their radios. "And it looks like you're about to have company. Predator feed shows a lot of dismounts, all stirred up and headed your way."

Nate swore under his breath. It had taken a lot of arm twisting and favor calling to get a Predator tasked to their mission, and he was grateful for it now.

But this news wasn't good. A lot of Tangos on foot—dismounts. While they'd planned for it, he still didn't want to deal with a slug of bad guys.

"Looking like we might need some help headed our way," Nate told Crystal.

"Roger that. Already on it," she replied. "Stand by."

Contingencies were in place if the whole thing had dropped into the pot, but his team being out here was so off book that Nate wasn't sure he could count on the military coming through—even if they did find Albert. DOD's repeated deniability mantra wasn't merely lip service. If it started to look as if they were going to buy the farm, they would suddenly be on their own.

For more reasons than one, he hoped they found Albert in that house. Then they needed to get out of here. Fast.

He still hadn't heard from Bravo squad. "Bravo. You stop for a burger and fries? What the hell's going on in there?"

Chapter

25

Ty fought the controls, trying to assess where they'd been hit. Smoke boiled up in the cockpit, so thick he could barely see the multitude of warning lights blinking at him from the instrument panel. Beside him, Mike frantically hit switches, reset breakers, and changed over to backup systems.

Ty bore down hard on the right pedal and finally managed some semblance of control. The smoke started to clear, and he scanned his gauges. Not good.

"Everyone all right?"

"Fine," Mike and Waldrop answered.

"Want me to take back the controls?"

"I've got it, big bro. What the hell hit us?"

"My guess? RPG," Waldrop said, then yelled, "And shit, shit, here comes another one. Break left! Now, now!"

Ty continued to fight with the damaged controls; the bird moved sluggishly. "Brace!" he yelled. "She's not responding."

By some miracle of luck, timing, and fairy dust, the RPG missed them.

"We're clear!" Waldrop shouted. "Damn. Thank God and poor shots."

"That came up out of the valley we just crossed." Mike craned his head around, looking for more. "Don't know about you, but I've had enough. Can you keep her in the air?"

Ty clenched his jaw. "Does a one-legged duck swim in a circle?"

"Then swing back around. I'm going to get that sucker."

Ty let the right pedal loose a bit, and the helicopter miraculously responded and spun back toward the valley.

Mike flicked the weapons selector switch back to Missiles, took aim, and pulled the trigger, dumping half a dozen missiles toward the enemy guns.

This time, everyone was prepared for the flash, and they all closed their eyes as the missiles shot out of the pods.

When Ty opened his eyes, he saw the valley blow in a flash of fire.

"Nice." Waldrop high-fived Mike.

"Let's head back to the LZ and assess the damages," Mike said.

As Ty started to turn the chopper, a loud crash and

the sound of tearing metal rattled the bird. She started spiraling downward.

"Pull back! Pull back!" Mike yelled. "We're going down!"

★

THE LAST TIME Nate had looked, Reaper had been kicking ass and taking names as a massive series of explosions lit up the night. Then nothing.

"Reaper, do you copy?"

Nothing. Not even static.

He glanced at Green, then tried again. "Reaper, do you copy?"

More silence.

This was bad. Real bad.

Then Mike's soul-tearing words came over the radio. "Reaper is going down! Reaper is going down—"

The radio went dead silent.

Nate's stomach dropped. "Base, you copy that transmission?"

"Roger that." Crystal's voice sounded calm but filled with concern. "Eyes in the sky looking for the crash site now. Will advise. Out."

Nate pressed his cheek against his rifle barrel, then gathered himself. "All teams, sit-rep."

"Alpha, clear, moving toward your position."

"Bravo, where the hell are you?"

"Bravo targets secure. Repeat. Targets secure. Three subjects in custody. Hold fire. We're coming out."

Worried about the chopper crew but relieved to finally hear from Bravo, Nate walked toward the blown front door, with Green taking a covering position behind him.

Cooper and Taggart walked out first, leading three figures bound in flex cuffs with black cloth bags over their heads. The last one in line had a bad limp. He was almost as tall as Nate but was rail-thin beneath his Pashtun garb.

Nate's heart picked up a beat.

Santos and Carlyle followed, guns trained on all three figures. Santos, fluent in Pashto, ordered them to kneel on the ground. Two did as they were told, but the taller one stood, defiant.

Nate pulled the bag off his head. A tiny flash of recognition hit him. They all traveled with photos of Jeff Albert in their pockets. He'd stared at his so many times he'd memorized the man's features. The uniformed soldier they'd studied was in the prime of his life. His hair military-short, his face clean-shaven, his eyes bright with purpose and fire, his body buff and strong.

This man was dressed in typical Pashtun clothing. His scraggly beard had patches of gray, his face was as dark as that of an Afghan. He was shockingly thin and did not look as if he was in the prime of anything. In fact, he looked ill.

Still—there was something in his eyes . . .

"What's your name?" Nate asked, then asked Santos to repeat the question in Pashto.

The man looked at him and then at the rest of the team. "You're Americans," he stated with equal measures of wariness and hope.

Wasn't much point in denying it now. "We are."

The man's knees buckled, and Green quickly grabbed his arm and steadied him. "Thank God."

"Can you identify yourself?" Nate asked again, more gently.

"Sergeant Jeffery Robert Albert."

"I'll be go to hell," Reed muttered under his breath.

"Look," Nate said, "there's not a lot of time for introductions, but I need to verify you're who you say you are. What's your mother's maiden name?"

"I don't know."

"Name of your dog?"

"Did I have a dog?"

Puzzled, Nate tried one more time. "Name of the street where you grew up?"

"Look. I don't know. I took a hard knock on the head. I don't remember anything prior to deploying here with my unit."

"Give me some help, then," Nate said.

"I formed letters on the roof. My initials and the Special Forces credo. Rabia"—he motioned toward one of the people still bound and on their knees—"she took blood and hair samples to an Army patrol near Emarat . . . a Lieutenant Court spoke with her. I sent a letter explaining who I was and what had happened to me."

"Who held you prisoner?" Nate persisted.

"The ISI."

That soaked it. They'd found their man. This wasn't a wild-goose chase after all.

Nate extended his hand. "Glad to finally meet you, Sergeant Albert. Bet you've been wondering what took us so long."

"Every hour of every day, sir." His voice broke with emotion before he regained his composure.

Nate laid a hand on his arm. "How about we take you home, son?"

Albert nodded slowly, clearly overcome with relief.

Nate motioned toward the two hooded, kneeling figures. "Who are these people?"

"Wakdar Kahn Kakar, the *malik* of this village, and his daughter, Rabia. I wouldn't be alive if not for them."

Nate motioned for Santos to remove the hoods and cut them free.

"You're the one who contacted the U.S. patrol." Nate addressed the woman.

She nodded.

"America is in your debt," he said. "I don't mean to be impolite, but we've got to get out of here."

The old man rose slowly to his feet and spoke heatedly to his daughter.

"My father does not wish to leave." She glanced fearfully at Nate, then at Albert. "He says he is an old man. He is ready to die here."

Albert touched his hand on her arm and started speaking softly and respectfully to the old man in fluent Pashto. The *malik* continued to resist until Rabia's name came up.

He lowered his head, then finally appeared to concede.

The woman smiled gratefully at Albert, who reached out and gave her arm a reassuring squeeze. Nate found the exchange both interesting and poignant. Albert had been with this woman for almost four months. He imagined a lot had happened between them.

Crystal's voice in his headset interrupted his thoughts. "Charlie to Lead, we have located Reaper's crash site—approximately five-zero-zero meters from your current position, north, along the road. No movement from the site but numerous dismounts moving rapidly toward it."

They had to get to that bird and his men. Nate keyed his mike. "Roger that, Charlie. Advise that we will be moving toward Reaper. Repeat. Moving toward our downed team. Advise the brass that we have Beckwith. We have Beckwith and have verified. Need air assets now."

Beckwith was the code word for Jeff Albert and the last name of the founder of Delta Force, Charlie Beckwith.

"We also have the two additional evacuees," Nate stated.

"Roger that. You have Beckwith and two additional evacuees, and you need air assets at your position. Stand by. Charlie out."

Nate turned to his team. "Let's scramble up some ground transpo."

"Rabia has a car, sir," Albert said. "An older-model Toyota."

"Not going to do it. Not big enough. Santos and Cooper. Go see if you can find a working vehicle large enough to transport all of us. We need to get to Reaper and check on our guys. We'll take cover in the house until you return. And hurry your asses up. Reaper's in trouble, and so are we."

Crystal broke in again. "Lead, be advised that we are experiencing a slight delay scrambling air assets."

"How much of a delay?"

"Working it out. Will notify when ready. Charlie out."

Nate looked at his men, then at Albert. "Looks like we might get to fight our way out of here yet. Don't suppose you've got any weapons to add to the mix?"

"No, sir."

Perfect. They were up shit crick in a leaky boat with no paddle. With a nod from Nate, Bravo team along with Green and Alpha team moved into the house, posting up at windows and doors and watching for bad guys as they waited for Santos and Cooper to show up with their ride.

✳

RABIA SCRAMBLED TO change from her night clothes to her day wear, thankful that Jeffery had asked this favor for her. Still catching her breath, she sat on the floor, low along the inner wall of the cooking room, as the Americans had instructed her. Her father sat on one side of her, Jeffery on the other. Both were silent. Her father's silence came from anger. Jeffery's, she suspected, was prompted by disbelief. And relief.

They had come for him. He would now go home.

For him, she felt happy. For herself, in the aftermath of the terror when they had burst in with guns and bound their hands and placed hoods over their heads, she felt a numb sense of loss.

He was leaving. Just when she had convinced herself that somehow he would stay. It had been a foolish notion, she knew that. But the grief she felt at the thought of losing him seemed as huge as the night that swallowed the world in shadows.

In the dark, in the silence, as the Americans watched for resistance, she felt Jeffery's hand seek hers. She clung and tried desperately not to cry.

"I'm so sorry," he whispered. "I'm so sorry I brought this to your door."

"This is not your doing. This is Allah's will. You were destined to leave here."

"Come with me," he whispered urgently. "Rabia . . . you can come with me. Your father, too."

The tears did come then. For the hope in his voice and the impossibility of it all. "I cannot go with you any more than you can stay."

He said nothing. Because he knew the truth as surely as she did.

If they all got out of here alive, she and her father would go to their family in Kabul, as Jeffery had wanted. They would be safe there. She would return to teaching.

And there she would be alone, surrounded by family and friends.

She listened to the night, the cadence of breathing of the armed men guarding them. And she thought of the roof and wished with all her heart that they could have had one more night together beneath the stars.

✴

Ty came to slowly. Pain throbbed through his head and back. And his arms—what the hell? It felt as if a pair of vise grips had clamped around his biceps. That's when he realized he was being dragged.

Fight-or-flight instincts kicked in, and he started flailing. He'd be damned if he'd let some Taliban jihadist take him alive.

"Easy, bro. I've got you."

Mike. Thank God. "What happened?"

"Remind me never to get into a helicopter with you again, Crash."

Right. They'd taken a hit. Which would explain

why his back was killing him. Now that he was marginally with the program, he could see the smoking wreckage of the bird Mike had dragged him away from.

"You OK? Waldrop? Where's Waldrop?"

"We're fine. Both of us. Waldrop's setting charges to blow the chopper. Sit tight."

Mike pulled a radio from his vest pocket. "Lead, this is Reaper. We are down, minor wounded, but are functional. Chopper is toast. Awaiting orders."

"No shit, you're down," Nate replied, sounding uncharacteristically rattled but clearly relieved. "Damn happy to hear your voice. But you've got a bigger problem than a broken bird. Base advises numerous subjects approaching your position—assume they are enemy. Multiple dismounts, and a couple of trucks have joined in. Take cover and defend. We'll be there as soon as we can to extract."

"What about Albert?"

"We got him."

Mike glanced at Ty and nodded, letting him know they'd found Albert.

If Ty had known what to say, he would have, but he didn't have a clue. If they lived through this, life for him had changed irrevocably, no matter what.

Waldrop sprinted up beside them right then and pointed down the road. "Company. Coming full steam."

"Crystal still have that Predator circling overhead?" Mike asked Nate.

"Roger that."

"Yeah, well, we've got a truck zeroing in, and I don't think it's pizza delivery. Be real neighborly like if you could do something about it."

"Charlie copies direct."

"Bless you, Crystal, darling." Mike breathed a sigh of relief when he heard Crystal's voice, clearly happy as hell that she'd been monitoring their commo. "Party's about to start, sweetheart—now would be a really great time for the punch to arrive."

"Ask and ye shall receive. Shot out," Crystal advised urgently. "Duck and cover. Duck and—"

A fireball streaked across the sky, then exploded with a loud boom, drowning out the rest of her commo. The missile smashed into the Taliban truck, lighting it up like an oil-rig fire. Bodies spilled out onto the road. Men climbed from the wreck and scrambled into the shadows.

"Nice shot, babe!" Mike crowed.

Crystal's relieved breath preceded her voice. "Roger that, flyboy."

"Can you walk?" Mike asked Ty as he handed him an M-4 and a bandolier of loaded magazines.

Ty wasn't even sure if he could crawl, but his brother didn't need to know that. "Hell, yeah, but I'd rather run." He checked to see that the M-4 was loaded, that the magazine was fully seated, and then, gritting through the pain, he trotted after his brother and Waldrop to a low berm, where they hunkered down and waited for the bad guys.

Chapter

26

*N*ate was still digesting the news that the helicop-ter crew was safe but the chopper was out of commission when Cooper and Santos pulled up in front of the house in a "jingle truck," a garishly painted pickup about the size of a U-Haul.

He stepped outside.

"Did we deliver or what?" Cooper grinned, reached out the driver's-side window, and patted the door panel as if it was a prize bull at a county fair.

"Nice score," Nate said. They might fit everyone onto it.

His radio crackled. "Charlie to Lead. I've got an AC-130U gunship locked and loaded and in the air. All we need are coordinates, and we can handle some of that ground resistance for you and Reaper. Over."

Oorah! He was going to owe Crystal, B.J., and the Specter pilot flying the gunship a steak dinner with all the trimmings if they got out of this. The AC-130U gunship was basically a cargo plane stuffed full of guns, including—*Lord have mercy*—a 105mm howitzer plus 25mm and 40mm cannons. This ship was the closest equivalent of the hand of God, carrying ordnance capable of smashing things to pieces in seconds. And thanks to Crystal and B.J., it was five minutes away.

"Roger that, Charlie, and please know that if I didn't love my wife, I'd run away with both of you. As soon as I figure out what we need, you'll be the first to know. Stand by."

It had been a while since Nate had called in an air strike, but he'd done it enough that he could rely on muscle memory. Once he knew exactly where the bad guys and the good guys were, it was a matter of pointing them out and letting them loose.

He called the team and the evacuees out of the house and over to the hood of the truck. After laying the map out, he gave a quick briefing. Although everyone knew the details of the backup plan, there was little harm in reaffirming it.

"Cooper, you good behind the wheel?"

"As gold, sir."

He looked at Rabia. "Can you navigate for us?"

She glanced at the map. "Yes. But my father," she added hesitantly. "He is not well."

Nate understood. "We'll take care of him. He can ride in back with the team. He'll be protected." He turned to Albert. "You ready?"

"I am."

Nate watched with interest as the SF sergeant limped heavily, favoring his left leg, then eased carefully up into the truck bed.

"How bad is he?" Nate asked Rabia in an aside.

"It is the vertigo," Rabia said. "From a head injury. Movement often makes him violently ill."

This was going to be a tough ride for Albert.

"You going to be all right back there, Albert? I can make room for you in the cab."

"I'm good," Albert insisted, but even in the moonlight, Nate could see he'd turned gray around the edges.

When everyone was onboard, Nate climbed into the shotgun seat. "Let's move out. Ma'am, you keep down. Way down."

Cooper ground the gears, and they made their way down the road toward the edge of the village.

Nate keyed his radio. "Reaper, we're heading your way." He heard gunfire in the background.

"Roger that. I was just telling the boys how much I missed your ugly faces. Sir," Mike added as an afterthought.

"Any cover you can give us will be appreciated."

"Taking heavy fire here, sir. Got all we can handle."

"Roger that. Hang on. We're on the way."

✳

NATE HEARD THE gun fight over the radio, confirming that Reaper was under attack. Here on the road as they rolled toward them, it was surprisingly quiet. A sure sign that all hell was about to break loose.

They made it about a hundred more yards before it did.

Tracers suddenly flew at them from all directions; bullets cracked and whined around their heads as Tangos shouting "Allahu Akbar!" charged out of the ditches at the truck.

Ten M-4s fired at will, shooting at anything that moved. Cooper jammed on the brakes, almost throwing them from the back as an RPG rocketed past the front of the truck. Nate shot a suicide gunner and beaded in on other targets.

In the midst of the melee, he heard the smack of a bullet striking flesh. He jerked his head around and watched Green drop. He would have rolled out the back of the truck if Albert hadn't grabbed him.

"How bad?" Nate yelled.

In answer, Green got back onto his feet and, shouldering his rifle with one hand, shot a charging Taliban fighter.

"Got it covered." Coulter knelt beside Green, quickly opened his medical field kit, poured some QuikClot on Green's wound, and wrapped it tight.

About that time, Cooper gunned it, and the truck

started rolling again. Faster this time. Speed was their only ally. If they could make it to Reaper, they could hope to consolidate their position and call in that air strike.

Gunfire, screams, and the roaring of the truck engine were all that Nate could hear as his senses threatened to overload. Through it all, he shot, reloaded, and shot again, as his team did the same. Another smacking sound of a bullet hitting flesh had Taggart clutching his arm. He swore before shouldering his rifle again, pain and determination etched on his face.

Nate leaned around the woman and yelled at Cooper as they ran the gauntlet of enemy fire. "Blow the cobs out of this bitch!"

★

"HOW'S YOUR AMMO?" Ty asked Mike. Ty was down to three loaded rounds and one more mag.

"So low that that I might have to start calling them names and hope they'll run home crying to their Mommas."

"I'm low, too." Waldrop zeroed in on another suicide runner.

They were fairly well protected behind the berm— until the baddies put two and two together and figured out that they could surround them and pick them off like carnival ducks.

They were also outmanned and outgunned, and right now, the only thing that stood between them and a very bad day was for Nate and the boys to come rolling up and call in the air strike. And soon might not be soon enough.

Ty had heard the radio commo. He knew Nate and the team had Jeff Albert onboard. He'd wanted to be there when they found him. At the least, he'd wanted to be in the cockpit when Albert boarded the bird. Wanted to be able to look him in the eye, see that this man had gone through hell, and know he'd done the right thing coming after him and bringing him home to Jess.

Helluva deal. Now it looked as if he was the one who might not come home alive.

"Hooah!" Waldrop crowed. "Lookie lookie who came to play."

Ty poked his head up to see an overloaded truck barreling toward them, the muzzle flashes of Alpha and Bravo squads lighting the way.

Relief shot through his blood. They were a long way from home-free, but things were finally looking up.

Mike keyed his radio. "Lead. Friendlies at your twelve."

"Roger that, Reaper. Get ready. We're coming in."

Ty loaded his last magazine, and when the truck roared up in front of the berm, he, Mike, and Waldrop jumped up firing and leaped into the back of the truck.

"Gentlemen." Reed snagged Ty's hand with a grin. "The conductor will be by soon to check your tickets."

The charges on their downed chopper blew just as they cleared the blast radius.

Mike grinned. "Let DOD try to take that out of my paycheck."

★

"THIS HORSE IS going to pull up lame any minute now!" Cooper yelled as they bounced over the rough terrain. The truck was so overloaded the shocks kissed the ground every few feet, as they put as much ground as possible between them and the advancing Taliban fighters.

"That's what happens when you try to stuff two tons of rocks into a one-ton box," Nate agreed.

Damn. He was happy as hell they'd hooked up with the Reaper crew. Now he could call in that much-needed air support. His radio cracked just as he reached for his mike.

"Charlie to Lead. It looks bad down there, Nate. You ready for that air support?"

Nate flipped an IR strobe back to Reed, who tapped it to the roof of the truck's cab. "Charlie, see our strobe?"

"Roger that."

"Then give Striker permission to light up anything he sees moving within a quarter-mile radius of us."

"My pleasure. Lead, stand by."

Moments later, a faint sound of propellers hummed overhead. Next came a chainsaw-like buzz from what he figured was the gunship's 25mm cannon, followed by an explosion that shook the ground beneath their wheels. Two more explosions followed in quick succession.

"Charlie to Lead." B.J. this time. "Three trucks scratched."

"I'll thank you properly next time I see you."

"The hell you will," Mendoza groused from the back.

"See, boss," Reed put in. "I'm not the only one who gets twitchy where my wife is concerned."

"I'm not twitchy," Mendoza groused. "I'm damn weary of getting shot at."

Because they were two of his best and because he knew this kind of nonsense was how they let off steam, Nate ignored them. "Charlie, be advised, our transpo isn't going to last much longer. What can you do for us?"

"Way ahead of you, Lead. There's a significant force at Firebase Shaker."

"Say again." He'd thought that all FOBs had pulled out of the province.

"What the mainstream media doesn't know can't hurt us and all that," B.J. replied. "They're already on the move to meet up with your team. ETA your position thirty mikes. You can radio contact them on channel seventeen."

"All right!" Mendoza crowed, overhearing the commo. "You now have my permission to kiss my wife, sir. Reed's, too. They have saved our sorry selves yet one more time."

For the first time since things had started going south, Nate smiled.

"Roger that, Charlie. You two better pucker up. You're both going to be mighty popular when we get back."

If the team could only hold on for a little while, the cavalry would arrive, and they were golden.

"Don't get too comfortable," Crystal advised, sounding worried. "We're seeing multiple dismounts headed your way. Danger close. Too close for air strikes. You're going to have to roll out fast or hunker down and hang on until Firebase Shaker arrives to evac."

"Roger that." Nate turned to Cooper. "Let's roll."

They rolled all of twenty yards, and the truck groaned, gasped, and stalled.

✷

TY HAD BEEN looking for a meeting with Jeff Albert—J.R.—and he'd finally gotten it. When he'd jumped into the back of the truck, he'd landed across from him. And damn, the shape the man was in, made his own back pain seem like a tickle.

He was a shadow of the man in the photograph that hung behind the register in Jess's store. At first glance, he'd thought they'd picked up a Taliban captive. He was dressed like a local, at least eighty pounds lighter than his photo, and sporting a beard that covered half of his face. His cheeks were sunken, his eyes barely slits. And clearly, he was suffering.

Yes, he said to himself. Yes, he'd done the right thing. But Jess . . . there was no way in the world Jess could be even remotely prepared to see this man who was her husband.

He was not going to be her husband. Not now. Maybe not ever.

"That's it." Cooper's voice carried from the cab to the truck box after attempting to turn over the engine several times. "She's dead."

"Everybody out," Nate ordered. "This is where we make a stand."

Wincing against the knifing pain in his back, Ty climbed out with the rest of them, ashamed of himself for an instant of hesitation before reaching for Albert's arm and helping him and the woman and her father out of the truck.

Albert nodded his thanks and leaned heavily against the tailgate.

"You doing OK?" Ty asked. Albert was sheet-white as he slid to the ground.

"Holding up," Albert said through gritted teeth.

Poor sonofabitch, Ty thought. A stand-up soldier. He was amazed that he'd made it three and a half years with the ISI and come out alive.

"How's your father doing?" he asked the woman, who had moved beside the old man, her arm linked through his in support.

"He will be fine."

Ty had to look away then. He couldn't look at Albert without wishing for something that was no longer his.

He scanned the area. There was minimal cover here. Open ground.

Nate moved up beside them. "What do you think?"

"I think we'd better start digging."

Ty grabbed a shovel from Taggart's gear. Neither Taggart nor Green would be digging with those bullet holes in their arms. Instead, the two of them provided cover while the rest of the team started digging shallow Ranger graves.

They had barely enough time to dig a long, shallow trench when a shot rang out, too close for comfort.

"Take cover!" Nate shouted.

Ty helped Nate get the woman and her father away from the truck and into a Ranger grave. Once he had them settled, he went back for Albert, who leaned heavily on him, stumbling across the ground like a drunk. When they reached the small berm, both of them dropped behind it. "Hold on, bud."

He'd just scrambled in beside him when he caught his brother's eye.

A mix of pride and sympathy accompanied Mike's sharp nod.

Ty couldn't bear looking at him. Couldn't bear knowing that Mike was wishing the same thing he was. That everyone came out of this alive and got what he wanted.

Right now, Ty figured the best he could hope for was the alive part.

✳

THE TRIP FROM the village to pick up the Reaper squad and run like hell had seemed like an eternity. In fact, it had been all of fifteen minutes. The next thirty minutes, however, as they fought off Taliban and waited for ground support, were among the longest Nate had ever lived. He was down to one magazine for his pistol. His rifle was empty, despite taking ammo from dead Taliban.

Everyone else was in pretty much the same state. They grouped tightly together to provide as much mutually supporting fire as they could, given their ammo situation.

Beside him in the trench, blood trickled down Jones's temple and splattered Mendoza's fatigues.

"How bad?" Nate asked.

Mendoza grinned. "Not mine. The big guy here stuck his head in front of a bullet and decided to bleed all over me."

"Hard as a steel plate," Jones assured his boss. "Relax. It's a scratch."

"Coulter," Nate called, as AK-47 fire continued to zip around them.

"Right behind you." Hunkering low, Coulter removed Jones's helmet and checked out what, fortunately, turned out to be a flesh wound. "You make my life so hard."

"I make your life complete." Jones grinned at him. "We all know that."

"I thought *I* made your life complete," Reed protested.

"I know this goes against the grain," Nate cut in, "but now might be a good time to stay focused."

Out of the dark, directly in front of them, a horde of Taliban fighters ran screaming toward them with one goal in mind.

This is it, Nate thought, seeing his wife's face as clearly as if Juliana were beside him. This was where he was going to die.

Then he heard it. The distinct sound of MK19 40mm grenade launchers and Browning M-2 fifty-caliber machine guns bombarding the air.

He glanced over his shoulder. Three Stryker armored fighting vehicles rolled to a stop directly behind them, their big guns blazing.

Beside him, his men let out a whoop, and faced with the intimidating guns mounted on the Strykers, the Taliban fighters who were still alive turned and ran in the other direction.

The cavalry had indeed arrived.

Chapter
27

Jeff was alone in the hospital room when he woke up the second time. A machine blipped softly in the background. He lifted his arm, let it fall. A plastic tube ran into an IV port inserted into the back of his hand. A cuff on his arm tightened, measuring his blood pressure and pulse. The plastic clip on his finger measured his blood-oxygen levels.

He vaguely remembered someone telling him they were treating him with IV fluids that dripped from a bag hanging somewhere behind him.

He specifically remembered Nate Black assuring him that they'd made it. That he was safe. Once again, he didn't remember everything that had happened to him. He remembered that the rough, hot, dizzying ride inside the belly of the Stryker had kicked up the vertigo with a vengeance. He'd puked his guts out and then gotten the dry heaves. Long before they'd made base, he'd been barely conscious despite the team medic—Coulter—hanging an IV to rehydrate him.

He didn't remember much after that, including the flight to the AFB or his admission into the hospital.

"The NATO-run hospital at the Kandahar Air Force Base is a forty-plus-million-dollar facility," Black had assured him, as he'd helped him into the ambulance that had met their air transport from FOB Shaker. "The medical staff will do everything humanly possible to get you squared away again."

Everything but one. They hadn't let him see Rabia.

"Rabia." He could barely speak, his throat and mouth were so dry. He didn't know how long he'd been out this time, but he was frantic to know what was happening with her. "Rabia." He tried again. Her name came out as a hoarse croak.

"Well, hello, soldier. Welcome back to the land of the living. How you feeling?"

He opened his eyes. A tidy Air Force nurse in a prim white uniform stood by the side of the bed.

"Rabia," he croaked again.

"I'm sorry, I can't understand you." She turned away, then came back with a wet sponge swab that she gently wiped over his lips. "See if this helps."

He sucked on the swab like a man dying of thirst.

"Better? How about an ice chip? It's not much, I know, but we don't want to overdo it."

He nodded, then regretted it as the room began to spin.

"The vertigo should settle down a bit for you soon." She laid a sympathetic hand on his arm. "Doctor prescribed both antinausea and antivertigo meds. That's why you conked out on us again. Stuff makes you sleepy, but I guess you already figured that out. We're pumping fluids to get you rehydrated. In the meantime, try to stay still and let the meds do their work. If you continue to progress, I wouldn't be surprised if they authorize a flight home to a hospital in the States tomorrow."

She went on, checking his IV bag, then fluffing his pillow. "Normally, they would ship you to Ramstein AFB in Germany, but since you're a special case, you're going straight home."

He was a special case, all right. He still didn't know where home was. He had so many questions. No one had come up with any answers.

He opened his mouth for the ice chip, let it melt, then reached out and grabbed her wrist. "Where. Is. Rabia?"

"Rabia? Is that the Pashtun woman who came in with you?"

"Yes. Where is she?"

"She's down the hall."

"I want to see her."

She carefully removed his hand from her arm and laid it on top of the pristine white sheets. "Let me go see what I can find out, OK?"

He closed his eyes, afraid to feel too much relief. "Thank you."

"I'll be right back. You rest."

★

NATE ADDRESSED THE team once Albert had been turned over to the medical staff. "It goes without saying, we need to keep the mission and Sergeant Albert's rescue quiet, for national security reasons and for Albert's privacy. The last thing the guy needs is for his story to blow wide open on an international scale. He'd be bombarded by the press. Hell, his story has blockbuster movie written all over it. But for now, he has a lot of recovery ahead of him. A lot of healing physically and emotionally. A lot of adjusting to do."

For that reason, Nate asked for a volunteer to stand guard outside Albert's hospital room.

Despite the fact that his back was killing him, Ty had stepped forward without hesitation and now stood at parade rest outside Albert's door.

For the same reason that he couldn't articulate why he needed to be a part of the rescue mission, he couldn't explain, even to himself, why he'd volunteered for this duty.

"Why are you doing this to yourself, bro?" Mike had asked on the plane from Minnesota to Virginia before they'd deployed to Kandahar.

"What would you do?" Ty had asked. "If you suddenly found out the woman you loved had a husband, a war hero, a man who has to have been through hell and back . . . wouldn't you want to know? Wouldn't you want to see for yourself if he was alive and, if he was, face him so you'd know firsthand what kind of man she's leaving you for?"

"You don't know that she'll go back to him."

Unfortunately, he did know. Now that he'd seen Albert and knew what sad shape he was in, he knew exactly what she would do. "I know Jess. She's loyal. She doesn't quit on anything. If he needs her, she'll be there for him. And we both know where that leaves me."

So yeah, maybe in a way, he was doing this more for Jess. He sure as hell wasn't doing it for himself. Was he glad Jeff was alive? Of course. That didn't mean he wasn't dying by degrees knowing he'd lose Jess because of it.

So here he stood, making sure he knew that Albert was a stand-up guy. Making sure he wasn't so far off the deep end emotionally and mentally after his ordeal that Jess wouldn't be safe with him. And making sure he had an impression of the man to remind himself that Albert had Jess first, so he would always remember where his place was.

He overheard Albert and the nurse speaking. Sensed Albert's distress when he'd asked about the Pashtun woman, Rabia. After observing the two of them together in the back of the truck and then in the Stryker, Ty could see there were very close ties between them. What kind of close he wasn't even going to speculate. She had saved his life. He'd depended on her for his very existence for months. They'd been through a lot together. Now she and her father were homeless, and Albert got to add guilt to the pile of things he needed to deal with.

The nurse slipped out of the room, gave him a quick smile, and headed silently down the hall in her soft-soled shoes. Not long after, footsteps brought his head around to see Nate Black escorting the Pashtun woman toward Albert's room.

The hospital staff had helped her clean up and given her a pair of scrubs and a scarf to replace her dirty clothes. Her head was down, but he could see enough of her face to know she looked drawn and exhausted. In shock, no doubt. She'd been through a firefight. She'd lost her home. Now she was going to lose Albert. Regardless of what they meant to each other, everything in her world had turned upside down in a few hours.

"You're relieved, son." Nate nodded to him. "Go find Reed to replace you, then get someone to look at your back and get some shut-eye. As soon as the base commander and the medical staff release him, we'll see Albert the rest of the way home."

It wasn't exactly relief Ty felt as he nodded and walked away.

It wasn't exactly anything. Physically he was in pain. Emotionally, he felt numb. He felt as if his body and his mind were operating on two separate planes. And it felt as if his heart was back home in a cabin by a lake, in a big log bed where he would never lie with the woman he loved.

✹

TY FOUND REED, but instead of finding a doc or bunking down, he located the commo room, talked someone into letting him use a SAT phone, and dialed Jess's number.

"Hello?"

"Hey."

"Ty. Thank God." It hurt to hear her voice, expectant, scared, relieved.

"We found him, Jess. I wanted you to hear it from me before you got the official word. We found him. He's coming home."

✹

"I'LL BE RIGHT outside the door, ma'am."

Rabia acknowledged the man named Nate Black, who had been so kind to her and her father. Then she walked slowly into Jeffery's hospital room. Wanting to see him. Needing to see him. Knowing it would be the last time.

Her heart squeezed tightly at the sight of him lying in the bed, tubes coming out of his arm, intricate machines with pulsing lights making soft swishing sounds. He looked so pale. His eyes were closed, and he lay so still she did not know if he was awake or sleeping.

Then, as if sensing her there, he opened his eyes.

She walked hesitantly to his bedside. When he lifted his hand, she folded it in both of hers. "How are you, Jeffery?"

"I'm fine. Just . . . weak as a damn baby."

She knew well how difficult it was for him to have his strength desert him. "You were very ill. The ride . . . was difficult for you. But I am told you are stable now."

"Are you OK? Are they taking care of you and your father?"

She nodded, focused on their joined hands because she could not look him in the eye. "Yes. Yes, we are fine. They have treated us well."

"Is your father still angry?"

She managed a small smile. "I could not say that he is happy. But he has accepted. What did you say to persuade him to come with us? I could not hear your conversation."

He rubbed his thumb over the back of her hand. "I told him he had to think of someone other than himself. That he had to think of you. I told him that he was the sun and the moon to you, and without him in your life, your days would be as dark as your nights."

Tears filled her eyes. How could he have known so well what was in her heart? Could he possibly know that he also was the sun and the moon to her?

"Come with me, Rabia. Come to the States with

me. Shh." He raised their joined hands and pressed a finger to her lips when she started to protest. "You can return to teaching there. There's a huge Muslim population in the States. We'll find a mosque you and your father can attend. You can live in peace."

This hurt so badly. But she must be strong. "We will be fine, Jeffery. Family in Kabul will make my father soon forget why he ever wanted to stay in the village. I will go back to my job."

"What about the Taliban? They lost a lot of fighters last night. They lost a lot of face. They'll retaliate. They'll search for you. They'll know when they return to the village and find you gone that you were the one who hid me."

"How will they know? People abandon homes all the time. Salawat is a poor village. Many families leave to seek work in the city. It is not an unusual occurrence."

"It's unusual to have your front and back door blown off," he said desperately. "They'll know you didn't leave because you wanted to. They'll question your neighbors. Someone will have seen what happened. They'll talk."

He was right. And she knew she was in possible jeopardy. But she had no choice. "Kabul is a large city, Jeffery. They could not find you in a tiny village. They will not find us among three million people."

"But they'll search. They won't quit."

"They will search, yes. But they will not find us.

There are many, many people named Kakar in Kabul. They do not know what I look like. And they will quit. Kabul is not Kandahar. The Taliban are not welcome there. You do not need to be afraid for me."

He closed his eyes again, and for a moment, she thought he had fallen asleep. Then he squeezed her hand hard. "Please come with me. Please."

Would life always be about loss? Would Allah continue to test her? Would she never be allowed to keep something—someone—so close to her heart that the thought of living without him left a huge hole inside her?

She must not question. She must only do what was right. She must do the only thing that was possible.

"You know that cannot happen. I cannot go with you. Even if it were possible to persuade my father, I cannot go."

"You can."

It physically hurt to look into his eyes and see her own pain reflected there. "Jeffery. Did they not tell you?"

"Tell me what?"

She searched his face through a blur of tears and knew what she had to do. She had to tell him what she had overheard Nate Black tell the American doctor.

"Jeffery. You have a wife waiting for you to come home."

Chapter

28

San Antonio, Texas, early November

*H*e'd had this ridiculous notion that once he was rescued, his life would make sense again. He'd get health care. He'd be relieved of the stress of the constant threat of death, and he'd remember. He'd be safe. He'd be home.

But he didn't remember. He didn't remember that the last post he'd been stationed was Fort Bragg—which was why he'd ended up at Brooke, the closest large Army medical center at Fort Sam Houston in San Antonio.

He didn't remember that he had a brother named Brad, who had apparently flown in from Minnesota to see him and was due to arrive within the hour.

Along with his wife.

The thought sent a rush of terror and shame straight to his gut. He had a wife. Apparently, they'd been childhood sweethearts. Her name was Jess. And he didn't remember what she looked like.

What he remembered, what he couldn't get out of his head, was Rabia's face when she'd said not only the last words he'd expected but also the last words he'd ever hear her say.

You have a wife waiting for you to come home.

If the rescue and his triage and initial medical assessment at Kandahar had been a blur, the next twenty-four hours and the subsequent flight home felt as though someone else had lived them.

But he sat up in his hospital bed and went through the motions, shaking hands with the members of the team who had accompanied him to Texas and had crowded into the room to wish him well and tell him good-bye.

Their names he would always remember. Those men had risked their lives for him, and he had no idea on earth how he could repay them. He'd said his good-byes and given his thanks to Jones, Reed, Green, Mendoza, and Coulter in Kandahar, grateful to know that they would personally escort Rabia and her father quietly to Kabul, then head home from there.

Cooper, Taggart, Carlyle, Santos, Waldrop, and the Brown brothers, Mike and Ty, stood back as Nate Black extended his hand.

"Good luck, Albert. Proud to know you."

"Thank you, sir." He clasped Black's hand firmly in both of his before letting go. "That goes both ways."

"I'm sure you'll be briefed after the doctors clear it," Black went on, "but I want to assure you again that the lid's on tight. No one's going to get word that you're back. Not from the military. Not from our end. Two people know. Your brother and your wife. How you handle it on your end is up to you. Mr. Kakar and his daughter are safe with their family in Kabul. No one will know of their connection in any aspect of the operation or of the aid they provided you—which, in a way, is unfortunate, as this country owes them a great debt."

"The best way to repay them," he said somberly, "is, as we discussed, never to acknowledge their existence."

How strange that it was so easy to say those words, when everything in him wanted to reach out to Rabia. To talk to her. To know that she was safe.

To touch her. To see her face.

"Good luck, son." Black's voice brought him back to his new reality. To a world and a life that, ultimately, was as foreign as the life he'd just left.

★

NATE HAD A buddy he wanted to catch up with in San Antonio, and when the rest of the team decided to find a local watering hole and have a quick beer, Ty begged off.

"You guys go ahead," he said. "I've got to make a few calls. I'll meet up with you at the airfield."

Mike hung behind, his eyes full of concern. "You're waiting for Jess."

"Yeah," Ty admitted. It would be pointless to lie to his brother. "I'm waiting for Jess."

"And then what?" Mike asked as the guys stood at the end of the hall, holding the elevator and waiting for him. "Why torture yourself?"

"Go," Ty said, understanding that Mike was worried about him. "I'll be fine."

Only he wasn't fine. He was never going to be fine again.

Mike gave him a hard stare, then lifted a hand in surrender. "Call if you need me."

Ty nodded and watched Mike walk away.

He thought about going in to talk to Albert. And say what? *Hey, man. Glad you're home safe. And by the way, I'm in love with your wife.*

Yeah, that would be a real stand-up thing to do. Hit the man while he was down. Albert didn't even remember Jess. He didn't remember anything about his life before he was captured. How could a man forget a woman like Jess?

By going through hell. By suffering untold horrors.

That could have been him . . . or a thousand other men or women who'd gone off to war. Any one of them risked being killed or captured every time they signed up for service. How would he feel if he'd lived through that kind of mental and physical terror, if everything in his life had been taken away from him for more than three years, and then come home to hear the news that, oh, yeah, by the way, your wife is in love with another man and had planned to marry him until you showed up and screwed it all up.

He had to let it go. He had to let her go.

Mike was right. He shouldn't be here.

He headed down the hall toward the elevator and had almost reached the nurse's station when he heard her voice.

Jess. Asking for J.R. Albert's room.

Oh, God. He wanted to see her.

He couldn't see her.

He ducked quickly into the men's restroom and held the door open a crack so he could see the hallway.

Brad walked by first. Looking big and happy and anxious.

Jess followed. Slower, hesitant, brave.

Seeing her face, the uncertainty, the guarded hope, and the pain in her eyes, was all it took to make him realize he couldn't go to her. Not without hurting her more. Not and still be the man he'd been raised to be.

He had no place in her life now.

So he left without saying hello.

Without saying good-bye one last time.

                        ✶

IT FELT ODD walking into Brooke Army Medical Center for more reasons than one. Womack, the Army medical center at Fort Bragg, was the last hospital where Jess had worked as a nurse. Brooke very much reminded her of Womack—except on a larger scale. And it was at Bragg that she'd last seen J.R. It was at Womack, while on shift, where she'd been told he was dead.

"Mrs. Albert?"

Jess swung around to see a doctor walking toward her, his white coat flapping around his legs as he rushed down the hospital hall just as she and Brad were about to walk into J.R.'s room.

"Mrs. Albert?" he asked again with a lift of his brows when he'd caught up with her.

"Yes. I'm Jess Albert."

"I'm Dr. Jasper. I'm overseeing Jeff's care."

He extended his hand, and Jess shook it. "This is J.R.'s—" She stopped, corrected herself. Only family and friends at home knew him as J.R. "Jeff's brother, Brad."

The two men shook hands.

"I wanted to catch you before you went in to see your husband. Do you mind? Can we talk a bit first? We can use the waiting room down the hall."

She looked at Brad, who nodded, and they followed the doctor toward the waiting room. Jasper looked to be in his mid- to late fifties. He was trim and fit and reminded her a little bit of Tommy Lee Jones.

"Has anyone briefed you about Jeff's condition?" Jasper asked after they'd found a quiet corner in the waiting room.

Jess shook her head. "Not yet, no. I know only

that he has multiple medical issues that need to be addressed. And that I need to be prepared because he's lost a lot of weight."

Jasper offered a kind smile. "That's true. He has lost weight. When he arrived, it was immediately clear that Jeff suffers from severe malnutrition. According to his military records, his weight upon arrival in Afghanistan was two hundred pounds. He's now down to one hundred thirty."

Jess sucked in a breath. Beside her, Brad swore softly.

"He's lost a great deal of muscle mass, and his metabolism has been damaged by chronic malnutrition—basically, a starvation diet. The NATO medical facility in Kandahar did a triage of sorts, stabilized him, and sent along their findings, but we're still in the midst of a more thorough physical and mental evaluation. We'll know better how to help him with his issues as more test results come in.

"In the meantime," Dr. Jasper went on, "what we're trying to do is replace what we can with IV fluids and medications and work to get him eating right again. We'll have to do this slowly so as to not cause more damage to his system."

"But he'll recover from that, right?" Brad asked.

"In time, yes." Jasper nodded. "Unfortunately, there are certain conditions he won't recover from. Jeff suffered a detached retina in his right eye. Had he had medical assistance available immediately, it could have been treated. Since it wasn't, unfortunately, the blindness in that eye appears permanent. Of course, we're consulting with our best ophthalmologists, and their assessment is not yet complete, but in situations such as these, the sooner medical treatment is given, the better the chances for recovery."

"So you're saying there's little chance he'll regain his sight in that eye," Jess said shakily.

"Unfortunately, that's correct. I'm sorry. But we'll wait for the final word before we assume the worst."

"His other eye. It's OK?" Brad sounded anxious.

"Perfectly fine. He's already adjusted remarkably, considering the circumstances."

"What else?" Jess needed to know.

"At some point—at least three years ago, according to the X-rays—Jeff incurred a broken left tibia."

"Tibia?" Brad scowled.

"The main bone in his shin," Jess explained, interrupting Jasper's reply. "I'm sorry. I didn't mean to interrupt. I'm a nurse, Dr. Jasper. The last place I worked was Womack."

"Well, that's great news for Jeff." Jasper smiled kindly, then went on. "The bone was never set; consequently, that leg causes him a deal of pain. There's also a loss of function in that extremity. It's not life-threatening, but it will have to be dealt with later, most likely with surgery. The concern is that he's currently not strong enough to tolerate the procedure, so we will have to wait until he's recovered some of this strength."

Jess felt physically ill. Starvation. Detached retina. Broken bone. In an attack? During torture? She wanted to know. She didn't want to know. "What . . . what else is he dealing with?"

Again, Dr. Jasper smiled gently. "Another concern is his diagnosis of positional vertigo. He's fine unless he moves his head the wrong way or he's jostled, and then it manifests itself. His vertigo is most probably a result of a traumatic brain injury. A blow or several severe blows to the head," he clarified when Brad looked puzzled. "The TBI also causes him intense headaches. There are several good noninvasive treatments including physical therapy and medications that can help treat both the vertigo and the headaches. We're conducting a complete neurological workup to find out exactly what we're dealing with. The good news here is that they started him on medication in Kandahar, and he's already seeing some relief on both counts, so that's very positive."

Jess nodded and attempted to smile at this bit of good news, but she suspected she hadn't heard the worst of it yet.

"That's the extent of his physical issues, although you must be prepared. He was tortured. He has scars from injuries that, fortunately, did not result in long-term health issues but will affect him emotionally for years to come."

"PTSD," Jess whispered, and closed her eyes. She'd been prepared for this diagnosis, but still a wave of nausea hit her.

"Yes, I would be very surprised if Jeff doesn't exhibit some manifestation of post-traumatic stress disorder. Regardless, it's going to be difficult for him to adjust to the real world again. Medications can help, if it's determined that he needs them, but he will most likely require extensive therapy to regain some semblance of normality. We won't know how much until we perform further evaluations. Which leads us to the final concern." He faced Jess somberly. "Jeff's memory has been affected by all he's been through."

"His memory?" Brad leaned forward in his chair. "What's wrong with his memory?"

"Jeff advises us that it was only recently that he was able to recall his name, his unit and battalion, and what happened to him the night his team was attacked."

"Because of the TBI or emotional trauma?" Jess asked.

"At this point, we don't know. RA, retrograde amnesia," he clarified for Brad, "can also be induced by either physical or severe emotional trauma. So what you must both keep in mind during the coming months is that the brain is very complex and malleable, and everyone is different in his course of recovery. How well Jeff does will only be known as time passes."

"Wait—you're saying Jeff has amnesia?" Brad asked in disbelief. "That there are things he still doesn't remember?"

"Unfortunately, yes."

"He . . . he doesn't remember me? Or . . . or Jess?"

"I'm sorry. No."

"What does he remember?" Jess asked, shocked and suddenly fearful of the doctor's answer.

"Only portions of the last three and a half years. He basically remembers nothing of his life that predates the attack on his convoy. It's only been within the past month or so that he remembered that."

She must have looked as though she were in shock, because the doctor reached out and covered her clasped hands with one of his.

"He's going to get through this, and so are you. It will take time and patience and ongoing medical care, but he will get through this."

Jess couldn't sit any longer. She stood and walked over to the window, stared out at the autumn-bare trees planted in neat rows in a failed attempt to break the barrenness of the concrete parking lot.

"I'm sorry I didn't have better news for you," Dr. Jasper said. "If you have any questions, at any time, ask the charge nurse, and she'll get hold of me."

"What . . . what happens next?" Jess asked, pulling herself together and facing him again. "I mean, when he's well enough to be discharged, what comes next for him?"

"You're going to have to speak to his commanding officer at Fort Bragg to get complete information, but in my experience, what generally happens when a warrior returns home with medical issues is that after he's released from the hospital, he'll need to be debriefed about what happened to him over there. In Jeff's case, since he was held in captivity for so long, they'll want to gather as much intel from him as they can.

"But please don't worry. Treating and addressing Jeff's emotional and mental stability are as important to us as his physical well-being. We won't let him undergo any questioning we feel he's unprepared to deal with. But you have to remember, until a panel can convene and determine the ongoing extent of his disabilities, he's still in the military."

"You don't think he'll be medically discharged?" Brad sounded angry.

"Oh, I absolutely do. In the meantime, he'll be on leave—needless to say, he's accumulated a lot of leave—and you'll be able to take him home. I also want to reassure you that once his discharge comes through—which may be several months—his treatment won't stop then. We'll get him hooked up with the VA medical center closest to where you live so he'll receive plenty of follow-up care."

Brad had grown very quiet. Jess felt for him. His brother had left whole and had returned a badly damaged man.

"I'll leave you to process all of this," Dr. Jasper said gently. "You can go in and see him whenever you're ready. My suggestion would be to take it slowly with him. All of you will have major adjustments to make. Patience is your friend."

Then why did she feel friendless? And as barren as that parking lot?

She was married to a man who didn't remember her.

She was in love with a man she needed to forget.

She felt confused and guilty on both counts. But there was only one thing she could do right now.

On a deep breath, she gathered herself, then made the longest walk of her life.

＊

JESS STOPPED HESITANTLY outside the door of J.R.'s room, steeled herself, and, as Brad hung behind, walked inside.

Oh, my God, oh, my God.

She covered her mouth with her hand to smother a gasp. She barely recognized the man asleep in the bed. His hair was long and threaded with gray. He had a beard. J.R. had hated it when he'd had to grow a beard for a mission.

Tears filled her eyes, and she walked closer and better saw the ravages his captivity had done to him. A pressure squeezed so tightly in her chest she could barely breathe.

Emaciated.

Withered.

Gaunt.

Destroyed.

Those words cycled over and over in her mind as she studied him in stunned disbelief.

And pain. *My God,* the pain he had to have suffered.

What the years and the war had done to him crushed her heart. And what love she'd had for him revitalized and swelled as she remembered the man he had been—now as much a stranger to her as she was to him.

Any question she'd had about whether she could do this, whether she could walk away from a man who loved her and toward a man who didn't even know her anymore, had been answered in the few seconds since she'd walked through that door. She could not turn her back on this man. This broken, damaged man. She could not be that selfish.

Then and there, she made a promise to do whatever it took to help heal him and heal their marriage.

Filled with new determination, she went to his side, folded his limp hand in hers, and softly said his name.

Chapter

29

Minnesota, late November

*J*eff sat in front of the TV in the new recliner Jess had bought for him, the dog asleep by his feet.

"To keep that leg up," she'd said with an overbright smile when the chair had been delivered shortly after she'd brought him home to this apartment above a store he'd apparently frequented but didn't remember. "Don't think I don't notice that it swells up on you if you're on it too much."

He'd been back in Minnesota for two weeks. And everything about the Crossroads General Store and the lake where he'd grown up fishing and hiking and hunting and camping remained as foreign to him as a moonscape.

"Did we live here?" he'd asked Jess after he'd

painstakingly climbed up the stairs from the store to the apartment for the first time.

"We didn't, no. I lived here with my parents. You spent a lot of time here, though."

"Why? Did I work here?"

"No. I did. You hung around so you could flirt with me," she'd said easily and with a shy smile. "After we got married, you and I lived on several different Army posts. We were at Bragg when you deployed and . . ." She let the thought trail off.

And went to Afghanistan and got killed, was what she was going to say. Maybe he should have gotten killed. Maybe he should have died over there.

"But then you already know you were at Bragg," she added inanely.

Yeah. He knew. After he'd been discharged from the hospital three weeks ago, they'd put him and Jess and his brother up at the Fisher House that had been built specifically for rehabbing soldiers and their families so they'd all have someplace to stay during his debriefing. All of them had been relieved when there'd been three bedrooms.

He'd hoped returning to Bragg would help jog his memory, that maybe he'd remember the good times. Instead, it had been pure hell. The debriefing sessions exhausted him. Worse, though, was when his teammates—the ones who weren't deployed—dropped by to see him. Men he'd fought side-by-side with, drunk beer with.

Men he didn't remember.

He didn't know who had been more uncomfortable, them or him.

Maybe I should have died there.

He stared blankly at the TV. Look at the lives he'd ruined by living. Rabia. Her father. His brother, Brad. Jess.

It hurt him to watch her try so hard to be natural with him. So he didn't watch. He watched TV instead. For hours and hours on end, even though he couldn't say what he'd seen an hour ago, let alone the day before. Mostly, he watched it so he wouldn't have to deal with the pain in the eyes of a woman who was still a stranger to him.

Sometimes he looked out the window. He couldn't see much except the tree line, but he passed time watching the wind blow and the snow fall. In northern Minnesota, the snow fell early and often. The fact that he knew that didn't count.

What counted was what he didn't know.

At first, she'd brought him high school yearbooks and photo albums. It made his head hurt to look at them, to see himself as a boy he still didn't recognize. So he asked her not to bring them anymore.

With a patient but sad look in her eyes, she'd understood. "Sure. No problem. I didn't mean to bombard you. I thought maybe . . . I don't know. Maybe I hoped seeing the photos might trigger a memory."

"It's OK. It's nice of you. I appreciate it. But nothing's happening. I'm sorry."

She'd knelt down beside him, covered his hand with hers. "You don't have to be sorry. It'll either come or it won't. There's no pressure, J.R."

But there was pressure. Every time she looked at him that way, every time she drove him to a doctor's appointment in Hibbing or a counseling session in Duluth, or every time she called him J.R. in that automatic way that said she'd called him that since they'd both been little kids, he felt the pressure.

I can't come with you, Jeffery.

Rabia.

Another pressure. One he couldn't get out of his head.

He rose stiffly from his chair. "I think I'll turn in."

That hurt look again. "Don't you want dinner? I fried chicken. Your favorite."

Maybe it was. He didn't know. "Sorry. It'll still be good tomorrow, right?"

"Sure. You go ahead and go to bed."

So polite. They were so polite to each other. Like strangers meeting on a train, passing through each other's life to get back to their own lives. Only the train never stopped and dropped him off where he was supposed to be. It kept going and going, and he kept searching and searching.

He forced a smile for her, because she tried so hard, then got up and walked into the bedroom that was supposed to be theirs. Only he slept there alone, and she slept in another room on another bed.

Two strangers on a train.

He lay down, covered his ears with the pillow so he couldn't hear the soft sounds of her weeping, and thought of Rabia again. Always. On a rooftop under the stars. Bringing him back to life with her soft hands and healing heart.

The soft clicking of paws on the hardwood floor, then the slight dip of the mattress, told him the dog had followed him. Eyes closed, he reached out and found the Lab's soft muzzle. Bear immediately moved in next to him, lay down, and, with a contented sigh, laid his doggie head on his chest.

"You don't care, do you, buddy?" he whispered into the dark bedroom. "You don't care who I am or if I remember. You're a good dog, Bear. A good dog."

★

"WHERE'S J.R.?"

Jess sat down with Brad at her kitchen table after pouring them each a mug of coffee. He'd brought the scent of fresh snow and winter cold with him, even though it was only early December.

"He's in the shower."

"Any change?"

He asked the same question every morning when he stopped by to check on J.R. It was the same question her mom and dad asked every day when they called to check on her and on J.R. And Shelley, who'd been so generous to keep Bear for her while she'd been in Texas.

"Physically, yes. The vertigo and the headaches are much better. But mentally, no. Basically, he sits in his chair and watches TV. And he hasn't remembered anything."

"He just needs time, right? Just like he needs a lot of sleep. Like the doc said." Brad nodded his head as if trying to convince himself as much as her. "He's put on a little weight, though, don't you think?"

"A little, yes. I think he's up five to ten pounds since they brought him back to the States."

Brad glanced over his shoulder, as if checking to see if J.R. was in earshot, but the shower was still running. "I want to thank you, Jess. I . . . I've been meaning to say something. I know this is tough for you . . . what with your plans with Brown and all."

Last week was Thanksgiving. She and Ty were to have been married then. Instead, she and J.R. had been in Hibbing, at the VA medical center there, spending the night Thursday so they could be on time for his early-morning battery of medical exams and evals Friday morning.

"J.R. is my husband, Brad. Did you really think I'd turn away when he needed me?"

"I didn't know," Brad confessed. "I got to tell you, I don't know what I'd do if it was me in this situation."

"I know what you'd do," Jess reassured him.

"Well, I want to thank you. I love my brother." Tears welled, and Brad quickly looked away.

"I love him, too, Brad. I'm going to be here for him."

She got up to get the coffee pot and to give Brad some time to compose himself. J.R. wasn't the only one struggling. She could sense how tense and fragile and raw Brad felt around his brother. She could sense it because it was exactly how she felt around J.R.

"Maybe today he'll be ready to get out of the apartment for something other than a doctor's appointment," Brad said when she returned to the table. "I can take him down to the shop, let him hang around with me for a while."

"I don't know. You can ask him."

"We can't keep his return a secret much longer," Brad said, sounding worried. "It's been three weeks. People know something's up."

They knew something was up because she'd closed the store for almost two weeks without notice and left the state. They knew because Ty was gone. A dull ache swelled in her chest. Everyone had known they'd planned to get married at Thanksgiving. She tried not to think about him. She tried not to wonder about him. She had a husband to heal. A marriage to restore. And she was going to do everything in her power to make things work. But the dog, it seemed, gave him more comfort than she did.

"I know," she said, pushing thoughts of Ty from her mind. "But that's a major issue for J.R. It's not only that he's uncomfortable seeing people. He wants to keep his entire story secret. The family who helped him, the woman and her father? He's worried that if the press gets hold of his story, their names will come out, and the Taliban will go after them in retaliation for hiding him."

Brad considered his coffee cup with a dark frown. "Wish we could thank them some way."

"You can thank them," J.R. said, limping into the kitchen, Bear padding along softly behind him, "by never mentioning them again. The way you thank them is to keep quiet."

Brad nodded quickly. "I know. I know that, bro. No one's going to hear about it from me. But I was thinking. Like I was telling Jess, people are starting to wonder what's going on. You know, this store is like the watering hole for everyone who lives around the lake."

"So I've been told," J.R. said.

After a brief hesitation, he joined them at the table.

Jess knew he was still not comfortable around either one of them, but she tried to act natural so that maybe it would start to feel natural to him.

"I've got water hot for tea. I'll get you a mug."

Jess sprang up from the table, then slowed herself down, so J.R. wouldn't see how unsettled she felt. He used to be a coffee drinker but had developed a taste for strong tea and honey. The woman who hid him got him started on it, he'd explained.

"Thanks," J.R. said absently.

"So," Brad began again, "how about we tell them the partial truth? You were held captive all these years and managed to escape. End of story. People aren't going to pry, J.R. They'll respect your privacy, especially if we put the word out that you're still recovering and don't want to talk about it. To anyone."

"He's right, J.R." Jess returned to the table with his tea and honey. "Yes, they're going to be excited for you. In fact, they'll probably want to throw some kind of a party. But we'll make it clear you're still recovering, a party is out of the question, and privacy is essential, to keep it under their hats until you're back on your game."

She covered his hand with hers and blinked back tears when he slowly withdrew it, rejecting her touch, still so very, very uncomfortable with physical contact.

Bear, it seemed, was the only thing to have breached that barrier. J.R had loved the dog on sight. The feeling had been mutual. Jess had read that Labs had very sensitive radar concerning human feelings. She was fully convinced it was true. The dog rarely left J.R.'s side. Whether he felt protective or sensed J.R.'s fragile state, she didn't know. She was glad the dog had penetrated the wall J.R. had built around himself and his feelings and had given him an outlet for affection.

"Do whatever you have to do," he said, not looking at either one of them.

"Thought maybe you might feel up to a drive today," Brad said hopefully. He had been suffering, too, not knowing how to reach his brother. "Take a loop around the lake, maybe? Stop by my shop, show you my business. You used to help me guide, you know. We had some good times and real laughs on some of those fishing trips."

"Maybe another day," J.R. said, not unkindly but with a tone so dismissive Brad knew not to coax. "Thanks, though. I appreciate the offer."

"No. No. It's OK. I understand." Brad stood then, trying not to look like a little boy who hadn't been picked for a team. "Guess I'd better get moving. You, ah, you let me know if you need anything, OK?"

"Sure thing," J.R. said without looking at his brother.

"You, too, Jess," Brad said, and headed for the door.

The kitchen felt suddenly empty and a little scary. She wasn't afraid of J.R. She was afraid for him. She was afraid for them.

She stared at the walls Ty had painted for her, and a memory of him making love to her on the kitchen table flashed, so vivid and real her abdominal muscles clenched.

"I'm sorry," J.R. said, still staring at his untouched tea. "I don't mean to hurt him. I wish I could respond to him. He . . . he tries so hard."

"He understands," Jess said, even though she knew Brad didn't understand. He wanted his brother back. He'd pinned all his hope on some miracle happening to jog his memory once they brought J.R. home.

"I wish I did. I wish I understood any of this."

Tears formed in his eyes, and her heart went out to

him. "I have an idea. After breakfast, why don't I cut your hair and shave off that beard for you? Maybe . . . I don't know. Maybe a change would be good for you. What do you think?"

He gave her a half-smile, then looked down at the dog who had parked by his feet. "What do you think, Bear? Think maybe it's time you're the furriest critter in this house?"

Bear wagged his tail.

J.R. looked up at her with a hint of a light in his eyes. "Bear says it's time."

"Then we have a plan. First I feed you. Then we do a makeover."

And for the first time since she'd heard the news that her husband was alive, Jess's smile wasn't forced. For an instant, a very brief instant, she'd seen a glimpse of the old J.R. That half-smile, that silly sense of humor, and it made her heart glad.

Chapter

30

J.R. watched Jess from his recliner as she hauled boxes of Christmas decorations out of the hall closet, even though it was only the first week in December.

"Business drops off drastically in late autumn," she told him, chattering away as she always did. It wasn't that she annoyed him. He understood. She was simply attempting to fill him in on her life, which was now his life.

She really was a very attractive woman. Kind. Attentive. He wished he was attracted to her. It would make it so much easier for both of them.

He appreciated that she didn't try to smother him. It would have been easy to do, since she was a nurse, but she kept it in check, asked necessary questions, and otherwise assumed he'd let her know if he had a problem.

"I cut store hours from November first to April thirtieth, opening at eight A.M. and closing at five. I also close up on Sundays," she explained, then stopped and had to put some muscle into dragging down a heavy box. "During the summer, I have part-time help, and believe me, I need it."

She didn't hear him come up behind her and jumped when he reached above and around her to help.

"Thanks," she said with a surprised smile.

"Where do you want this?"

"Over there on the table with the rest of them."

Again, he appreciated that she didn't make a big deal out of the fact that he actually did something other than take up space.

"This time of year, though," she continued, smiling at him, "running the store is a one-woman show."

The fact was, she often spent the better part of the day upstairs in the apartment and only headed down when the bell above the door alerted her that she had a customer.

"Go ahead," she said, when she caught him eyeing the boxes. "Open them up. I've kept everything over the years. There are some decorations in there you made when you were in Boy Scouts." She laughed. "I'm sure you'll figure out which ones they are."

Because he was up and because she seemed to

want him to, he opened the first box. Garland, lights, glittering glass balls . . . and at the bottom of the box, another smaller box. Inside were three old pine cones sparkling with glitter; old-fashioned gold curling ribbon had been glued onto the stems, then looped so they could be hung on a tree. A picture of a boy who looked to be about eight years old had been taped to the middle of a bell that had been sloppily cut out of red construction paper. Another length of gold curling ribbon had been threaded through a hole made by a paper punch, then tied, making a loop to fit over a tree branch.

She walked up beside him, smelling clean and healthy and like a little bit of the maple syrup she'd served with his pancakes this morning.

"Guess I found my decorations."

She smiled. "I always loved that picture of you."

He studied the boy in the photo, wishing he could conjure up some connection. "He looks like an ornery little twerp."

She laughed this time. "You were hell on wheels. You had this old bike you used to ride on the roads all around the lake. Cars would come up behind you, and you wouldn't get out of their way—just to tick them off."

"Sounds like I was a candidate for juvie hall."

"Nah. You were never mean-spirited. Besides, Brad never let you get too far out of line."

"What happened to my mother?" he asked abruptly.

She looked at him sharply. "You . . . you remember about your mother?"

He lifted a shoulder, then pulled a kitchen chair out and sat down. "I know she wasn't around. That's the one thing that came to me over there. That I hadn't had a mother."

She touched a hand to his shoulder, and for once, he didn't feel like shrugging it off.

"She left. I won't defend her, but your father was an alcoholic. I guess she couldn't take it. Why she left you boys with him, I'll never know."

"How old was I?"

"When she left? You were five, I think. Brad was ten. Your dad tucked into the bottle even deeper then. You were fifteen when he wrapped his truck around a tree one night."

"So Brad . . ." He let the thought trail off.

"Pretty much raised you."

They talked then for the better part of an hour about his high school days, sports, and dating, and for once, he asked the questions instead of relying on her to offer information.

"What are you going to do with all this stuff?" he asked when he'd absorbed as much as he could about the boy who had become the man he didn't remember.

"Hang it on the tree . . . as soon as I get one."

He glanced out a window. The sky was brilliant blue, but the indoor/outdoor thermometer by the sink said it was twenty-eight degrees Fahrenheit outside.

"Do you want to go with me?" she asked, with a hesitance he completely understood. He'd been back three weeks, and he hadn't once left the apartment. "There's a tree farm between here and the Falls. I usually go cut my own."

She'd been trying so hard. His brother had been trying so hard. Maybe it was time *he* tried. "Maybe we should call Brad," he said. "See if he wants to go with us."

Her smile was too happy, too bright, for such a small concession on his part. "Great idea. We'll go as soon as I close the store at five."

★

"I DON'T HAVE a wife."

A fist hit him in the gut, doubling him over. Another slammed into his kidney. His knees buckled, and he fell on the dirt floor, covered in mud from the water they threw on him to revive him. Mud mixed with his blood.

Every day for longer than he could remember, they had dragged him in here, threatened him, and beat him, and when they were through with him, they dumped him back into the box. Four feet by four feet by six feet. Too many marks on the earth walls.

"Tell us her name. Tell us her name so we can find her and tell her what a hero you are."

"I don't have a wife." Through the pain, he felt himself being hoisted by pulleys attached to the ropes that were tied around his bleeding wrists.

"Tell us what Americans were doing in Pakistan."

"*We got lost.*"

Pain exploded through his jaw, and his knees buckled again. Only the ropes held him upright. He couldn't see out of his right eye. Blood burned his pupil and dripped onto the dirt.

"*Tell us about the Americans' latest weapons system.*"

"*Rock . . . slingshot.*"

Another blow to his head.

Another round of questions.

Over and over and over.

"*What is your wife's name? Tell us, and we will stop. We will feed you. You don't have to hurt anymore.*"

"*I don't have a wife. I don't have a wife!*". . .

"I don't have a wife!"

"J.R. Wake up. You're having a nightmare."

"I don't have a wife!" he yelled again, as hands held him down.

He reared up swinging . . . connected with flesh . . . heard a cry.

Not his.

A woman's.

"Rabia? Oh, God, Rabia."

He frantically looked around. He wasn't in an interrogation shed. He wasn't in a box.

He wasn't on a roof under an Afghan moon.

Rabia.

He was in a room. With soft light. A soft bed.

A dog whined and scratched at the door from the other side.

Another muffled cry.

Not a dream.

Jess.

"Oh, God. Jess."

"I'm OK," she whispered from the far side of the bed.

"Did I hit you?"

"It's OK. I'm OK. I'll . . . I'll be right back."

The door opened, and she hurried out.

And all he could do was sit there in the bed, his hands braced behind him, his heart pounding wildly . . . and relive the nightmare that had been his life in captivity.

✴

JESS RUSHED INTO the bathroom, flipped on the light switch, and walked directly to the vanity. One look at her mouth, and she turned on the cold-water faucet. Blood pooled between her teeth and her split lower lip and trickled down her chin.

She groped for a washcloth with a shaking hand, wet it under the stream of water, then winced when she pressed it to her swollen lip.

Oh, God. She breathed deep to steady herself.

"Jess."

Her head snapped up. She met J.R.'s eyes in the mirror.

He stood in the doorway behind her, his eyes filled with anguish.

"It's OK," she reassured him.

"It's *not* OK. You're bleeding."

"It looks worse than it is."

"I hit you. I hurt you." If pain was a sound, it came out in his voice.

She shook her head. "I shouldn't have woken you like that. But you were having a nightmare. I . . . I don't know. I wanted to wake you. To get you away from wherever you were."

It all crashed down on her then. From hearing the news that he was alive. To telling Ty good-bye. To seeing J.R. in the hospital, broken and defeated. To bringing him home and trying so hard to give him his space and hoping so, so hard that he would remember . . .

A sob wrenched out unbidden, and then the floodgates broke.

She sank to the floor, helpless to pull herself together. All the years without him, all the pain of adjusting, and now, less than a month with him, and she'd hit the wall.

She'd thought she could help him.

She'd thought she could heal him.

She'd thought they could begin again.

For him, she *needed* to begin again.

But it was never going to happen. She couldn't reach him. She couldn't have Ty. She couldn't stop crying. Couldn't catch her breath. Her chest hurt. And still she cried, her tears mixing with her blood and her helplessness and her shame.

She felt his hands grip her shoulders. Felt him lift her, wrap her in his arms, and hold her as she unraveled.

After several long minutes, he walked her into the living room. He sat down with her on the sofa and wrapped them together in a big soft comforter, with Bear anxious and confused at their feet, the soft lights from their new Christmas tree gently twinkling.

And despair crowded around them like darkness crowded in on dusk.

Chapter
31

*S*unday morning, Jess woke up on the sofa, the comforter still tucked around her, her head on J.R.'s lap. Bear, curled up in a tight ball, slept soundly at her feet.

Her head hurt. Her eyes and throat burned from crying, and her lip felt as if it had swollen to the size of a basketball.

Then J.R. finally started talking, and none of that mattered anymore.

"During the beatings," he said hesitantly, "they used to tell me they would find my family and kill them if I didn't talk."

She didn't speak. She couldn't speak.

"So I told them I didn't have a family. I told them I didn't have a wife."

She sat up slowly and found him looking at her.

"I didn't remember . . . until last night. Maybe . . . maybe that's why I don't remember you . . . maybe I said it so often to protect you my mind made it true."

She hadn't thought there were any more tears left inside her. "I am so, so sorry for what they did to you."

"Yeah," he said. "Me, too." His brows furrowed, and he took her hand. "Was I a good husband, Jess?"

"You were a good man, J.R. You're still a good man."

He grunted. "Tell that to your lip. And do *not* say that you're OK one more time."

"I wasn't going to say that."

"Was I a good husband?" he persisted.

She stretched to cover her discomfort over broaching this subject, then got up and walked to the kitchen to make coffee, put on water for his tea, and figure out what she was going to say.

He was still on the sofa when she came back. And he was still waiting for an answer.

"You were as good as you were capable of being." She sat down beside him again and gathered the quilt over her, tucking it around her bare feet.

"What does that mean?"

They'd gone past the point of whitewashing and tiptoeing around each other's feelings last night. When the dam had broken on her tears, so had her ability to cushion the truth. "It means we were kids when we started dating. It means we fell in love and became a couple before we figured out what it was like to be friends. It means," she went on gently, "that when you enlisted, I suddenly had competition. You loved me, but you loved the Army more. Everything about it. Were you good to me? Yes. But the Army came first. I knew that when I married you. I figured at some point . . . I don't know . . . I guess I figured you'd eventually decide you'd had enough, and then we could be one of those couples who came first in each other's life."

"Sounds like I was a jerk."

"No. Not a jerk. A very principled man with a very big passion and sense of patriotism."

"At your expense."

"Nothing's ever perfect."

He stared straight ahead for a long moment. "Did you ever think of leaving me?"

"Yes," she said honestly. "Right before your last deployment. I begged you to promise me it would be your last, that you'd put in for an instructor position here in the States. We fought about it. You left without saying good-bye." The next word she'd heard was of his death.

He looked sideways at her. "Would you have left? If I'd come back then, would you have left?"

"I honestly don't know. I loved you. But the deployments, the danger, being alone all the time . . . it wasn't easy for me." She pressed a palm to her forehead. "God, that sounded horrible. All you've been through, and I'm complaining because I had it bad."

She got up suddenly and headed back to the

kitchen to check on the coffee. When she returned with her mug and tea for him, she decided to risk asking him a question.

"Is Rabia the woman who helped you?"

He stopped with his tea halfway to his mouth.

"You said her name. Last night. When you woke up from the nightmare."

He exhaled heavily. "Yes. Rabia and her father. He was the village *malik*. The liaison between the people and the *jurga*, the religious and governmental council."

She hesitated only briefly. "Can I ask how you ended up with them?"

At first, she thought he wasn't going to respond. But then he started talking. About the mission. The attack. His captivity. His escape. How Rabia had found him.

While he'd been reluctant at first, the longer he talked, the more she could tell he'd needed to get this all off his chest.

He told her about how ill and helpless he'd been, about the opiate addiction, hiding under the floor from the Taliban, and how he constantly worried that he was placing Rabia and her father in danger. How he would have left if he could, but he could barely walk.

He talked through a pot of coffee and several cups of tea and honey and breakfast and continued talking after lunch until he was finally exhausted. For that matter, so was she.

It was all so horrific. So terrifying. That he was

alive was a testament to what a strong man he was. And to the bravery of two very special people.

She felt closer to him now than she ever had. He was open and unguarded. It felt like the time to break another barrier they'd both been avoiding.

"Let's . . . let's go to bed," she said hesitantly. "We could both use a nap."

He looked at her, and she could see both anxiety and indecision in his eyes. Her heartbeat quickened.

Finally, he rose, took her hand, and led her toward the bedroom.

✳

CLOSE TOGETHER. UNDER the covers, Jeff held this sweet, kind woman who was his wife in his arms. Her heart beat rapidly against his. She was nervous. Hell, so was he.

But he owed her this. She wanted a husband, not a houseguest. So when she turned her face to his, he pushed back thoughts of another woman's face, another lifetime ago.

It was not unpleasant kissing her, taking care for her poor split lip, taking pains to be gentle and responsive when she tentatively kissed him back.

She turned fully in to him, warm and petite and covered only in her soft flannel gown.

She touched his face and deepened the kiss. He touched her hip and drew her closer.

And he couldn't.

He couldn't do this. Not yet. Maybe not ever.

"I'm sorry." He rolled onto his back and stared at the ceiling.

Beside him, she lay achingly still. He'd disappointed her. He'd humiliated her.

"It's not you, Jess. You're . . ."

"Still a stranger. It's OK." She sounded childlike and fragile and, though it might have been wishful thinking on his part, a little relieved. "Just sleep, OK? We both need to sleep."

✱

ONLY JESS DIDN'T sleep. She lay beside her husband in the quiet afternoon light, afraid that she could never do this. She'd tried. She'd even initiated. But it hadn't felt right. It had felt like a lie. How could she ever be a wife to him again? Not the kind of wife he needed her to be. Even if they finally breached this barrier and made love, it would be a lie.

The tears came again. Soft and silent.

She cried for all he'd lost. For all she'd lost.

She cried for Ty and let the ache of missing him finally take over.

She turned away, had to get out of the bed, but J.R. stopped her with a gentle hand on her arm.

"I'm sorry," he whispered, and pulled her against him again, then held her while she wept.

✱

"THIS ISN'T GOING to work, is it?" Jess asked two weeks later, after several more dismal attempts to be intimate.

They were in bed again; he'd reached for her again. Nothing happened. Again.

They'd both tried, but every time, it ended up with one or both of them in tears—him consoling her or her consoling him or both of them consoling each other.

Yet, inexplicably, in the midst of all their pain and confusion, they formed a bond that they'd never shared when they'd been married. Through the trial, through the despair, they recognized and respected each other as survivors. Battered, bruised, and confused, they comforted each other, cried for each other, even laughed at the unrelenting irony of fate getting them this far and then putting on the skids.

They'd found trust. They'd found confidantes. They'd become friends.

And they could now be brutally honest with each other.

That's why she'd finally put it out there on the table. It wasn't going to work. She thought she knew the main reason.

They'd talked a lot. Late into the night. Early in the morning. He, in particular, talked a lot about the Afghan woman and what life had been like there. His eyes softened when he spoke of her. His voice became melancholy and sad. And it had finally occurred to her.

"What aren't you telling me, J.R.?" They sat side-by-side in bed, pillows propped behind their heads, Bear snoring softly at their feet.

"What do you mean?"

"Rabia," she said gently. "Was she more to you? More than a woman who saved your life?"

He looked down, clenched his jaw.

"Talk to me. Whatever it is, it's OK. I know you don't want to hurt me. But I know your heart isn't here. Amnesia or not. Memories or not. Your heart is never going to be here again, is it? It's back there. With her."

He finally looked at her. Tears filled his eyes, and she put her arms around him. "Tell me about her."

So he did, finally admitting that he'd fallen in love with her. "But it doesn't matter," he said dismally. "She won't leave Afghanistan, and I can't go back there."

Jess's heart went out to him as it never had before. Because she understood. "Come on." She urged him out of the bed. "I'll make some hot chocolate. I've got something to tell you, too."

★

WHILE JESS WAS downstairs handling a customer in the store, J.R. stood in front of the Christmas tree, absently thinking about what she'd told him about her and Ty Brown and looking at the motley collection of ornaments she'd hung along with old-fashioned tinsel and popcorn garland.

"This was from our first tree," she'd told him, as she lifted a tarnished and scratched silver and blue ball carefully out of a box.

She knew where every decoration had come from and how long she'd had it. It was not one of those designer trees he remembered seeing in fancy department stores. She called it her memory tree, because so many of the decorations were homemade, some from when she was a kid and some, like his Scout craft projects, from pine cones.

She was a very special woman, he thought, as he heard the bell ring downstairs signaling that the customer had left. And Ty Brown was a stand-up man. He still couldn't get over that Brown had volunteered for his rescue mission. But he did understand why Jess might love him.

Telling her about Rabia had been the right thing to do. The relief they'd both felt after their mutual confessions had actually been the catalyst for a special sort of love between them.

It felt good to have someone like Jess on his side. But he couldn't hold her life up forever.

He heard her walk up the stairs and turned when she opened the door. "You need to tell him, Jess," he blurted out. "You need to tell Brown. You need to go to him."

Her brows drew together. "Where's this coming from?"

"You love him. It's that simple."

She smiled sadly and shook her head. "I think we've both figured out that nothing in our lives is simple." She walked over and sat down on the arm of the sofa. "I hurt him. You can understand that. I can't expect him to forget that I walked away from him. Look. Don't worry. If things are supposed to work out with Ty and me, it will. Right now, you're my priority."

"I think maybe I might be the fool in this mix." He limped over and drew her to her feet and into his arms. "Our marriage may be too broken to fix, but I do love you, Jess."

She hugged him back. "I know. I love you, too. And I'll always be here for you if you need me."

They were going to get through this, he thought, actually believing it for the first time. Somehow, they were both going to get through this.

Then Jess's cell phone rang and turned his world upside down again.

*

"PUT US ON speaker, Jess," Mike Brown said after saying hello and asking if Jeff was there. "You both need to hear this."

"What's wrong?" Jess glanced nervously at J.R.

"Just put us on speaker, sweetie."

"It's Mike Brown," she told J.R., as she switched the phone to speaker mode.

"Jeff," Mike said by way of greeting. "Look. I've got some bad news."

J.R. frowned at the phone. "How bad?"

"Word just came down that your story's been leaked."

J.R. went pale. Jess touched a hand to his shoulder to steady him.

"How much of the story?" she asked, hoping maybe it wasn't as bad as it sounded.

"More than should have been. Apparently, some genius working in Army's public relations section ferreted it out, decided it was time a branch of the military other than the SEALs got some glory, and he let it all out."

"How could that even happen?" Jess asked as J.R. limped to the sofa and sat down heavily.

"How does any secret get leaked?" Mike said in disgust. "Somebody talked who shouldn't have, and word spread from there. The only thing that seems to have escaped exposure is the black team's involvement. The after-action report fudged on our connection and substituted Special Forces."

"Did they name names?" J.R. wanted to know.

"I'm afraid so, yeah," Mike said. "It hit the AP wire earlier today. It's going to hurt, but you'd better turn on the TV. It's all over the news."

Jess scrambled toward the TV, turned it on, and switched to a twenty-four-hour news station. She muted the sound and kept one eye on the TV, watching for coverage of the story while Mike talked.

"You'd better be prepared. There'll be reporters from every local and national outlet clamoring at your door anytime now."

"Rabia?" J.R. asked, looking ill.

"The press got a hold of her picture, man. I'm sorry. Apparently, they found it in a roster of teachers in her school in Kabul."

"My God." Jeff dropped his head into his hands. "She's dead. Now that the word's out, the Taliban will find her, and she's as good as dead."

"We're not going to let that happen. Between me and Nate Black, we've been on the phone nonstop to the brass at DOD, chewing ass and pointing out the facts. They're going to have egg all over their collective face if something happens to her and they know it. As news spreads, any American who's seen and heard about her part in your rescue will call her a national heroine. Hell, if she was a Catholic, she'd be canonized for what she did for one of our own.

"So trust me," Mike continued emphatically. "Every U.S. asset available in Kabul is currently on the hunt for her. They'll find her and get her out of the country long before the Taliban can close ranks and get to her. They'll get her out of there just like we got you out. I want you to believe that, OK? You need to believe that."

J.R. didn't look convinced.

Jess sat down beside him and put an arm around his waist. "When will you know something?"

"It doesn't matter," J.R. interrupted dismally. "Her father won't move again, and she won't go anywhere without him."

"The old man left before when he thought it would save his daughter's life, right?" Mike pointed out. "As soon as he knows she's in danger, he'll agree to go with her. Look, guys, I'm sorry, but I've got to go. The minute I hear something, I'll call, OK? Hang in there."

The line went dead.

Jess stared at her phone, then at J.R. "Mike won't let her down, J.R. He'll do what he said. He'll get her out."

But J.R. had tuned out. He had that look in his eyes. The thousand-mile stare. He'd gone to that place in his head where he went sometimes when life became too difficult to deal with.

Only in this case, he was staring thousands of miles away, where the fate of the woman he loved was in the hands of faceless, nameless strangers.

Chapter

32

*T*he open-air market teemed with life and scents and colors. It was the life that Rabia needed. She had mourned long enough. It was time to renew the process of living again with an open heart and get past the grieving.

She pulled her heavy coat tighter around her to ward off the December chill and, with a small basket handle looped over her arm, browsed through the market. Taking her time, she soaked it all in as she walked among the vendors, searching through racks of dresses and lovely, colorful scarves. She even stopped at the food vendors and bought loaves of fresh-baked bread and tender nut meats. Kabul markets had one hundred times as many vendors as Salawat.

Thoughts of the little village where she had spent

time with Jeffery and her father came unbidden, reminding her of what would never be again.

Not only had she lost Jeffery; twenty days ago, she had lost her father.

"It is his heart," the doctor had said, after her father had collapsed and she had rushed him to a hospital. "His condition has been left untreated for too long. I am sorry. There is nothing we can do but make him more comfortable."

Two hours later, her father was gone.

Her last link to Salawat had died with him.

So Allah wished it.

As Allah wished for her to go on. Her life was rich here. She could walk freely without covering her face and hands, drive her car without fear of punishment. She could teach. The imminent threat of the Taliban was far away in Kandahar Province.

And here she had family and friends. She had renewed her ties with the Afghan women's movement and worked to reach out to outlying villages to encourage more fathers to allow their daughters to attend school.

So yes, she must look toward the future now. This she reminded herself daily. For while the past held her heart, the future held her promise.

She added a daily newspaper to her basket, then stopped and stared in disbelief when she saw her own photograph on the front page.

Heart slamming, she looked up and around to see if anyone was watching her, if anyone had recognized her as the woman in the news. Then she ducked into a small alcove and quickly scanned the article. Each word accelerated the beating of her heart and added to her sense of doom.

It was all there. How she had harbored Jeffery, alerted the Americans of his existence, and helped them with his rescue, and that she now taught school in Kabul.

Panic, huge and breath-altering, stole the blood from her head. Sent it all to her heart, which pounded so hard she felt it in her fingertips. She swayed on her feet and would have fallen had someone not reached out and taken her hand.

"You all right, ma'am?"

Through her racing thoughts, she recognized the voice as that of an American.

She looked up and into his eyes, just as he glanced away and nodded to someone behind her shoulder.

She followed his gaze. Another American. And another. She quickly counted six in all.

"Ma'am," the first one said, nodding to the photograph of her in the paper. "We've been turning this city upside down looking for you."

✴

IT TOOK A little convincing before Rabia accepted that they had been sent by Nate Black to help her. It took little persuasion, however, to make her realize that her only option was to get out of Kabul.

The next thing she knew, she was in a vehicle. Shortly after that, she was on a plane.

Everyone treated her well and kindly. They provided her with food and a pillow and a blanket and told her it would be a long flight, so she might as well sleep.

She was going to America. Where she would be safe, they assured her. Where she could start a new life. She would not be on her own. She would have help. She would have support.

Yet there were certain truths that could not be ignored. She was a woman, a Muslim, in a foreign land. There was no war in America. Not with guns and bombs. But there was a culture war. She had read of it. Because of the Islamic jihadists, Muslims were often regarded with suspicion and ostracized in the United States. She understood why that would be so. As she understood that no matter what they said, she was alone.

But she was alive. Something she would not be in Afghanistan.

Weary and wary, she did everything she was told by the people who had pulled her off the streets and then boarded the plane with her. They stopped once. To refuel, they told her. Then they were in the air again.

She slept again because she was exhausted. She slept because in sleep, she could avoid the questions that plagued her about where she would go. How she would live. Whom she could trust.

She slept because she could escape from the sadness of knowing she would never see her homeland or her family and friends again.

And she slept because she could then avoid the truth that every worry, every concern, every fear, was attached to the impossible hope that somehow, some way, she would see Jeffery again.

Her selfishness shamed her. Jeffery did not belong to her. He had a wife. And he had a life she had no part in.

Only the grinding of the landing gear woke her. She looked out the window at the snow-covered fields and city below.

"Welcome to America, ma'am," someone said as the wheels touched down on the tarmac.

She touched a hand to her abdomen, where the child she and Jeffery had made slept.

"Here it begins," she whispered, and prayed to Allah that her baby would grow as safe and as strong as the father it would never know.

✳

SHE NOW UNDERSTOOD how Jeffery must have felt to have been totally dependent on and at the mercy of strangers. Upon landing, she was escorted to a car with dark-tinted windows. After they'd ridden almost two hours over winding roads and through gently rolling snow-covered hills, it had grown dark.

Houses dotted the countryside, most of them

adorned in brightly colored lights. Many with nativity scenes in the front yards. Most with evergreen trees— the first time she had seen any—draped with more lights. Evergreen wreaths hung everywhere. She had read of the Christian Christmas tradition and had even seen photographs of elaborate light displays. Nothing had prepared her for the grandness of the spectacle that played out on house after house. While she did not fully comprehend the connection of colorful lights and Christianity, she found herself mesmerized by the twinkling lights and the festive mood they created.

Soon, however, there were fewer houses, the traffic became nonexistent, and she noticed tall, industrial-strength fencing bordering either side of the road.

She saw lights ahead—not Christmas lights—and concluded that they were security lights when the vehicle slowed, the driver rolled down his window, and a uniformed guard checked his identification.

"We've been expecting you, sir," the soldier said, and then advised him which building to approach.

Fighting a slight measure of unease, Rabia told herself it would only be expected that she would have to undergo some sort of military questioning to ensure that she was not, in fact, a jihadist. There would also be paperwork, she assumed, authorizing her entry into the country.

So she did as she was politely asked and followed another uniformed soldier into a building and down a long hallway.

"These are your temporary quarters," the young soldier said. "Someone will be in to see to your needs momentarily. Have a good night, ma'am."

He left her standing in the hallway, watching him walk away. Off-balance and disoriented, she finally looked through the open door, then gingerly stepped inside.

It was a roomy apartment. She stepped immediately into a sitting area with a sofa, chairs, TV, and artwork on the wall. Very uncertainly, she explored the rest of the apartment, which consisted of a small cooking room that opened into the sitting area. There was also a modern bathroom. A single bedroom housed a huge bed with soft pillows and a pristine white bedcover.

For a long moment, she stood there, looking at the bed. Then she walked into the sitting room, wondering what it meant that she had been left here. Was she to go to bed? Was she to find food in the cooking room and prepare a meal? Was she free to go where she pleased?

The open door said so. But where would she go?

Feeling suddenly exposed, she crossed the room and closed the door. Then she walked around, touching things. The fabrics were of fine quality. The wall colors were soft and comforting.

She sat down on the sofa, folded her hands on her lap, and stared at the dark TV. She considered turning it on to fill the emptiness of the room with some noise, but a knock sounded on the door before she could figure out the remote control.

The door was not locked. Whoever was out there could come in at will, so although she was apprehensive, she walked over and opened it.

And there stood Jeffery.

She raised her hands, pressed them to her heart, and stared, not certain she could believe her eyes.

But it was him. He had gained some weight. His hair was short, and his beard was gone. But it was him.

He smiled at her, and her heart rocketed into the clouds.

"How? What? I do not—"

Then he pulled her into his arms and kissed her. She did not care that it was wrong; she kissed him back. Not thinking about his wife. Only reacting to the loneliness, the missing him, the fear and the love she would always and forever feel for this man.

✶

JEFF COULDN'T BELIEVE he had Rabia in his arms again. The waiting had been hell. The worry that they wouldn't get to her in time was crippling. Then Mike had called with the news.

"They've got her, Jeff. She's on her way to the States now."

"Thank God, thank God." Jess had teared up with joy beside him. And for the first time in a very long time, he thanked God, too. "Where will they take her?" he finally had the presence of mind to ask.

"That's up in the air for now."

Jess had gotten on the phone then and told Mike the way things were. "Now, *you* figure out how he's going to get to see her," she'd ordered like a drill sergeant.

So now here they were. In some top-secret military facility, one of several in the U.S. that only the top brass and immediate personnel knew about. Sharing a bed in an apartment that was generally reserved for the men with stars on their uniforms.

Jeff didn't even know where the post was. Mike had sent a plane to International Falls. Between Brad and Jess, they'd managed to run interference with the press that had been camped out at the store since about two hours after the story broke. Using a couple of Brad's buddies as decoys, Brad had driven him to the airport and put him on the plane—but not before he'd said his good-byes to Jess.

"You're an amazing woman."

"I know," she'd said with a grin. "And you, my dear friend, are going to be just fine."

He'd hugged her hard.

"You haven't seen the last of me," she'd promised, as more tears threatened. "No matter what, we're family. Now . . . go to her. She must be scared half to death."

Yes, she'd been scared and confused, he realized, as he watched Rabia sleep beside him in the bed that, in her eyes, was larger than any man and woman would ever need.

She wasn't afraid anymore. She was thoroughly loved and blissfully sated. And now she slept in his arms, and all the missing her was behind him. She was here now. She was his now, and he was never letting her go.

He'd told her about Jess. There would be paperwork, but since he'd been declared legally dead, they weren't even certain if they were considered married at this point. They would work it out.

Then he would be free, with Jess's blessings, to marry her.

"Marry me?" Her onyx eyes had glittered with happy, bewildered tears as he'd brushed the hair away from her face.

"In America, we marry for love. I love you, Rabia."

"Yes, I will marry you, Jeffery."

Then, to his amazement, she'd fallen asleep. Just like that. Because she felt safe and because she could finally give in to the exhaustion and let him share in the sorrow over her father's death that she'd carried by herself for too long.

With her sleeping peacefully beside him, he, too, finally gave in to the pull of exhaustion.

★

WHEN JEFF WOKE up several hours later, Rabia was lying on her side, watching him.

"Hello." He smiled into her eyes.

She found his hand, brought it to her lips, and kissed it. Then she lowered it to her abdomen, pressed it against her. "Someone else would like to say hello."

Her expressive eyes relayed both excitement and uncertainty. And as she held his hand there, spreading her fingers wide over his, her meaning finally dawned.

"A baby?"

She nodded, still uncertain.

He felt a smile spread from his heart to his eyes. "We made a baby?"

Seeing his happiness, she smiled, too. "On the roof. Under the stars."

It humiliated him that he cried so easily these days. He'd done enough of it in the past month to last a lifetime. But these tears didn't bother him. These tears were born in wonder and steeped in joy.

These tears celebrated the hopeless improbability that in the midst of such suffering and terror and ugliness, something as beautiful and miraculous as life had been created.

Chapter

33

Key West, Florida, December 20th

*Y*ou know," Ty said, surprised when his brother, who he hadn't seen in several weeks, walked into his office as if he did it on a daily basis, "last time you showed up, you brought bad news."

"Hey, little bro. Nice to see you, too. How've I been, you ask? Why, I'm just dandy. Eva? Yep. She's fit and fine."

"Sorry," Ty said, feeling like an ass. "Been a long day." It had been a long freaking month. He missed Jess. He missed the life they had planned to have. He felt sorry for himself. But that wasn't anything his brother was going to find out.

He rocked back in his desk chair as outside his office window, a small cargo plane taxied down the apron toward the runway, heat shimmering off the concrete under the hot Florida sun. "Folks OK?"

"Talked to 'em last night. They're doing great. Worried about you, though. What's this about not coming home for Christmas?"

He regarded Mike thoughtfully. "Until the past two years, you hadn't been home for Christmas or birthdays or—wait—you hadn't been home at all. For eight long years. I'm not allowed to miss one Christmas?"

"I'm the black sheep. I'm supposed to be a jerk. You're the good son."

Ty knew perfectly well why Mike had disappeared for eight years, and it wasn't because he was a jerk. His brother was the best man he knew. But Mike had been in a bad place back then—which, most likely, was the reason he recognized exactly where Ty was right now.

"So how's business?" Mike sprawled in a chair across from Ty's desk and made a big show of checking out the whiteboards and the full schedule inked in with erasable marker.

"Banner year." Ty still wondered why his brother had shown up but figured it had little to do with Christmas, which was less than a week away. "What do you want, Mike?"

Mike propped a boot heel on the corner of Ty's desk, linked his hands over his belt, and regarded him with a wise-ass smile. "I think I might let you worm it out of me."

For the first time, Ty laughed. "Sorry. Not playing."

"Oh, you're going to want to play this game."

The Cheshire Cat smile was getting irritating.

"I'm not coming to work for you, if that's what this is about."

"Nah. I knew that was a pipe dream."

More of that ridiculous toothpaste-ad smile.

"You look really stupid, you know that?"

This time, Mike laughed. "And you're going to *feel* really stupid if you don't get your head out of your ass and ask me why I'm smiling."

"OK, fine. Why are you smiling?"

"The reason rhymes with guess—which is kind of ironic, since you're going to have to guess to find out."

Ty tilted his head and glared at his brother through narrowed eyes. "You are so close to getting punched."

"OK. So you need another clue. It also rhymes with mess—which is the condition of your head since you left Minnesota."

Ty clenched his jaw. "I don't want to talk about her."

Mike dropped his foot and leaned forward. "OK, fine. Then I'll talk. You listen until I'm your favorite brother again."

✻

DECEMBER 21. THE first day of winter, had blown in with a vengeance in Minnesota. Dressed in old jeans, a turtleneck, and a heavy flannel shirt, Jess hugged her arms around herself and looked out the apartment window as snow drifted down in huge, heavy flakes. The wind was supposed to come up later tonight, and the storm threatened to dump eight to twelve inches across the borderland by morning to add to the five or six already on the ground.

Even though it was barely five P.M., in less than fifteen minutes, dusk would give way to dark. This storm was on track to match another winter storm almost two years ago, when Ty had blown in with his friends, saved two lives, and changed her life forever.

"What do you think, Bear? Should we go out for a quick walk before it gets any deeper?"

On cue, the dog started dancing in excitement at the word *walk*. She laughed and headed for the closet to get her coat and boots. Her phone rang, stopping her and, quite honestly, saving her from thinking morosely about how different this Christmas season would have been if she and Ty had gotten married at Thanksgiving as they'd planned.

"Hello?"

"Hey, Jess."

"J.R. Hey." Warmth flooded her chest, banishing her melancholy mood. "How are you?"

"I'm well."

She and J.R. had talked often since he'd reunited with Rabia last week. Jess couldn't be happier for them, although she couldn't help but worry about his health. He still had some healing to do, both physically and emotionally. But she had to believe he was in a good place now. A place where he would continue to seek the help he needed.

"And Rabia?" She was so excited about the baby.

"She's fine, too."

While she would love to meet Rabia, she understood that now wasn't the time. She didn't want to make Rabia uncomfortable.

"So what's happening?" she asked cheerfully, as Bear bounced by the door like a puppy—all eighty pounds of him.

"A lot. Too much to talk about. So I'm taking a breather. And I started thinking about you. About how lucky I am to have you in my life. I wanted to call and let you know that."

Tears pooled in her eyes. "I feel the same way. And I'm so glad you're happy."

"Have you called Ty yet?"

He asked each time they talked. "No," she confessed.

"Ah, Jess."

"I'm not ready."

"You're scared."

"That, too," she admitted. "I need to get myself together a little better before I call him."

"Because you think he's going to reject you."

"I would, if I were him. He's suffered losses, too, J.R. He lost his Navy career. He's lost people he loved. What if I was the last straw? What if he's reached a point where he's afraid to risk losing again?"

"The man loves you so much that he risked his life

to save mine, because he needed to be sure you were happy. I don't think a man like that is afraid of much of anything."

She stared at the Christmas tree and hoped J.R. was right. The part of her that doubted, however, had a stronger hold on her than the part that believed.

"Nothing to say to that?"

"I'll call him. I will," she promised. "I just need a little more time."

"The man is suffering, Jess. Like I suffered without Rabia. Put him out of his misery."

"I'll work on it, OK?"

"You do that. Look, I've gotta go. I just wanted to check in. Take care of yourself. And give Bear a hug for me."

"He misses you."

"I miss him, too."

"You're going to have to come back and visit us when you're both up to it. Thanks for keeping in touch with Brad, by the way. It means so much to him."

"He's my brother. I may not remember him yet, but it didn't take long to figure out that he's a good man. Don't worry. We aren't going to lose touch. None of us. I'll call again before Christmas."

"Take care."

She disconnected, then stared at the phone for a moment, the melancholy creeping in again as she thought about Ty being as miserable and alone for Christmas as she was.

But then Bear whined pitifully and snapped her out of it. She bundled up in her boots, down coat, a stocking cap, and gloves and took him outside into the snow.

✳

JESS TOOK BEAR on their usual route down the blacktop toward the lake and into the woods, but she cut the walk short at the halfway point. She'd barely made it out the door when the promised wind had picked up and the temp had dropped. The snow drove against her with such force it peppered her bare cheeks, and walking against it, she had to keep her head down to keep it from stinging her eyes.

"Sorry, buddy, we're heading back."

The blowing snow and deep drifts didn't faze the Lab, but he changed course when she did and, energized by his romp in the woods, loped ahead of her down the road.

Normally, she would have kept him closer, but there was no traffic tonight on either the blacktop or the highway where the two roads intersected in a T. Anyone with half a brain would be tucked up tight at home, warm by the fire, waiting for morning, when they'd start the task of digging out.

In fact, the last time she'd seen the snow plow go by had been around four, and the local news reported that road crews would be called in early because of the severe weather conditions.

So when she saw headlights cutting through the snow and bearing east on the highway, heading toward the store, she not only marveled at the stupidity of the driver but also figured she'd soon be dealing with a stranded motorist. It wouldn't be the first time. Some people had more balls than brains, her dad used to say.

Oh, well, she'd take them into the store and call Shelley, and then Darrin would come after them on a snowmobile and put them up for the night at the lodge.

She was still half a block away from the store when, sure enough, the headlights veered off the road, and the vehicle pulled into the parking lot and stopped under the light of the fuel pumps.

Bear, who never knew a stranger, trotted right up to what Jess could see now was an SUV.

"You're a heck of a watchdog," she grumbled, and tucked her chin deeper into her scarf to ward off the icy cold.

The driver's-side door opened, and a man stepped out. She wasn't close enough to make out his features, even under the security light, but something about him seemed familiar. Apparently, Bear thought so, too. The dog started jumping in happy circles and crying as if he'd found a long-lost friend.

The man went down on one knee to ruffle the dog's coat and give him a hug. Bear jumped on him as if he was fresh meat, licking his face, nudging his hands, practically tackling him.

The man laughed then . . . and she stopped mid-stride, twenty yards away.

She knew that laugh.

She loved that laugh.

This was no stranger. Ty knelt in the snow, watching her, snowflakes dusting his hair, his cheeks fiery red from the cold.

She started running.

She didn't care that snow stung her face, or that the happy tears running down her frozen cheeks blurred her vision, or that her lungs burned like fire. She needed to be in his arms, kissing him.

He was still on his knees when she reached him, and she didn't stop. She flew at him and tumbled them sideways into six inches of snow.

His arms wrapped tightly around her, and they rolled until she ended up on top of him, smiling down as snow fell around them and crept inside her coat collar.

"You're here," she whispered, breathless and deliriously hopeful and happy. Still disbelieving, she framed his cheeks in her gloved palms.

"I'm here," he said softly, searching her face, making it infinitely clear that he'd missed her as much as she'd missed him.

"You know? About J.R.?"

"And Rabia? Yes. Mike told me."

Damn, she was going to cry. "You don't hate me?"

His eyes softened. "I could never hate you."

She did cry, then. "But can you still love me?"

He pulled her head down to his and kissed her. "If you'd be kind enough to get me inside, out of the frozen tundra, I'll show you how much."

✱

TY GRABBED HER hand, and they scrambled to their feet. The bell he'd missed so much dinged wildly as he jerked open the door, made sure Bear managed to squeeze inside, then shoved it closed behind them.

"I need your mouth." He pushed her up against the door and slammed his mouth over hers. "I need to be inside you."

He felt primitive, feral, as, with a low groan, he broke the kiss and led her up the stairs. They frantically stripped off their clothes, leaving a trail from the doorway to the bedroom. He was hopping on one foot, cursing, and trying to get his boot off, when he looked up and saw her. On her knees. In the middle of the bed. Naked. Arms outstretched.

Screw the boot. He flew to the bed, dragged her against him, and tossed her onto her back.

Then he found the heart of her, the heat of her, and buried himself deep inside.

He'd missed her for too long. Had been certain he would live his life without her . . . for too long.

No more. He was here now. She was his now. Her sweet, responsive breasts. Her soft, giving body. Her wild, hungry mouth.

Her pure, giving heart.

Finesse could come later. The way she moved against him told him she didn't want finesse right now. Told him it was the same for her as it was for him.

This union was about lonely nights and hopeless longing and a crippling fear that they'd never be together this way again. This was about desperation and regret, about promises that would never again be broken.

This was about staking claims and coming home to a woman he was never going to leave again.

Epilogue

Minnesota, December, the following year

Kabetogama is one of the memories that came back first." J.R. stood in front of the log cabin's massive picture window, Bear sitting beside him. The Lab had divided his lavish attention between Ty and J.R. since he and Rabia and the baby had arrived two days ago. "Yet every time I see it, it's like I've forgotten how beautiful it is up here."

A fire crackled softly in the stone fireplace as Jess walked up beside him, sharing the view outside the dream home Ty had bought for her.

"Like a postcard," she agreed.

The frozen lake spread out like a moonscape to the north, while the snow-heavy forest nestled around them.

Since she and J.R. were sharing a rare moment

alone, she took advantage of it to make sure all was well.

"Ty's not pushing you too hard, is he?" Yesterday, Ty and Brad had insisted that J.R. go snowmobiling with them. This morning, they'd gone ice fishing.

"No. I'm good. Those guys are crazy wild on those machines, though," he added with a laugh.

"Please don't take too many chances with the leg," she cautioned him.

"Yes, Mom." He grinned at her.

Nine months ago, the VA's best surgical team had successfully repaired the break. J.R.'s rehab had been remarkably fast—mainly because of his determination—but Jess didn't want him pushing too hard.

It was clear, though, that he was doing fine. This was his and Rabia's second visit to the lake since she and Ty had gotten married last spring, and she was thrilled with how much progress he'd made since she'd seen him last. He looked like the old J.R. again, except for the touches of gray in his hair. He appeared healthy and robust and whole. Most of all, he was happy.

Jess credited Rabia and the baby with much of that. And the gradual recovery of his memory. Since that huge void in his life had been filled, he was better able to manage the PTSD. He still had headaches and nightmares but not as often, and he handled them better now.

"We did the right thing," he said, smiling down at her.

"We did," she agreed, and hugged him. They'd both be miserable right now, and so would Ty and Rabia, if they'd stayed the course and tried to force their marriage to work.

"So you think you got a big enough tree?"

She laughed. The oven timer dinged then, and she walked across the great room to the open kitchen to take another batch of cookies out of the oven.

"You know Ty. Go big or go home."

The tallest Christmas tree Ty could find fit in the center of the great room and rose almost to the peak of the eighteen-foot ceiling. He hadn't stopped there. A huge wreath hung on the wall between the ceiling and the top of the cabin's front door. Outside, another wreath glistened with Christmas lights. He'd strung more lights on a perfectly shaped white pine in the front yard and draped garland on the porch posts.

"Much more fun than decorating pineapple palm trees," he'd said with a grin.

They'd decorated the inside tree together with more twinkling lights and both her old, sentimental ornaments and the new ones she'd had to buy to fill up the gigantic tree. Beneath the tree, Jess had placed lovingly wrapped gifts for everyone she cared about. Shelley and Darrin. Mike and Eva—Ty was meeting their plane in the Falls right now.

There were gifts for Brad and for her mom and dad and for Mike and Ty's parents, who were all arriving tomorrow. She'd bought presents for Kayla, Blake, Lane, and Hailey and her other part-time help, and she'd even found something special for Boots and Marcia.

And while she didn't want Rabia to feel as though she were forcing Christian traditions on her, Jess had also bought her a gift in the spirit of friendship and goodwill when she'd gone shopping for J.R. But the lion's share of the ribbons and bows were wrapped around pretty little packages for the beautiful baby girl who napped upstairs while Rabia took advantage of the downtime by catching a much-needed nap herself.

Little Farishta—"Angel"—had her mother's black eyes and gorgeous olive complexion and her daddy's determination, especially when she wanted attention.

"We got the word last week that the book has been optioned for a movie."

She blinked across the counter at him. "You're kidding?"

"Doesn't mean a movie's going to happen, but the option money will go a long way toward college tuition."

As if J.R. had any financial worries. Once the story had broken last year, he'd had book offers flying at him like bullets. Only after he and Rabia had given it hard and serious consideration had they decided to engage a literary agent. The subsequent bidding war for the book about his ordeal had made J.R. a wealthy man.

He hadn't taken the book deal because he'd wanted to get rich, though. He'd taken it to help fund Rabia's cause. They'd eventually settled in D.C., where

Rabia actively lobbied for awareness of the need for continued support of Afghan women's rights. A film documentary was also in the works that brought attention to the plight of women and girls in her homeland. All because Rabia had a voice that would not be silenced.

Jeff had enrolled in college. His goal was to become a counselor for veterans suffering from TBI and PTSD.

"I'm so proud of you," she said, "but I've got one question."

"Shoot."

"Who's going to play me in the movie?"

He grinned and snagged a warm sugar cookie off the tray. "Someone with a smart mouth."

The front door opened then, bringing a gust of crisp winter air and the laughter of the man she loved.

✱

"WILL YOU QUIT smiling?" Ty teased the next night, as they snuggled side-by-side on the sofa in front of the fire, after everyone had retired to one of their five bedrooms.

Jess nestled deeper against Ty's chest. "I can't help it. I'm happy. Most of the people I love in this world are safe and warm under our roof tonight. We should have worked a little harder to persuade Brad to stay and sleep on the sofa."

"I think that confirmed bachelor was more than

happy to retire to his man cave for a little peace and quiet."

"You've got to admit, when you Brown boys get together, things do get a bit out of hand. Your poor mom. You two gave her fits when you were growing up. Some of the stories she told me!"

"You don't want to believe that sweet, apple-cheeked woman. She lies."

She laughed and gave him an elbow in the ribs. "Shame on you."

"She does," he insisted, with a hint of a whine that made her laugh again. "We were angels. Like the one on top of the tree."

As much as she enjoyed these quiet moments together, she couldn't stop a yawn.

"Speaking of angels," he said, "I know another one who needs to go to bed. You're beat."

"I don't want to move."

"You don't have to." He gathered her in his arms and stood.

"You'll hurt your back."

"You let me worry about my back."

He carried her upstairs, Bear padding along behind them, and laid her down. Then he undressed her while she watched his eyes in the dark.

"Thank you," she whispered, when he crawled under the covers with her.

"My pleasure." He drew her into his arms and nuzzled her neck. "And I should be thanking you."

"For what? Having your family here?"

"No. Because I would never have this without you," he murmured.

"This?" She lifted her head so she could see his face in the soft shadows. Unexpected emotions welled up inside her when she saw the sheen of moisture glistening in his eyes.

"Home." He pressed his lips softly to hers. "I never thought I'd find this sense of home." He kissed her again with a tenderness that humbled her. "Thank you for showing me the way."

Author's Note

*L*ake Kabetogama, where a good portion of this novel is set, is a very beautiful, very magical place. Kabby represents a treasure trove of special memories from when I was a child vacationing at the lake with my parents, to the present where our children and extended family and friends join us to make more memories. It was truly a joy to write about the area.

The Crossroads General Store is fictional, but locals and frequent visitors to Kabby will recognize that Crossroads bears a marked resemblance to The Gateway Store, a landmark that has stood for decades and accommodated so many travelers. The Whispering Pines Resort is also fictional, but its depiction could match any of a number of beautiful resorts on the lake.

Although the names have been changed, some among you (cough Boots cough Marcia cough) may recognize characters loosely patterned in your image.

All other landmarks, including The Walleye, are real.

Any mistakes in either the Kabetogama or the Afghanistan locales are mine and mine alone.

Acknowledgments

I'm blessed with amazingly talented and giving friends, many of whom also happen to be writers and who share my insecurities and their wisdom :o). Rob Browne, Debra Webb, Glenna McReynolds, Le-Anne Banks, Susan Connell—thank you for helping me find my way through this book.

Maria Carvainis—agent without equal—thank you for guiding my way.

Micki Nuding—editor and friend—thank you for the unflagging support and lovely edit.

Louise Burke—publisher extraordinaire—thank you for the amazing opportunities.

And to Joseph Francis Collins—fellow author, firefighter, paramedic, expert on all things military, I thank you, friend, for the invaluable contributions you've made to this book in the form of time, research, and counsel. *The Way Home* has been special from the moment the story made itself known to me and, with your help, it turned into everything I hoped it would become.

Turn the page for a sneak peek
at Cindy Gerard's next military romantic suspense
set in the world of the Black Ops, Inc.
and One-Eyed Jack series

Running Blind

Available in Spring 2015 from Pocket Books

*M*onday's *were so not his thing. And this damn* early on a Monday morning was so far out of his comfort zone that Jamie Cooper felt as if he'd landed in a different time zone.

All because of a woman who wouldn't give him the time of day.

Grumbling under his breath over his stupidity, he sat at a large table and looked around the restaurant. He was the first one to arrive at Brewed Awakenings, a good fifteen minutes before the other team members were due to show up. He opened up a menu, quietly sizing up the twenty or so other customers enjoying breakfast. He'd give it a ninety-nine percent probability that none of them represented a threat. Even off the clock, situational awareness was key. He never dropped full-alert status.

Right this moment, however, he was alert for one team member in particular: Rhonda "Bombshell" Burns.

The recently hired head computer analyst/security expert had thrown him way the hell off his game. In the six months she'd been on board, the woman had single-handedly elevated the stereotype of computer nerd to computer sexpot. That was Taggart's term, but he damn sure agreed with the assessment, PC or not. The woman was a walking, talking wet dream.

God help the man who called her that to her face, though. Her smackdown would be swift and brutal. And hot, he thought with a smile—then told himself to get his head out of his ass and recalibrate.

The bombshell was strictly "look but don't touch." And if the fact itself that they were teammates didn't make touching taboo, she'd be happy to make it painfully clear herself.

Yet here he sat. Waiting for her. Though the woman barely spoke to him.

How screwed up was that?

If Taggart or Mike knew he'd turned stupid over a woman, they'd laugh their asses off. Would want to check his temperature.

Maybe they'd be right. Maybe he was sick—in the head. He'd actually set his alarm so he could be here to watch Rhonda make her grand entrance. It was so high school of him. But with Rhonda, the entrance was always grand, so he cut himself a little slack. Especially when he spotted her walking past the plate-glass windows fronting the restaurant.

He might have stopped breathing, because it felt like he had been kicked with a combat boot in the center of his chest when she sashayed through the door, a bitter blast of the February morning air entering with her.

What a sight. Slashes of pink painted cheeks flushed with cold; her baby blues sparkled; and her thick, glossy blond mane framed her face like the angel hair his mom used to drape on their Christmas tree.

Only Rhonda Burns was no angel. She slipped off her coat and hung it on the rack by the door, and the sight of her in her skin-tight pink sweater, short, ass-hugging skirt, and nose-bleed high heels had him conjuring up thoughts that could send him straight to hell.

A wisp of Obsession drifted across the room and he felt an involuntary tightening in his groin. He didn't know where she got those sweaters—soft, fuzzy angora in colors that made him think of the sweet, gooey marshmallow chicks that always showed up in Easter baskets—but he hoped she didn't run out of them anytime soon. Just like he hoped she never changed the way she dressed, the way she smelled, the way she walked, and the way she radiated confidence, sass, and attitude.

Bombshell Burns was one tasty marshmallow chick, oozing a simmering sexuality. With her luscious curves and "look all you want, enjoy, but don't touch" bravado, she made his day every time she walked into a room.

✷

RHONDA BRACED HER palms on the bathroom counter in her hotel room and glared at herself in the mirror. Jamie Cooper was impossibly gorgeous—even when he was annoyingly surly, rock-jawed, and silent. She worked with a boatload of gorgeous alpha males, yet he still stood out. Flying out here, sitting beside him on the cramped commercial flight, she'd felt his undeniable sexuality radiate from his body in pulsing waves.

And she'd dreamed about him again last night, even though she knew she would never get involved with him. The vibes he'd been giving off, however, suggested he might think that she should.

Not happening. She dug a brush out of her bag and went to work on her hair. She wasn't opposed to good, healthy sex, although you'd never know it from her recent dating history. Or her not-so-recent history, for that matter. Sex was one thing; a conquest was another—and that's what a man like him would consider it.

Well, she'd never been, and would never be, some

man's spoils of war—even if it was simply a war of the sexes.

But oh, she did wonder what a night in bed with him would be like.

She tossed the brush onto the counter in disgust. She was as guilty as he was. She hadn't been able to put that damn kiss behind her, either.

But she would. She had no time and no desire to let someone like Cooper interfere in her life, or get too close. She had to cowgirl up and let him know he was wasting his time and hers.

A sharp knock drew her out of the bathroom and toward the door to her room, and she reluctantly thought that they might have that talk right now. Because it could only be Cooper knocking. She looked through the peephole anyway to confirm it.

There he stood. Arms folded belligerently over his chest, feet planted wide apart, looking as gorgeous as ever and as combative as a submachine gun.

Ready or not, she swung open the door.

When he saw her, his expression of grim resolution slowly turned to disgust.

Forget the talk, then. She did not want to deal with his damn hostility right now.

Irked with him for being such a dick, and with herself for not making him own up to it, she turned away. "Let me grab my coat; then I'm ready."

"For what? Speed dating?"

His clipped, judgmental tone, as much as his words, had her turning back to him with narrowed eyes. "What exactly does that mean?"

He lifted a hand in an encompassing sweep of her body. "We're going to a military facility, for God's sake, not a photo shoot. Must you always be camera-ready?"

Rhonda knew she sometimes pushed the "acceptable" limits of professional attire. It was who she was and she didn't intend to change for anyone. Today she wore this particular white sweater, red skirt, and black heels because she needed to feel powerful enough to match whatever grief Cooper might send her way. And apparently he planned on sending plenty.

And she was now officially pissed. "What are you? The fashion police?"

He gave her another contemptuous once-over. "Forget it. I want to get to the base and get a few hours under my belt today. Let's just go."

"You know what? I'm not going anywhere." Guess they were going to have that talk after all. She crossed her arms beneath her breasts and stood her ground. "Not until you tell me who shoved that stick up your ass."

★

DAMN, STUBBORN, BULL-HEADED shrew of a woman. Short of dragging her out of the hotel room by her hair and shoving her into the elevator, it looked like they were going to have that "talk" Coop had hoped they could avoid for—oh, the next decade or so.

"Look. I don't want to be here, okay?" Not lying, but not exactly telling the whole truth.

She snorted. "Alert the media. I never would have guessed."

He walked to the window and glared out over the parking lot. "I need to be back at Langley, working on the investigation."

"I figured that out," she said from behind him. Which was where he needed her to be, because damn and damn again, she looked so hot, all he could think about was the fact that they were alone together, in a hotel room. With a king-size bed.

"I want to be back there helping out, too. But there's more going on with you than that."

Oh hell, yeah.

She pressed, "You think I'm not up to the assignment? Is that what this pig-headed silence is all about?"

She was like a dog with a bone. He shook his head. "I don't think that, no. I think you'll do fine."

"Then that only leaves one thing."

When she didn't explain, he finally turned around. She looked like a runway version of an Amazon priestess. Expression hard and unbending, body lush and curvy, legs long and . . . man oh man, he wanted them wrapped around his waist.

"You kissed me," she announced, cutting right to the heart of the matter. "If you're having trouble with that, then it's on your head—not mine. So if you want to be ticked off at someone, look in the mirror and quit taking it out on me."

One thing no one could accuse him of was not admitting when he'd been called out. She was right. He was taking it out on her. And she wasn't finished clearing that up for him.

"And grow up while you're at it. It was a kiss—big deal. We were happy for Mike and Eva. We were relieved she was alive. We were relieved that we were alive. It was instinctual; it didn't mean anything."

He stared at her, wanting to agree with everything she said. But he couldn't. Because she was wrong. She was dead wrong.

That kiss had meant something. It had meant a helluva lot of something. And that's why he was so angry.

Talk about getting slapped in the face with the truth.

He wasn't upset about kissing her. He was upset because he wanted to kiss her again, and again. And . . . because he might want a lot more than a kiss. Maybe even . . . a lot more than sex.

He dragged a hand through his hair, stunned speechless. Then he met her eyes and, with a single beat of his heart, shot from bewildered to total clarity.

That kiss had meant something so huge, he'd been afraid to qualify it. He was still scared. But so was she. That's why she'd lied about it being nothing. He'd felt the way she'd melted into him. He'd sensed, with every instinct he'd ever relied on to keep himself alive, that the significance of that kiss scared her every bit as much as it scared him.

Well, he'd never run away from fear in his life before, and he wasn't about to start now.

She wanted to be pissed? Maybe he'd just give her a reason, then.

He stalked toward her. "If that kiss didn't mean anything, then this won't mean anything, either."

She read the intent in his eyes as he reached for her, but it was too late—for both of them. He banded one arm around her waist, cupped the back of her head with his other hand, and pulled her flush against him.

"What the hell do you think you're doing?"

"I think that I'm about to ruin your lipstick. But don't worry. It doesn't mean a thing."

Then he covered her mouth with his . . . and dove off the prow of a ship into a hundred fathoms of ocean.

He never acted like this. He didn't go off half-cocked and reckless over a woman, and he'd never resorted to manhandling one. Fortunately, after the first shocked few seconds, he didn't need to manhandle this one.

She melted against him like butter, met the heat and intensity of his kiss with all the fury that had prompted him to go caveman and drag her into his arms.

Pursuit. Another first for him. Women came after him; he didn't go after them. Now he knew why. Other women weren't her.

And he'd wanted her to be just another woman, like the ones who had danced in and out of his life until he didn't want to dance with them anymore.

Like he wanted to dance with her.

Because she wasn't just another woman.

Oh, man.

Pretty much terrified by the track his thoughts had taken, he abruptly broke the kiss and set her away from him.

She looked dazed and unsteady, and he wasn't real solid on his own feet, either.

He cupped her shoulders in his hands and walked her backward the two steps to the bed. When the back of her knees hit the mattress, they gave, and she sank right down.

"I'm sorry I've been such a jerk. You didn't deserve it," he said, meaning it. "And I'm sorry . . . about what I just did. I was out of line. Way out of line."

She had yet to speak. It was the most unhinged he'd ever seen the bombshell.

It was the most unhinged he'd ever felt.

"Better touch up that lipstick." Before he could stop himself, he reached out and brushed the pad of his thumb over her lower lip.

She blinked—a "what the hell just happened?" blink that had him backing toward the door.

What the hell *had* just happened?

"I'll meet you in the lobby in ten." Then he high-tailed it out of her room as fast as he could.